USS Hoquiam PF-5:
Hocky Maru

USS Hoquiam PF-5: Hocky Maru

Mark Douglas

Order this book online at www.trafford.com
or email orders@trafford.com

Most Trafford titles are also available at major online book retailers.

Printed in the United States of America.

ISBN: 978-1-4269-6437-4 (sc)
ISBN: 978-1-4269-6435-0 (e)

Library of Congress Control Number: 2011905977

Trafford rev. 04/26/2011

 www.trafford.com

North America & international
toll-free: 1 888 232 4444 (USA & Canada)
phone: 250 383 6864 ♦ fax: 812 355 4082

This story is dedicated to
all the KIA and MIA of the Korean War

U.S.S. HOQUIAM PF-5: Hocky Maru

To the "small boys" especially, it was a dreary and often dangerous campaign of constant blockade and bombardment, essential to the war effort and necessary to the support of the fighting ashore.

The Sea War in Korea, Chapter 9, page 283ff

JANUARY 1951

"THIS IS A F R S TOKYO WITH THE MORNING NEWS, JANUARY FIRST NINETEEN FIFTY-ONE, AIRMAN MIKE DILL REPORTING. UNITED NATIONS COMMAND IN KOREA REPORTS THE CHINESE COMMUNIST FORCES HAVE MOUNTED AN ALL OUT OFFENSIVE ALL ACROSS THE ENTIRE FRONT WITH OVER A HALF MILLION SOLDIERS."

0815, January 1, 1951
Sick Bay
USS Hoquiam PF-5
Dry-dock #1,
SRF Yokosuka, Japan

Stewart strode up to the gray door and froze, staring apprehensively at the six-inch Red Cross emblem centered on the door. Stewart pulled his white hat off, hesitating because he just knew that somehow he had magically gotten VD on the cruise to North Korea and Doc was about to give him a shot of penicillin with a thirty-day medical restriction. Seaman Apprentice Stewart shrugged and knocked twice on the doorframe with his knuckles.

What a way to start a new year!

A muffled voice growled an unintelligible response through the door.

Stewart took a deep breath, opened the door a crack, and peered around its corner. A whiff of sick bay alcohol puffed out at him. Chief Farmer, known as Porky behind his back, was dressed in clean, albeit wrinkled, wash khakis. He squatted on his short, steel piano stool facing two angry sailors who were holding their love lives in their hands. Both were smearing the heads of their penises on small, rectangular specimen glasses.

Porky didn't even look up as he pointed his finger at Stewart. "I don't want to hear it. Take this specimen glass," he growled, handing him a clean one, "milk down and smear the end of your penis onto it. I'll check the specimen under the microscope to see if you have gonorrhea."

"Chief, how the fuck could I have the clap? Ain't had a chance to use it since we left here last October," complained Stewart.

"Stewart, I don't want any shit outa you. Just do it. I got twenty-seven sailors to check after a hell of a celebration at the Chief's Club last night."

Stewart took a closer look at the Chief and noticed that the damp towel draped across the back of his neck was nearly sopping wet. His face was a little redder than usual and his eyes were pretty bloodshot.

This is not a day to get a shot from him.

Lee did as instructed. He was careful to hold the glass by the edge as he'd seen the Chief do and wiped the head of his penis on it like the other sailors had done. The Chief grunted, removed the first specimen from under the microscope, made a note in the deck ape's Medical Record, and set in the second specimen. Refocusing the microscope, he grunted again, removed that specimen, and made a note in the Laundryman's Medical Record. Then he took Stewart's specimen and set it under the microscope. Grunting softly like a pig, he leaned over the desk and made a note in Lee Stewart's Medical Record, too.

Then he straightened up and looked at the three sailors.

"You ever hear the joke about good news bad news?"

The three sailors nodded hesitantly not sure where this was going.

"The good news is you guys don't have the clap! You can put your toys away now."

He beamed and smiled at them as he said it. Three sailors looked at him in disgust as they stuffed their joy toys back in their pants and buttoned up.

We know that!

He closed their Medical Records and handed them to Webb for filing. "What you have is a strain brought on by physical stress—say lifting very heavy things. Were any of you on the Depth Charge detail yesterday?"

They looked at him and frowned at each other as they thought about it. Stewart recalled seeing the Laundryman but not the deck ape. They all nodded reluctant agreement.

"Lifting Depth Charges is not the best exercise in the world. Your bodies rebelled at the weight and leaked a little bit. That's in way of an explanation. So, you are not infected with a venereal disease and you don't need a shot of penicillin. However, the bad news is you men have to stay aboard until the leakage stops."

He held up his hands as three angry sailors sucked in their breaths to scream.

"Wait. Hold it a second, sailors. You are on light duty today. Come back at liberty call and I'll check again. If the leakage is absent, you get your card if you don't have the duty." He looked at them with a smile in his eyes as he handed them each a light duty chit. "Fellas, it really is in your best interest. Now, get the hell outa here. Webb, send in the next three."

Stewart jammed his white hat back on his head as he left sick bay and headed back to the Radio Shack, taking it slow and easy on the ladder to the 01-deck.

What a low blow! Bust my ass to get all the ammo off then gotta stay aboard because I busted my ass. Fat chance of that happening again soon.

Stewart walked a little stiff-leggedly into the Radio Shack, grumbling about the injustice of it all. His Leading Petty Officer, Radioman First Class Jimmy Bob James, glanced at him.

"I don't want to hear about it. Liberty call is going at 1100 this morning and I want this placed squared away. Take down all this Christmas tree shit and them Christmas cards, too. Oh, better yet, stack those cards by name and let the guys keep 'em or toss 'em. Also, the bright work is shitty." He paused and looked Stewart up and down. "What the hell are you smiling at?"

Stewart handed him his light duty chit with a flourish. "No heavy work, boss, 'till this leak disappears."

James studied the chit and handed it back. "Okay, scratch the bright work. But get hot on that Christmas stuff, then route the fuckin' board."

Stewart nodded in understanding. "Anybody want to take a picture of it before I take it down?"

"Don't worry about that shit, Stew. Just get it down and over the side."

"Right, James."

As Stewart unplugged the spruce branch from AC power, spruce needles began dropping from the branch onto equipment, people, and the deck. Three trees had been delivered at sea just before Christmas during their last replenishment off Hungnam. This branch almost had dropped on his head when it fell from one of the trees. The Radio Shack guys had been proud of their unique Christmas decorations.

Very carefully, he pulled the string of official U.S. Navy colored indicator lamps from the tree and placed them on the ET's workbench. Needles were going everywhere.

"Dammit, Stewart, I told you to get rid of that shit. Now do it!" Stewart had started to remove the bright bits of tinsel that had been Christmas wrapping paper. One look at James convinced him. He gently placed the entire branch in the trashcan to stop spreading needles all over the deck.

Checking the glowering James again, he hastily pulled Christmas cards from the filing cabinet, bulkheads, and overhead, sorting them into piles for the other guys to pick over.

There's my three: Mom and Dad, Ruth—and Betty, of all people. Still don't understand why she sent me a card, after all the legal crap she's started.

Stewart picked up the clipboard and sorted through the messages that needed initialing and delivery. "James, I'll route the board first and hold field day afterwards, if that's okay with you."

James looked up from the message traffic he was checking and pointed to the door.

"Go."

Stewart closed the door behind him and checked to see if Lt.(jg) Forsythe was in his stateroom across the passageway. He always wanted to check the board before anyone else saw it. He next picked up a couple of signatures in the Officers' Wardroom and then left for the Bridge. He grabbed the quick release wheel bar on the Starboard hatch and rotated it opening the hatch, stepped into a cold, light rain and latched the hatch shut. Covering the board, he made a dash for the ladder, pounded up to the Bridge, realizing too late that he shouldn't do that while recovering from that strain. Puffing a little, Stewart leaned back against the Flag Bag and watched the Signalmen at work.

Looks like the Chief has them holding field day before liberty.

Chief Swenson stood six foot two inches from his shined brown shoes and pressed wash khakis, to his combination cap, which was beginning to drip water from its shiny brim. Light grey eyes in a lean, square face smiled at Stewart.

"Hey, Stew, how's the drip coming along?" he laughed.

"Not funny, Chief. Junior is still leaking. Don't think I'll get to make liberty again tonight and I've got the duty tomorrow."

"Well, look at the bright side."

"What bright side?"

"You're not spending all that loot."

"Shit!" Stewart looked down at his clip board and back at the Chief. "You got a daily weather forecast and a Hydrographic floating mine warning on the board, Chief. Wanna sign for them, please?"

Chief Swenson took the clipboard into his cubby, extracted his copies, and read them both at his leisure.

Stewart, waiting for the Chief to return his clipboard, watched his friends at work. The rain stopped for the moment and there was a frantic effort to polish brass and chrome bright work. Red Curry, Signalman Third Class, stopped washing the bulkhead long enough to chuckle a hee hee at Stewart. "How long do you think that leaking will go on, Stew?"

"Damned if I know. I can feel it sort of seeping right now. But with this light duty chit today, maybe it'll be gone by liberty call tonight. Any word on Kiki, yet?" Red had introduced Stewart to Kiki in September, a marvelous Japanese girl who spoke near perfect English. It seemed a match made just for them.

Red shook his head. He had had a great night with Kimiko and knew that Stew was hurting.

Chief Swenson still had a smile on his face. He said, "Alright, quit bothering these guys. They have work to do," as he handed Stewart the board.

Time to go.

"See you guys at chow, maybe."

As Stewart turned to leave, he blinked. A snowflake had landed on his cheek.

I didn't think it was that cold.

But looking around as he slowly went down the ladder, he could see a lot of snow beginning to fall.

Opening the door to the Radio Shack, he saw everyone there except Coyle who was sleeping off the mid-watch. "Okay, liberty hounds, better draw your snow shoes before you go ashore. It's snowing pretty good out there." James and Masters groaned and shook their heads.

"On top of that, my girl friend has had the rag on since we been back, I really need this," growled James.

Ah ha! So that's why he's off his feed—no pussy. Well, join the crowd, boss.

Stewart smiled and began humming as he dusted and swept up.

0930, January 2, 1951
USS Hoquiam PF-5
Dry-dock #1
SRF, Yokosuka, Japan

Stewart stood on top of the dry dock looking down at his ship's hull. Long twelve by twelve inch timbers were jammed between her hull and the walls of the dry dock to keep her upright in the waterless dry dock. Looking up, his eyes swept over the small superstructure with all the bamboo scaffolding fitted around it.

After seventy-three days of being underway, it's hard to believe no smoke or steam is coming from the stack.

He stared around at the stark snow-covered gray and white buildings with splotches of black cinder piles between the buildings and muddy roads. The falling snow muffled the sounds of Japanese workers on the ship and in the dry dock under the ship.

Doc said since it wasn't the clap, I could make the regular Comm Center unclassified runs.

He could take his time on this run because of the light duty chit. Stewart strolled along the dry dock, crunching the fresh snow with his feet as he remembered back to his first bus ride here.

Jeez, that was less than four months ago! What on earth is going to happen in the next four months? I know this next ten days is going to be a bitch for most of the departments. Lots of work. The Radio Shack is in pretty good shape, though.

Lee Harrison Stewart had been a sailor for nearly two years and was a lifer, to the disgust of his recalled Naval Reserve shipmates. He intended to stay in the Navy and make it his career. Stewart was just a shade over six feet tall and weighed 155 lean pounds. His eyes seemed to have turned bluer since his arrival last September. Stewart liked to wear his blond hair in crew cut style. It was handy to wash; he didn't need any Wildroot Crème Oil or carry a comb around in his pocket to break.

Although it seemed he really just wanted a woman under him every waking moment, Lee Stewart was as curious as they come and wasn't adverse to joining a sight seeing tour so all his senses could be put to use. Part of his curiosity stemmed from his fascination with history. A bronze memorial plaque fastened to a building or along a road always caught his attention.

As a Radioman striker from Naval Station Tongue Point, Astoria, Oregon—the Navy calls all trainees strikers—he had brought a lot of new procedures, new since World War Two, to a Radio crew of bitter World War Two Retreads. But Stewart also harbored anger over events that did not allow him to advance to the next grade, Seaman.

He looked at his ship in Dry Dock One some more as he trudged along, reached inside his peacoat and pulled his Camels and Jap Zippo lighter from his blue chambray shirt pocket. Shaking the tobacco crumbs from a cigarette, he lit up, and walked over to the message center for their unclassified message traffic.

1815, January 2, 1951
Wardroom,
USS Hoquiam PF-5
SRF, Yokosuka, Japan

The quiet clatter of silver service on plates, spoons stirring coffee, and Steward's Mates' murmurs as they offered various platters of food to the officers around the wardroom table was relaxing and served to settle the Captain's mind. He went over his speech again in his mind to make sure he was covering all bases as he settled down to wait until everyone had been served and were eating.

Captain Brown picked up his fork and tapped the water goblet slowly for attention. Conversation instantly shut off and all heads turned toward him.

"You may have heard, but for the record, Bill found out today his brother is safe in Masan, South Korea, in the marine rest area, near Pusan. His outfit has been placed in reserve status for two weeks before going back up on the Line. We were already out in the stream at the Hungnam Sea Buoy when his outfit withdrew to one of the transports."

Grins and thumbs up, directed toward the Supply Officer, appeared around the table.

"So now, Bill, if I can have your undivided attention, you will learn how we are going to spend all that money you've been hoarding."

He smiled and casually looked around the table, gauging their tension.

"I found out today how effective our nightly meetings back in August and September turned out. We were the only PF that did that consistently: I have news for you—we are the only PF that hasn't suffered a major breakdown."

He paused to let that sink in and to allow them time to figure out what was coming next.

So much for sugar coating the pill.

"Starting right now, I am instituting after dinner status reports. All officers are required to be here. Chiefs or Leading Petty Officers will join us to participate in the meeting after the Stewards have cleared the table.

"Think of your division's problem areas as you enjoy your dinner, prioritize your problem areas. Once again, we'll go around the table listening to each other to discover any overlapping areas or something not covered. The DRT (Dead Reckoning Tracer) is an excellent example of how important items get overlooked because the people involved thought someone else was taking care of it."

He shot a quick, dirty look at Lt. Porter, the Operations Officer, and Ens. Hitchcock, the CIC Officer. He had placed them in hack for the first five days in port. Pausing deliberately to let them squirm, he then continued. "I'll be reporting to the Commodore on a nightly basis so he can press SRF the following morning. Now let's finish dinner." So saying, he leaned over his plate and began eating.

". . . And so to the sound dome itself." Lt.(jg) Carl Herbert paused to sip some water and catch his breath. "The SRF people and I inspected the sound dome very closely because of the list of problems. We found the sound dome to be in such poor condition that SRF has agreed to replace the entire dome assembly. And get this. The dome had several small pinholes, causing it to be filled with water—still leaking out as a matter of fact— and covered with barnacles. The starboard side was badly battered, as though struck repeatedly with a hammer, and the port side was rippled for its entire length. The condition of the sound head undoubtedly accounted for the past poor performance of our QBF sonar gear." Lt.(jg) Herbert leaned back in his chair with coffee cup in hand and waited for comments or questions.

The three senior underway Officers of the Deck looked at each other and back to Lt.(jg) Herbert. Lt. Porter spoke up. "The Hoquiam has never touched bottom and the prescribed practice of hoisting the sound dome when encountering heavy weather or when in shallow water has always been adhered to."

All other deck watch officers nodded in agreement.

"That had to be some more of the Russian's sabotage 'cause that's the way it was when we left dry dock in September. Remember, we complained the sound dome hadn't been inspected," injected Lt. Morgan.

Lt. Hansen raised his hand and was recognized by Lt.(jg) Herbert. He hesitated a second then said, "When we asked SRF why they hadn't inspected the sound dome, they said the dome's frozen mechanical train had taken so much time that ComNavFE ordered them to bypass the remainder of the dome inspection and get the PF-5 ready for commissioning."

The Captain raised a finger and cleared his throat, stopping further discussion.

"Okay, that's two that will be fixed before we get out of here. Let's adjourn until tomorrow night."

There was a scramble of junior officers standing as the Captain stood and smiled at them. He tilted his head to clear the overhead and walked forward to his stateroom.

1635, January 3, 1951
USS Hoquiam PF-5
Quarterdeck
SRF, Yokosuka, Japan

Barney was in ranks waiting for the Officer of the Deck to inspect him for liberty when he spotted Stewart hurrying aft to join the liberty party. Stewart had a very big grin on his face.

Barney waited for him on the pier. "Hey Stew, no juice coming out of your pecker, huh?"

"Not right now, boy-san, but there will be in a little while! You got plans or just making the gate?" asked Lee Stewart as they walked toward the Main Gate.

"Like we did the last time, Stew. I think I found a home in that little house. I'm trying out all the girls to see who's best. Then, I'll probably stick with her."

"Yeah, well don't forget what they are there for, Barney. They're supposed to blast the cobwebs outa your brain and soothe your savage brow. As soon as you leave, someone else is there pumping away. Nothing permanent, right?"

"You said it, Stew! You got that right."

After two and a half months at sea, the Hoquiam sailors still rolled a bit as they walked, trying to accommodate the rolling ship that wasn't there. It was good to walk on dry land again but it didn't seem to spring like a ship's deck. Barney and Lee didn't have much to say as they reached the Main Gate. Holding their ID and Liberty Cards for the Marine Sentry to see, they passed through into freedom.

Lee slowed and stopped before they got to the intersection. He stared at all the changes made since their departure last October. A Jap traffic cop was on a little stand topped with an umbrella, smack dab in the middle of the intersection. Standing there in his black hat and gray uniform with white gloves clear up to his elbow, he was a comical sight. One hand was held out stiffly holding traffic in one direction as the other hand waved in a vertical circle keeping traffic moving in the other direction. Every couple of seconds, the cop turned right, turned left, or even turned completely around.

Lee laughed, enjoying the sight. "You know, Barney, he reminds me of a target in a shooting gallery. Only thing missing is the pop of the rifle and the ding as the slug hits the duck."

Barney smiled and shook his head. "Bad, Stew, you're bad, you know that?"

Barney waved to a pedicab and gave him a card as they got in. The cabbie studied it for a minute and looked at Barney.

"You wan go heah?" he asked shaking his head. "Dis bad place. Ahl gir hava vee dee, you unnastand?—Vee Dee!"

Barney motioned for the cabbie to give him back his card and began to get out of the pedicab.

"No no, you stah. I take you."

Failing to change their mind so he could interest them in the house he had arrangements with, the cabbie stood up on his pedals and started pumping. Barney didn't say a word, just smiled at Lee and watched where the cabbie was taking them.

"Hey, boysan", Barney called, nudging the cabbie with his shoe, "you go there!", he said pointing to a side street. The cabbie had not turned on Barney's street.

Lee ignored Barney and the cabbie. After waiting through two days of juice and a day of duty, it was his first liberty.

Man, there're a lot of changes along the street.

There were more little shops and stores catering to the sailors and marines than when they had left back in October. Every shop was playing a different American or Japanese song on a 45rpm record player. Lee didn't recognize some of them.

"Jeez, Barney, lot of different stores. And look at the girls, dressed like the girls back home."

"Yeah. They watch American movies with Japanese subtitles and beg sailors to bring movie magazines ashore so they can copy the latest styles. Wait 'til you get a load of the new prices. No more hundred Yen pussy now. Guess how much?"

"Crap, how the hell would I know, Barney?"

"Try five hundred Yen for short time, and a thousand Yen for all evening. The works will cost you eighteen hundred Yen, easy."

"What do you mean, the works?" asked Lee apprehensively.

"Steak dinner, sake, rub down, wash, dry and iron your uniform from the skin out, and an evening's worth of pussy. But no sukahochi girls."

"Suka what—what the fuck is that?" asked Lee.

Barney turned and started at Lee in amazement. He could see Lee was puzzled and didn't recognize the expression.

"Blow job! Only special girls give blow jobs and that's what they are called. Not many houses have them. Most of the other girls won't have anything to do with sukahochi girls."

"Oh yeah? Well tell me, Barney, when you eat these girls, do they give you a discount?"

"You s-s-shitbird, that's not even funny," he stuttered, glaring at Lee.

Lee flashed back to Ruth Verlock in Seattle and got an instant hard on. That wasn't the only thing she'd taught him. He grinned quietly in remembrance as Barney prattled on about the girls in "his" house.

The cabbie was puffing as they pulled up and stopped in front of the house gate.

"Pay the cabbie, Stew. It's eighty Yen now."

Stewart's eyebrows joined his hair.

Wow, it had only been thirty Yen when they left in October.

He fumbled with his wallet and pulled out a one hundred Yen note. The cabbie shook his head. "No changa," he protested still shaking his head.

Barney had been watching and knew from his previous two liberties what was going on. He reached out and took the hundred Yen note back from the cabbie. "Mamasan, mamasan," he called out.

The cabbie looked around uneasily while Lee watched Barney and waited. Mamasan appeared in her gray striped kimono. Barney started talking. "Mamasan, him say yo bad vee dee house. Him try to cheat Stew."

As he said that, the old woman's wrinkled face screwed up in anger and she really blasted the cabbie. She took Lee's hundred Yen note and ran into the house. In a moment, she was back with twenty Yen and threw it at the cabbie, all the while yelling at him. The cabby's mouth formed a perfect small letter "O" as he heard her out and left, peddling fast. The excitement over, Lee and Barney sat down and took their shoes off. Barney snickered at the cabby's loss.

We must be early; I don't see anymore shoes here.

"Hey Barney, we the only guys to come over here? No other shoes."

Barney shook his head. "Mamasan runs eight girls. If none of them are away or flying Baker, we should see eight girls when we go in. Besides, Mamasan will take the shoes away to shine them."

Mamasan trotted back to her kitchen, chattering loudly as she went. A shoji slid and banged open and five girls came down the hallway to the door. Another surprise: they were not in traditional kimonos; they were dressed as American bobby soxers with one variation: they wore tabi's—sort of sox with a split for a separate big toe. Lee was disappointed in the changed style and he didn't recognize any of the girls. The one he had been with wasn't there. So he would try a new one.

Barney pointed to one girl, crooking his finger.

"Bahni," another one laughed, "yo buttahfry boya."

"What's she mean, Barney?" Lee asked as Barney grinned.

"A butterfly boy is one who has to taste all the nectar, not just staying with one girl. Girls come and go. I told you I was going to screw a different one every liberty. This is a nice house and I gotta great room. Mamasan knows what I like to eat and drink. She even has some Asahi beer, Stew."

Lee nodded again and looked at the stocky, small girl who had come up to him. He didn't care so long as the rust came out.

"What's your name?" Lee asked.

"Mah namu Bet ti," she answered.

Aw for crying out loud, an American name.

"No, what's your Japanese name?"

"You no can say it. Mah namu Bet ti!"

"Okay, Betty it is. My name is Lee."

"Ree?"

"No, Lee!" Lee was smiling as he responded with a strong L.

"I no say Ree?"

"Forget it. Call me Stew."

"Okay, Stoo," she laughed, then chattered with the other girls.

"Lee, give Mamasan seventeen hundred Yen. Mamasan still has your hundred Yen note. She was horrified that cabbie tried to cheat you. Then, take your girl and go do your thing for a while. We'll get together later and eat steak and eggs with Asahi, okay?"

"Right, Barney. Don't forget to ask about a discount."

"Asshole!"

Lee laughed as he handed Mamasan the Jap money and followed Betty down the hall to her room. His urges were strong and he reached out to softly slide his hand along her bottom. She jumped as if he had goosed her. "Noni, Stoo, you no do dat. Everybody see—no good. You wait we get rooma—okay?"

"You mean I can't touch you until we're in your room?" asked Lee incredulously.

"Hai. Not nice. Japanese no do."

"But who's to see us here in passageway?" Lee was plainly puzzled by this turn of events.

What was going to happen when they got in her room?

"You no touch—okay?" she asked very firmly.

"Okay."

It was winter and cold. As soon as they got into the room and closed the shoji, he noticed it was warmer.

"Now you touch all you want, Stew. Dis private. No one see. No one come in hyah."

Stew reached out and began to play with her body and squeeze her small breasts. Holding her against his chest, he massaged her bottom even as he glanced around. He felt and saw what Charles and Kiki had described last fall. The habachi pot had no smoke coming out of it but plenty of heat. Betty pulled away and undressed. Lee hastily stripped to nothing as she giggled. He turned to Betty ready for some exercise and saw that she now had on a plain kimono.

"Stoo, giva yo u ni foma, now."

He was at the ready. Betty went to the shoji and called out. Someone took all his clothes from her. She closed the shoji and turned around, dropping the kimono.

"You rika me, Stoo?" she asked smiling.

CHARGE!

Barney and Lee sat with their legs under the short table feasting on small tough steaks, three very small eggs, and fried tomatoes. Their Asahi beer was warm with broken ice in the glass. Their girls rubbed their backs and chattered while Lee and Barney savored a wonderful late dinner. All too soon, Mamasan brought them their uniforms and the girls helped them dress.

The rain was icy cold and coming down in sheets pushed by gusty winds as Barney and Lee dashed out into the darkness to the pedicab waiting with its top up, and climbed inside. This cabbie was dressed in a black rain suit and hat to keep dry. He buttoned the top's front closed so they wouldn't get wet. Even so, water leaked through the buttoned openings pushed by a strong wind. Barney and Lee could see where they were through isinglass windows on all four sides.

When the cabbie stopped on the street outside the Main Gate, Barney paid him a hundred-Yen and they dashed through the rain for the gate. Flashing their cards with Barney in the lead, they jumped on board the bus just before it left.

Another change. We don't have to use a Pro Kit now before reentering the base. I wonder why?

After a ride all over the Base, the bus finally stopped at their pier. Their freshly pressed blues were soaked. Lee's peacoat was soggy with rain but as he knew from previous experience, he stayed warm inside.

"Request permission to come aboard, sir," he said, saluting the fantail and the Officer of the Deck, while showing his ID and Liberty Card to him.

"Permission granted. Put your Liberty Card in that box," he said pointing to a metal box with a slot in the top.

That's new, too.

Stewart dropped his salute and moved over to the box, watched carefully by the Boatswain's Mate of the Watch. He heard Barney reporting aboard in the background.

He waited until Barney dropped his card, and they clattered down the ladder by Sick Bay and headed forward and down to their compartment. Stewart looked at his watch and saw they had squeezed liberty dry. It was 2226. Liberty still expired on board at 2230 for non-rated men. Close, but he had made it in time.

As Lee undressed for bed he reflected on the evening's adventure. Betty didn't want him to butterfly in her house. If he came to her house, he was to stay with her and not any other girl. If he went to another girl, she would be humiliated—lose face—because she was not good enough for him.

Lee had argued she was seeing several sailors and marines every night, so she was already a butterfly girl. He laughed quietly to himself as he remembered her indignant reply. "Me no buttahfry gir—me biznesss gir."

But, it would be okay if he went to a bunch of other houses to different girls each time. She said no one in her house would know about that and that wouldn't hurt. It had been a great liberty, but five bucks a pop? Whew! Not sure about that.

0845, January 5, 1951
ComNavFE Legal Office
U.S. Naval Station,
Yokosuka, Japan

Stewart had the morning watch on Combat's Harbor Common voice circuit. His job was to listen for radio calls to the Hoquiam, write down any message for the Hoquiam, and ask the Radio Shack Messenger—usually him—to pick up the message for write up and delivery. He was bored out of his skull, which was why he was about half way through Zane Grey's western novel, "30,000 on the Hoof."

"Stewart?"

Stewart, in his dungarees, pivoted in his chair and scrambled to attention. The Executive Officer, Lt. Marston, stood in the open hatchway. "Yes sir, Mr. Marston. Can I help you?"

"Yes, Stewart." Lieutenant Marston entered Combat, closing the hatch behind him, and slid onto one of the stools facing Stewart across the plywood sheet where the DRT was supposed to be and motioned for Stewart to sit. He laid his combination hat on the plywood, glanced at the paperback and frowned saying nothing out loud. Stewart sat back down, just a shade uneasy.

"I have made arrangements for us to go to ComNavFE Legal Office so you can make a deposition about that girl, Betty Echols, in Astoria."

Lt. Marston pulled out his cigarettes and a real Ronson lighter. He lit up as he put his thoughts in order.

"Here's what will likely take place. Two Navy officers who are attorneys will question you for the record. They have the letters and the picture. Some of their questions are going to get right down to the smell on your pleasure finger. But that's their job. One will represent the Clatsop County District Attorney; the other will represent you. It's a standard routine as far as they are concerned."

Lt. Marston stopped for a second to drag on his cigarette, let the smoke trickle from his nose and then tapped his cigarette tip into the square aluminum ashtray. He pointed the cigarette at Stewart.

"Just you make sure you have your facts straight. Be absolutely as objective as you possibly can." Stewart nodded agreement. "Try to keep your emotions out of your comments and answers. They will send a transcript of the deposition, and a copy of the District Attorney's letter, as well as a copy of her letter, to the Navy Department in Washington, D.C., to the Naval Station Tongue Point Legal Office, and also to that Clatsop County District Attorney."

"Thank you, sir. When do I do all this?" Stewart asked.

"Masters is going to relieve you in a few minutes. You and I will go over in the ship's jeep and get it done. Okay?" Marston asked with a smile.

"Oh, yes sir."

"I'll be in my stateroom. You need to shift into undress blues, Stewart. Knock when you're ready."

"Aye aye, sir."

Stewart shook his head as he thought back to that letter from Betty, and the other one from the District Attorney.

The whole thing is unreal. I'm sure glad I never got a piece of tail from her!

Lt. Marston led the way into ComNavFE Headquarters. He hadn't been here before. He hesitated as he looked around for an office directory. "Where's the directory? Do you see it, Stewart?"

Stewart looked around but about the moment he spotted it, Mr. Marston touched his shoulder and motioned to the left wall. ComNavFE Legal offices were located in Room 217, the second floor. They turned and went up the stairs to the second floor where a sign on the wall pointed them to the left.

Stewart stepped around Lt. Marston and opened the door for him. Mr. Marston smiled at him, removing his hat as he did. Stewart hastily followed suit.

A civilian lady in a grey wool dress with a blue button sweater stopped typing as she looked up at them with a question in her smile.

Not bad. Nice perfume, too.

"Lt. Marston and Seaman Apprentice Stewart are here for a deposition," responded Mr. Marston.

"Certainly, Mr. Marston. If you will follow me, I'll get you set up in the conference room." She rose as she spoke and walked out of the office, checking to see if they were following her. Her high heels clicked on the highly polished green linoleum tile. Their feet thumped in unison as they followed. She stopped before double doors at the end of the hall and opened one. She looked at them and pointed inside. "There is coffee and tea, and of course, you may smoke. This will be an informal hearing. The others will be along in just a minute."

Mr. Marston thanked her and headed for the coffee. "Coffee, Stewart?"

"Yes sir. Thank you, sir," he replied and followed Lt. Marston to the table with coffee silexes on warmers. He took his coffee from Mr. Marston and looked around. There was a very long table with eight chairs on either side. Five-inch brass shell case ashtrays were placed between every two seats along the table. Stewart stood uneasily, waiting. Lt. Marston drifted over to the windows to look out upon Tokyo Bay and Yokosuka Harbor.

He beckoned to Stewart who joined him at the window. He pointed to their ship in dry dock. "It looks so small, doesn't it?" As Stewart was about to answer, the door was pulled open and three people walked in.

"Lieutenant Marston?" a Lieutenant Commander asked.

"Yes sir, John Marston, and this is Seaman Apprentice Lee Stewart," he responded while swinging his arm around to include Stewart.

The navy officer in sharp dress blues smiled at Stewart. "My name is Janus, and I will act for the District Attorney of Clatsop County, Oregon." Stewart and Lt. Marston nodded together.

Mr. Janus turned to look at the other officer and back to Lt. Marston and Stewart. "This is Mr. Allison who will be your defense attorney, Stewart. WAVE Yeoman Ware is the court recorder who will take down everything we say." He paused. "Any questions, so far?"

"Oh, no sir," Stewart replied.

"Good. This hearing is very important for you. So, take your coffee and sit down in that chair. You can drag out your cigarettes and smoke if you like."

Thank you, sir." Stewart did as told and pulled an ash try toward him. He looked around and discovered Mr. Marston had retired to a corner to observe.

Ware, WAVE Yeoman First Class, or YN1, had pulled a wheeled cart into the room with her. She set her operation where she had a clear view of Stewart and the podium to be used by Mr. Janus and Mr. Allison. Lee took his time looking her over, noticing her well stacked body held up by a pair of shapely legs.

Oh, she would be nice to get next to, I'll bet.

Ware laid out several sharpened pencils and two new steno pads, plus one she already had open in her hand. Pencil poised, she was ready. She looked at Stewart, raised her right hand, and said: "Stand and raise your right hand, Stewart."

Stewart jumped to his feet and raised his right hand as Ware was doing.

"You swear to tell the truth, the whole truth, and nothing but the truth, Stewart? Say 'I do'."

Visibly nervous, Stewart cleared his throat, darted a look at Lt. Marston, and said "I do."

Lieutenant Commander Janus stepped to the podium, looked at everyone, nodded to Ware, cleared his throat, and smiled at Stewart. "Stewart, be seated."

As Stewart resumed his chair, Janus began to depose Stewart. "It is ten oh eight, January fifth, nineteen fifty-one. I am Lieutenant Commander Arthur T. Janus, attached Commander, U.S. Naval Forces, Far East, in Yokosuka, Japan, as the senior legal officer, acting for the District Attorney, Clatsop County, Oregon. With me is Lieutenant James Z. Allison, also attached to ComNavFE, as a legal officer, defending Lee Herbert Stewart, Seaman Apprentice, U.S.S. Hoquiam PF-5, formerly assigned to U.S. Naval Station Tongue Point, Astoria, Oregon. WAVE Yeoman First Class Peggy Ware, ComNavFE, senior Court Reporter, will record these proceedings."

"I will now read into the record the reason we are deposing Stewart." He cleared his throat again. "This is an official letter from the Office of the District Attorney, Clatsop County, the State of Oregon. It is addressed to Lee Stewart, SA, Communications Department, U.S. Naval Station Tongue Point, Astoria, Oregon, and is dated November fifteenth, nineteen fifty."

He glanced at Stewart to make sure he was paying attention to him.

"A felony warrant has been issued for your immediate arrest. Three attempts have been made to contact you regarding the minor child, Betty Echols, and her unborn child. You are charged with Statutory Rape and contributing to the delinquency of a minor by serving her intoxicants."

Stewart shifted angrily in his seat.

"Miss Echols declares you the father of her unborn child, that you got her drunk, and made your way with her. Further, when she advised you of the consequences, you declined to respond to her telephone calls or letters. The County Children's Protective Service is making funds available to Miss Echols' family to pay for her prenatal care, the child's birth, and after birth child care. The State of Oregon is asking the Department of the U.S. Navy to withhold these funds from your pay until the issue reaches the age of maturity. It is signed A.J. Crowlane, District Attorney."

There was silence as Mr. Janus looked at Stewart. "Stewart, these are very serious charges. If true, you could go to Mare Island Naval Prison for a long time. Let's see. You, Lee Stewart, a minor, obtained some kind of alcoholic beverage."

Stewart squirmed in his seat wanting to say something. Lt. Allison caught Stewart's attention and slowly shook his head. His meaning was clear — Be Quiet!

"This is a fairly serious offense in itself." Janus nodded to himself and continued. "It says here you gave enough alcohol to Betty, a minor, enough of it she didn't know what you were doing. That's another more serious offense."

Stewart was beginning to back up tight against his chair, scared of these accusations. He began shaking his head.

"Don't shake your head at me, Stewart. I haven't finished yet. Having gotten her so drunk she didn't know what was going on, you removed some of her clothing— at least her underwear—and forced her to have sexual relations with you. That's not statutory rape: it is rape! Statutory rape is when she is under age but getting with the program. Do you understand the difference?"

"No sir, I mean yes sir, I know the difference. It was not me."

"I'm not done yet, Stewart. Your relations with her were strong enough to cause pregnancy."

"That's not my baby, sir."

"Be silent!" Janus roared, "I am not yet finished."

Lt. Allison stood, knocking his chair to the floor. "Mr. Janus, I'll remind you this is not a court of law, this is a deposition regarding the charges against my client." The two attorneys glared at each other, then Mr. Allison broke off to pick up his chair and sit down.

Lieutenant Commander Janus took a moment to slow his racing pulse and take count of where he was.

"Very well, Stewart," he said in a milder tone, "these are pretty serious charges. What have you to say for yourself?"

"That is not my baby, sir. I never screwed h…"

He glanced at Ware and blushed. "I mean I never had sexual relations with Betty."

Ware broke in. "I couldn't hear your reply, Stewart."

Mr. Janus answered for Stewart. "He said he never screwed her, Peggy. Pay attention." Mr. Allison snorted and Mr. Marston covered his mouth and tried not to make a sound but a muffled chuckle came out anyway.

"Yes sir," Ware smiled.

"Every red blooded young man wants to make love to every girl he goes out with. You did try, didn't you?" Janus asked.

Stewart squirmed in his chair. "Yes sir, but I never got there."

"Well, how far did you get?" Mr. Janus probed, leaning over the podium.

"Well, I just never got there," Stewart replied with a quick glance at Ware, and blushing as he remembered.

"Okay, let's take it one step at a time. Did you kiss her?

"Yes sir."

"Did you French kiss her?"

"No sir, she wouldn't let me do that."

"Hmmm. I'm sure you held hands. Did you touch any other part of her body?"

Stewart's voice dropped to nearly a whisper. "Yes sir."

"I'm sorry, I can't hear you, Stewart," said Ware.

He looked at her. "I said 'yes sir'."

"Don't make me drag this out of you body part by body part. Where all did you touch her?" prompted Mr. Janus.

"After we got to know each other, just about everywhere, sir."

"You have to be more explicit, Stewart. Did you touch her breasts?"

Stewart nodded.

Ware piped up, "You have to answer out loud, Stewart."

He turned beet red. "Yes, I touched her breasts."

"Good, now we are getting somewhere. Did you rub them or kiss them? What did you do?"

"Uh, sir, I just squeezed them through her brassiere. She wouldn't let me take her bra off or pull it aside."

"I see. So, you are saying you never actually saw her breasts, is that right?"

"Yes sir." In a rush he continued, "she did like me to pick her up by her bottom and to rub her cheeks when I was holding her close."

Mr. Janus looked at him for a moment. "Stewart, stand up and pantomime what you mean. I want to see if I understand you correctly."

Stewart glanced at Ware and shook his head. "No sir, I can't do that."

His voice was very cold as Mr. Janus ordered, "That was not a request sailor; do as you are told."

"Sir, I can't do it with Ware sitting there watching me."

Mr. Janus looked at him, then at Ware. "Get this through your head, Stewart. She is not a woman, she is my court reporter."

"Oh, no sir, Ware is very much a woman, sir!"

It was Ware's turn to have rosy cheeks.

Mr. Marston approached Mr. Allison and whispered in his ear.

Lt. Allison suggested that Ware close her eyes while Stewart was demonstrating his petting action.

Ware turned bright red.

Mr. Janus looked at Mr. Allison, then Stewart, and finally Ware. "Peggy, close your eyes so you can't see this fellow demonstrate, okay?"

Ware nodded, closed her eyes, and stayed bright red.

Mr. Janus looked at Stewart. "Stand up and show us what you did regularly."

As he stood, he said, "Well, it was in the dark and where we were alone." He closed his eyes and pantomimed holding Betty close and letting his hands slide down her back, following the curve of her ass and lifting her for a better kiss. Then letting her down and softly petting or rubbing her bottom.

It had to happen: he got a strong hardon.

"Thank you, Stewart. Now, we all understand—all of it."

Stewart opened his eyes and found Ware looking at him with a big smile on her face.

"You cheated!" He exclaimed indignantly.

"As you were, Stewart!" roared Mr. Janus. "Now, what else did you touch or feel?"

"I tried to touch her pussy, I mean..."

"Stewart, let me again explain the ground rules regarding Ware. She may be a female but she regularly hears and records all kinds of nasty and foul language in hearing rooms like this. This is impersonal. If you did or said some of those things outside this room, that would be personal. Do you get the drift of that?"

"Yes sir. Betty never let me touch her pussy directly. I could feel it through her dress or shorts, but that was all."

"You are still insisting you never had sexual relations with Miss Echols, is that correct?"

"Sir," he blurted out, "I never got that close!"

Lieutenant Commander Janus studied Stewart for a moment. He turned and stared out the window at Tokyo Bay before continuing. "Stewart, did Betty ever play with your penis?"

Stewart swallowed and cleared his throat nervously. "Well, she liked to stroke it and squeeze it, sir."

"In or out of your pants?"

"At first…"

"Louder, Stewart, I can't hear you." Both Mr. Janus and Ware spoke at the same time.

Clearing his throat, Stewart took a sip of coffee and lit a Camel, waiting for his own cheeks to cool.

"Stewart, I'm waiting for an answer."

"Uh, sir, at first she just brushed it with the back of her hand."

"And then?"

"Well, then she began touching it. A little later she started squeezing Junior…"

"Junior?" Ware snickered. Stewart turned beet red, realizing what he had said.

"Nothing sir. She began squeezing…"

"You said Junior, is that someone's pet name for your penis?"

Stewart's shoulders slumped. "Yes, sir, mine, sir."

"Very well, you were saying something about Betty squeezing Junior?"

"Yes, sir. And while I was feeling her breasts, she undid my side buttons and slid her hand in to play with him."

"Him?"

"Junior, sir."

"Her hand was ice cold, I remember that," he muttered.

Stewart was so rattled by this time he didn't realize he said that out loud until all three officers and Ware broke out laughing. When they calmed down and Mr. Janus could keep a straight face, turned back to the window and asked: "And, was this all on one date, Stewart?"

"Oh, no sir. I think this was the fourth time we went out walking at night, just to be alone."

"She wouldn't let you see or touch her breasts directly but you let her touch and masturbate—Junior. Is that correct? Did that seem fair to you, or did you try to make some kind of trade like," he paused for dramatic effect, "I'll let you see mine if I can see yours?"

"That's just the way it was, sir. I tried for a trade. She wouldn't go for that, and I liked it when she played with me, so why stop it?"

"Did you get any further with her?"

Stewart was aware his hardon had not diminished at all and was sure that Ware could see it. "A little bit. The next night I let her take it out so she could see it."

"You did say this was night and it was dark, didn't you?"

"Wasn't that dark!" He shot back, sullenly.

Mr. Janus whipped around from the window and came to stand directly in front of Stewart. "Mind your manners and military courtesies, Stewart." he snapped.

"Yes sir, Sorry, sir. She did lean over a little bit to take a good look at it."

"Did she kiss it or take it in her mouth, Stewart?" he asked, very evenly.

Stewart's eyes widened in shock and he straightened with a jerk. "Oh, no sir, nothing like that happened. She just wanted to see what one looked like. At least, I got to touch her crotch through her dress that time."

"Oh? Anything else happen that was interesting?"

"Well, sir. She played with Junior for quite a while and I came. That really made her mad because her hand was all gooey and the juice messed up the side of her dress pretty bad."

"I see. Was that all?"

"Yes sir. As a matter of fact, Betty used my handkerchief to clean her hand and dress. Wouldn't let me help at all. That was the last time she wanted to play around, sir."

Mr. Janus announced: "Let's take a ten minute break. When we get back, Lt. Allison will present the defense. Stewart was grateful for the break. He needed to get rid of a lot of coffee.

After the break, Lt. Allison stood and nodded to Ware. He held up a letter and photograph in his hand. "This is a letter from Betty Echols asking," he paused for emphasis, "asking Stewart to marry her because she was pregnant and scared. Let me read the letter into the record. It was written in cursive pen with blue ink on plain paper and is dated September first, nineteen fifty."

Stewart leaned back and looked out the window into the Yokosuka anchorage. He'd read this letter enough times he didn't care to listen to Mr. Allison reading it.

"'Dearest Lee, I haven't heard from you for the longest time. You told me your restriction was only for a month. Yesterday when I tried to call you, the sailor said he couldn't find you. I heard him calling you on the P.A. system, but you didn't come. I cried most of the night. I miss you so much. Why haven't you called me? I had hoped that after our wonderful Memorial Day weekend that you loved me a little. But you would never say that to me. If you had, I would have let you go all the way with me. Lee, please call me. I'm real scared and don't know what to do. A guy named Ralph was my date for the graduation party. He got me drunk and had his way with me in his car." Allison paused to drink some water. "Last Thursday, our family doctor told me I'm two and a half months pregnant. Mom and Dad don't know yet. When I told Ralph Thursday night, he said he would see me Friday afternoon after work. Saturday, I called Mrs. Rogers, his mother, and she said he decided to join the Air Force yesterday and has already gone to Texas. I need to get married soon. Won't you marry me right away? Everyone at church still thinks we're practically engaged. So, if we got married suddenly, no one would be shocked. Please Lee, I don't have much time. All my love, Betty. P.S. My girlfriend Sally took this picture in our back yard.'"

Mr. Allison stopped and looked around. "This poor girl only wanted a husband to protect her and her baby's name. She chose Stewart apparently because he was a nice guy and her parents liked him too, not because he was the father."

"She and Stewart did what most dating couples do. They petted each other but never went all the way."

Turning directly to Stewart, "Stewart, did you ever insert your penis into Betty's vagina and have sexual intercourse?"

Stewart stood and looked at Ware, Mr. Marston, Mr. Janus, and finally Mr. Allison. "No sir. We never petted after that last time when she got mad. A week later, her Dad announced to everybody in church that we were a couple. I decided I had had enough and never went back to Betty's house or saw her or talked to her on the phone after that. I avoided her completely." He sat down, drenched in his sweat.

Mr. Allison looked down at his notes and the letters from Astoria and spoke. "Let us take into account the weeks that passed from the mailing in Astoria until Betty's and the Clatsop County District Attorney's letters were received aboard Hoquiam. Why didn't Mr. Crowlane call the base Chaplain, the Captain, or some other officer at Naval Station Tongue Point? Why didn't Mr. and Mrs. Echols try to contact some navy official at Tongue Point?"

Mr. Allison shuffled his papers into neat alignment, slipped them into a manila folder and sat down.

Mr. Janus cleared his throat and asked, "Were those questions rhetorical or did you expect me to second guess what occurred in Astoria?"

"Rhetoric, Mr. Janus. I am finished," he said.

"Then, everyone, this hearing is adjourned." Mr. Janus tapped the table with his hand as though it were a gavel and looked around. "We are done here, people," sighed Lieutenant Commander Janus.

Stewart sagged in his chair.

It's over.

Lieutenant Commander Janus, acting for the District Attorney agreed with Lieutenant Allison, acting as Stewart's Defense Attorney, that Stewart had no problem at all.

"Stewart, this is what will happen. We, ComNavFE Legal Department, are going to fire off a letter with this deposition and copies of the other letters, to Naval Station Tongue Point Legal Office for them to take corrective action." Stewart nodded as he listened.

"You can expect to hear from Tongue Point and Clatsop County as early as the beginning of February. This will backfire in Miss Echols's face."

Even Ware nodded sympathetically. Stewart turned beet red when he thought of all the things he had said to the navy attorneys.

"You will probably receive a letter of apology from the District Attorney. If Miss Echols happens to write to you, let Lieutenant Marston open it, as a qualified witness."

Lt. Marston nodded to Stewart and looked back at the Lieutenant Commander.

"Then he will hand it to you to read before resealing the letter in the envelope in case there are further charges." Lieutenant Commander Janus looked at Lieutenant Allison and Ware, and at Lt. Marston and Stewart. "As I said before, if there is nothing further, we are done here."

"Thank you, sirs, for helping me out here," said Stewart. Mr. Janus smiled and nodded as he and Lt. Allison headed out the door. Ware stood up and stretched her arms up and out, wriggling a numb butt.

She really is put together rather nicely.

She caught him admiring her figure and smiled. "Stewart, she's not a nice girl. Good story. You won't have any problem at all."

"Were you supposed to say that, Ware?" Asked Mr. Marston.

She shrugged and tossed her head. "Nooo, but after what Mr. Janus put him through, Stewart deserves a little encouragement." She gathered her tablets in a neat pile and began pushing her roller table toward the door. Stewart hastily moved to the door and opened it for her.

"Thanks." She looked at him with a big smile and in a low voice with elements of laughter said, "Junior?" as she disappeared through the doorway. Stewart's face surged with a tinge of red embarrassment made worse as Mr. Marston chuckled.

"Come on, Stewart. She's not for you. We've got to get back to the ship."

"Aye aye, sir. Mr. Marston, you're not going to tell anyone, are you? I mean—you know . . . . "

Mr. Marston turned away with a grin and didn't answer. He thought it would make a great story in the wardroom.

January 8, 1951
USS Hoquiam PF-5
Moored Pier A-6
SRF, Yokosuka, Japan

It was amazing how hard those Japs worked down in the bottom of the dry dock. SRF had time to install a new Pitt Log—a very small propeller turned by the ship's movement through the water, to measure and record a ship's speed.

The ship's bottom was sandblasted and repainted again while the sonar sound dome was being removed. Meanwhile, the topside workers were prettying up the hull and superstructure again.

Three days after Hoquiam entered dry dock, she was floated and pulled back to Pier Able, Berth 6. The Radarmen were about to have a baby waiting for their new DRT and some new radio remote positions. Naturally, another trip into dry dock was scheduled to replace the sound dome.

Crew training on the base continued as the Ship Repair Facility worked around the clock to bring Hoquiam up to snuff. On an unclassified message run to the Yokosuka Naval Base Message Center, Stewart learned something of value and decided to test the waters.

"What the fuck is this shit, Stewart?" growled James. He had a frown on his face as he read again Stewart's request chit.

I thought it was pretty clear, myself.

"It says here you want to go to that candyass Morse code school over on the base." James stretched out the chit to Stewart, unsigned. "I can't afford to let you go, Stew. There's too much work to do here. Besides, you're almost up to copying fox"—CW broadcast to all ships—"solid and you get to sit on the Task Group Common"—CW circuit between ships within a Task Group."

He flashed a look of exasperation at Stewart, as Stewart looked back at him stonily with his arms folded across his chest, ignoring James' extended arm.

"James, if I'm that good, then why aren't I Seaman? You gave me good quarterly marks for the quarter. I've been doing a good job and haven't been in trouble. There's only three SA's in the department and I have a hell of a lot more time in grade than the other two in Sonar and Combat, and neither one of them was advanced to Seaman when they graduated from their schools. Not only that but I heard that the top two or three in the code classes are advanced to RMSN."

James waved his arm at Stewart again to take back the request chit and thought about what Stewart was saying.

It's true. He ought to be seaman by this time.

He looked up a Stewart, who was looking pretty het up at the injustice of it all.

"Tell you what, Stew. If you take this chit back, I'll talk to Mr. Forsythe about it this morning and see if we can set up a Seaman's exam for you. Really, I don't know what is involved here. Would you tear up the chit for that? We really need you right here."

Oh ho! I seem to have a bargaining point here.

Stewart thought about what James was offering against the chance to get additional training he thought ought to be important.

But damn it all to hell, I need to get advanced. This Seaman Deuce shit is getting old after almost two years.

A little nervously, he answered. "James, why don't you sign that chit and take it up to Mr. Forsythe. Then, talk to him. I think that Morse school at ComNavFE would help me and I sure as shit have earned the right to at least take the test for SN."

James glared at Stewart, laid the chit on his desk—the CW circuit Communications Position that he used as his desk—and pulled out his fountain pen. Unscrewing the cap rapidly, he checked off DISAPPROVED and signed his name.

"Okay Stewart, I disapproved your request and will give it to Mr. Forsythe after quarters. Now, sweep down and make another fuckin' pot of coffee!"

"THIS IS A F R S TOKYO WITH THE MORNING NEWS JANUARY NINTH, AIRMAN MIKE DILL REPORTING. UNITED NATIONS COMMAND IN KOREA REPORTS THAT MATTHEW B. RIDGEWAY, COMMANDING GENERAL OF THE EIGHTH ARMY, IS VISITING TROOPS ALL ALONG THE LINE IN AN EFFORT TO IMPROVE MORALE."

"Here's your chit back, Stewart. It has been disapproved all the way up but please read Mr. Marston's note."

Stewart sighed, took back his chit and looked at the disapproval by James and Messrs. Forsythe, Porter, and Marston.

Great, just jim fucking dandy!

He turned it over and began to read the Executive Officer's typed note.

1. SA Stewart's request for ComNavFE Morse code school is without merit. This school is designed for Deck or other personnel not yet designated strikers for any rating, who have no Morse code knowledge or speed. James, his LPO, states Stewart has reached a level of code expertise shared by most radiomen striker graduates, and better than a lot of Reserve fleet radiomen.

2. His LPO also noted that Stewart has not been given an opportunity to compete for Seaman since this ship was commissioned. Neither has any other FA nor SA had an opportunity to be examined for advancement.

3. Noting his practical factors examination is over a year old, Chief Billons will have to sign off his seamanship ability. If Stewart is ready by February 1, 1951, he may participate in the ship wide examination for advancement to E3 as Seaman. The written examinations, designed by senior petty officers and Division Officers, will be conducted Monday, February 5, 1951.

Holy Shit! Billy boy gets to set my Practical Factors test? He has to pass me? Mother Goose. Not a Chinaman's chance in hell!

Stewart looked up at James with wild eyes and was interrupted before he could start.

"I already know what you got in mind, Stew. Chief Billons is the Chief Boatswain's Mate on this ship. He does have the necessary knowledge."
Well, that's true enough.

"You have had your share of problems with the old chief."

Fuckin' A John, Lord knows I have.

"But he will write the Seaman's Practical Factors test, as Chief Dortas will write the Fireman's Practical Factors test. Everyone is going to be tested on the same day.

That's fair enough. Well, maybe I have a chance after all. I wonder if I get a chance to see what Billy boy is going to do before the test?

"Both tests will be based, in part, on the Hoquiam's equipment and layout."

Uh oh!

"Excuse me, James. When I took the practical factors on the Chilton I was a Sidecleaner. It included a walk-through of the after port twin 40mm anti-aircraft gun-tub because I was Pointer on that gun-tub. I had to pipe five different calls recognizably because they had me slated to be a Boatswain's Mate; tie eight knots and explain their uses; explain LCVP Whalen Davit operations; and be thoroughly familiar with U.S. Inland River and Harbor Rules of the Road." Lee swallowed and took another breath. "Now, you got any idea of what Billy boy is going to do?"

By the time Stewart had finished spouting off his old practical factors test, Coyle, Lloyd, and Griffin were staring at him in surprise. Masters beat the others to the punch.

"Stew, I understand the knots—makes sense—even the 40mm trick, but why the rest of that shit?"

That's right, no one except James knows what I was doing before this.

"Hank, this time a year ago, I was a qualified LCVP Assault Boat Coxswain on the Chilton, going to be given Seaman if I shipped over on board, and was already using my own Bosun's Pipe. But I didn't want to be a Boatswain's Mate. Problem is, I don't know diddly squat about Hoquiam's tackle (pronounced tay-kul) or the 3-inch gun mount."

"You mean you could drive our Motor Whaleboat?" asked Coyle.

"Shit no, but drop me into an LCVP and watch my dust."

"But what about the pipe, Stewart. Did you actually blow one of those things?"

Oops, when did Mr. Forsythe walk in?

Stewart twisted around to look at Mr. Forsythe.

"Yes sir. I gave my pipe to Deak, my P.O., before I left the Chilton, just about a year ago."

The 1MC opened and the 'wheezer' played Sweepers. Stewart grinned as he cocked his ear and listened to him. "A hell of a lot better than that, Mr. Forsythe."

Mr. Forsythe smiled, shaking his head the while, and picked up the board to check for new messages.

"THIS IS A F R S TOKYO WITH THE MORNING NEWS JANUARY TENTH NINETEEN FIFTY-ONE, STAFF SERGEANT DAN PETERSON REPORTING. UNITED NATIONS COMMAND IN KOREA REPORTS THE FIRST MARINE DIVISION HAS LAUNCHED AN ATTACK IN THE MASAN - POHANG - SONDONG - ANDONG AREA TO ELIMINATE NORTH KOREAN GUERRILLA FORCES ATTACHED TO THE N K P A TENTH DIVISION."

Stewart leaned against the lifelines, smoking in the chill air, and taking in the ugly Yokosuka harbor and waterfront low tide perfume.

Lord, Hungnam didn't smell this bad!

They'd been in port for almost two weeks now. He and his shipmates were beginning to relax as the tension eased off from being along the East Coast of North Korea where loose mines floated offshore. His belly wasn't as tight as it had been. Lee was getting used to getting a full night's sleep when he wasn't standing the midwatch.

Stewart looked up in the direction of Kimiko and Kiki's apartment with longing. He had asked Charles this afternoon to see if Kimiko had any news of Kiki yet.

It will be great if she comes back from Sendai 'cause she does love to fuck. Wonder if I'll ever see her again. Sure didn't last long though. One thing I'm not going to do is go over to Kimiko's with Charles just to torture myself.

He jumped as a cough behind him surprised him. Whirling, he was caught off guard by Chief Billons standing there.

What the fuck is this shit? Why did he sneak up on me like that?

Billy boy stood there looking at him intently.

"Stewart," he growled softly, "you gawd damned radio pussy. You just can't have done the things I've been hearing about. You and a pipe? Assault Boat Coxswain? Shee-it," he drawled. But he wasn't frowning—just looking at him very curious like.

Stewart relaxed and leaned back against the lifelines, studying the Chief. Finally, he smiled and held out his hand, palm up. Billons recognized a challenge when he saw one and unclipped his pipe from its Navy blue lanyard—Chief Billons had weaved several lanyards, one for each color of uniform—and placed it in Stewart's hand with a not quite friendly smile.

Stewart, burning with the heap of injustice, let his feelings get in the way of being smart, as he wiped off the mouthpiece.

"You want some lessons, Chief? Is that why you handed it over? Are you the wheezer?"

Oh shit!

Chief Billons had him hanging backwards over the lifeline, his feet off the deck, far enough that if the Chief let go Stewart was going to take a bath.

"Listen, shit for brains. I been hearing things about you, good things I just can't believe. YOU said YOU could play a pipe. Now before I think about the rest of the shit I heard, asshole, play me your pipe."

Chief Billons eased Stewart from the lifeline and let him stretch his back.

"Okay, okay, Chief," while he stretched. "I ain't piped in a year." The Chief nodded acknowledgment and waved to the pipe.

Stewart looked at the pipe, which just fell into place automatically. The Chief noticed that. Wriggling his fingers in nearly forgotten motions, he brought the pipe up to the side of his mouth . . .

Here goes nothing . .

and piped Turn To.

Not bad for first draw.

The Chief had a look of surprise on his face.

Next, he called a boat alongside the gangway. Closing his eyes and focusing, he blew Sweepers and shook his head. The Chief gave him a nod and smile of encouragement.

Hmmm, kinda ragged on that.

Then All Hands, Tattoo, Taps, and Knock Off Ship's Work—letting it ring out slowly.

No way was he going to start in on Chow call. Shove that in your pipe, Billy Boy!

He tapped the pipe and wiped off the mouthpiece before handing it back to the Chief. He looked the Chief square in the eye and waited while the Chief refastened the pipe to his lanyard. Out of the corner of his eye, he saw James in the shadows behind Billons, watching. Catching a motion, he glanced at their open porthole and saw three faces watching him.

Wonder how much of this Jimmy Bob heard?

Billons didn't say anything for a while. He seemed to be thinking as he paced up and down in front of Stewart with his hands in his back pockets. Finally he stopped and with a little bit different tone in his voice, he asked Stewart: "Well, now we both know you're better than that Reservist who wheezes. But there is nothing in your service record that says you are a qualified Assault Boat Coxswain. You give me a decent reason for that, Stewart?"

"Yeah, Chief, I can. There's also nothing in my Records that shows I was a Cub Scout, Boy Scout, and Sea Scout, either but that's where I learned a lot of those things, like Morse code, knot tying, respect, honor, duty, and other things that earned Merit Badges. And you know what?"

Billy boy shook his head.

"A lot of that stuff came in handy on the Chilton."

The Chief just nodded and motioned for Lee to continue.

"You see, my Dad's a Mustang Lieutenant. Used to be an IC electrician. Now, he is Chief Engineer on the Siboney, a baby flattop out of Norfolk."

Chief Billons nodded and leaned back against the bulkhead. "So you traveled around a lot, Stewart?"

"Yeah. Back and forth between Long Beach and Bremerton three times before the war, Columbus, Ohio, Miami, and New Orleans in the middle of the war and Long Beach and Bremerton after the war. Never stayed long enough to really get acquainted and have buddies and girl friends."

The Chief nodded in sympathy.

"Anyway, just like transferring school transcripts from school to school, I was able to do the same thing with the Scout stuff." He looked out across the bay at Yokosuka for a moment. Then with a wistful voice, "Except, never got to go to any of the scout camps 'cause we traveled during the summer when school was out. Joined the Sea Scouts in Long Beach and learned to sail in Long Beach Harbor. Moved to Bremerton and transferred into the Sea Scouts there. Learned to navigate around Puget Sound, play the pipe," he lowered his voice "and I could semaphore and stuff like that but don't tell Chief Swenson. Understand now, Chief?"

Chief Billons grinned. "Doesn't explain about being an Assault Boat Coxswain, though."

Stewart sighed. This is really getting into details I'd just as soon forget. "Well, I always figured on joining the Navy—Dad and all. And, I got into electronics in college..."

"You was in college, too?" asked the surprised Chief.

"Yeah, wanted to become a Naval Officer, but ran out of money and joined up. Before I joined up, I took a whole bunch of tests that were supposed to put me into ET school at Great Lakes. But, I couldn't get a hitch long enough to handle that, and had to settle for being a USN-EV, an Enlisted Volunteer.

"That made me an ordinary deck seaman on the Chilton. My boat handling skills were right there and soon the Chief had me practicing on the Silver Strand in a LCVP. Ran army troops and their supplies to the beach during an amphibious operation. Did some day and night ops, too.

"Came time to ship over for six, I wanted ET school and the Chilton offered seaman and designation as Assault Boat Coxswain, and in line to be examined for BM3. So I left."

"You mean you coulda been a BM3 regular by now?"

"Chief, I left the Chilton because I did not want to be a Boatswain's Mate, I wanted to be an ET."

"Then, you mind explaining Radioman to me?"

"'Cuz someone screwed up my reenlistment choices and had me down as an ET grad instead of waiting to go to ET school. I got sent to a Naval Station with one ET3 that was being discharged in a few weeks and I was expected to take his place. That was just too heavy."

"Then, I discovered I had a knack for communications, and settled there. Was supposed to go for Seaman six months ago, but fucked up and lost that chance. Asked for return to sea duty and here I am."

Damn it all to hell, I let this kid get away from me? Shee-it! William, you stupid shitbird.

"Listen Stewart, we need more good seamen in the Deck department. We could really use a good hand like you."

Stewart was taken by surprise.

Christ, I've never heard him talk this softly before.

"If you're interested, I could arrange with Mr. Dixon to have you transferred tomorrow if things aren't the way you like them in the Radio Division."

"Chief, no offense you understand, but making grunting noises on deck is not my idea of a Navy career. I know you like it, but I like the excitement you can only find in Operations. Radio, Combat, Sonar, and the Bridge are more to my liking, you understand that. And, Chief: you know in your heart you can't do 'without gawd damned radio pussy', right?"

Chief Billons nodded, half waved, patted Stewart on the shoulder, and headed forward to his hatch down to the Chiefs' quarters. Stewart watched him go and smugly wondered how much of that James had heard.

More to the point, what is Billy boy going to do to the Practical Factors test, now that he knows more about me? Could he convince Mr. Marston to transfer me to the Deck Department?

Stewart headed below to his sack with a troubled mind.

0755, January 11, 1951
U.S.S. Hoquiam PF-5
SRF, Yokosuka, Japan

A good Bosun's Pipe rang out. "Turn to. Turn to. All hands muster on stations." Then he piped Attention. "Officers' Call, Officers' Call. Assemble in the Ward Room."

After his chat with Billy Boy, Stewart visited Smith YN3, the Training P.O., to check out a Seamanship manual, NavPers 10939, to review. He hadn't thought about seamanship or tied one single knot since he left the Chilton, and this book had all the knots explained in pretty good detail. He begged a four-foot section of quarter-inch line from Hays to practice with. Right now it was warming in his back pocket until he had a chance to practice with it.

He stood there idly by the coffeepot flipping the pages of the manual to see if it was any better than the one he had used on the Chilton. It wasn't—it was older. Battleships were still king shit.

The door crashed open, startling everyone. Stewart leaned over and picked up his training manual. Lt.(jg) Forsythe stood there with a spooky look on his face. His eyes darted around until he spotted James and practically leaped to his side.

"James. We got a problem."

James closed his little green pocket notebook, tossed his head to clear the hair from his eyes, and raised his eyebrows.

"What's up, Mr. Forsythe?"

"ComCortRon Five and the Sausalito are conducting a surprise Administrative Inspection of our ship. They're already in the Wardroom, briefing the Captain, Mr. Marston, and the department heads. What kind of shape are we in?"

Jimmy Bob James smiled and swept his arm in a circle. "Let me see, now. All the brass and copper is shining, bulkheads are clean, the deck is gleaming, and the coffee is fresh. All files and publications are up to snuff. We've sort of developed an unofficial Allowance List since none is available. Right now, I'm filing current signed off traffic."

Then he began pointing to different items as he rattled off the Radio Shack problems that Mr. Forsythe should have been on top of.

"As you can see, the TBL is torn apart for a new oscillator section, the TDZ's autotuner clutch is shot, won't hold any channel in tune, and has to be replaced by SRF, who also has both our typewriters for repair. There is no more carbon paper on the ship—James held up a piece of carbon paper you could see through—all departments are waiting for the next stores run. The same applies to typewriter ribbons. From the last fuckin' typewriter repair trip to SRF, we learned to remove our ribbons before they go over. Last time they came back without any ribbons in them. Other than those minor details, we're ready to get underway right now."

Lt.(jg) Roger Forsythe, USNR, stared at James and slowly turned pale, and left the Radio Shack. "I wonder how many days in hack this will cost me?" James grinned behind his back.

Gotcha!

During an Admin Inspection, the inspectors scrutinize message files, currency of publication corrections, compare actual vs equipment allowance, and other records. Everything had to match. They couldn't give a rat's ass less, about the condition of the physical plant, so long as the paper work about the physical plant was up to date. Whoever came in would probably lay their clipboard on the opened TDE while they checked files and pubs. James continued grinning as he thought of Mr. Forsythe's agony.

We'll get close to a 4.0 on Admin. Thank the Lord this isn't an Operational Readiness Inspection — we'd be fucked!

"Stewart!"

"Suh!" he said, giving a credible imitation of a British soldier reporting.

"Route the fucking board."

"That's a roger, James—any particular thing, or just in general?"

"Go!"

Stewart grabbed the board and headed for the bridge.

No sense in trying the Wardroom. That would be a mess in there.

Grabbing the rail, he spun around and clattered up to the Signal Bridge with the most recent weather.

A ha! Red's got the watch.

Stewart flipped through the messages, pulling the weather copy for the Quartermaster, and had Red sign for it.

"Kiki will be back before April, if you're interested, Stew."

"Wow, that's great news. Any dope on how her mother is making out?"

"Dunno, Stew, Kimiko had a note from her. Kiki didn't go into much detail. If you want to write her a letter, give it to me tonight with a hundred Yen for postage. I'll have Kimiko mail it for you. You got any idea of what would happen if you tried to mail it from the ship?"

"Pretty sure it would go overboard," he said laughing. With a much better feeling in his heart, Stewart took the board back and continued to make his rounds of the offices.

The Captain looked at his assembled officers and smiled. He sipped his coffee and cleared his throat.

"ComCortRon Five awarded the Hoquiam a "Very Good" rating, overall. The highest individual ratings went to the Engineering Log Room and Radio Room."

Lt. Hansen and Lt.(jg) Forsythe grinned at each other with pleasure.

"For your information, most of the frigates received a "Satisfactory" rating, one received a "Poor" rating, and no one received an "Excellent" rating. The fact is, only the Burlingame and Hoquiam got a "Very Good". Let's hope for an "Excellent" rating at the next Admin inspection."

NAVAL SPEEDLETTER
Serial 5110814, January 14, 1951
Commander, Cruiser and Destroyer forces, Pacific
Fleet, aboard U.S.S. Dixie (AD14)
Commanding Officer, U.S.S. Hoquiam (PF5)
Copy to: Commander, Escort Squadron Five,
aboard U.S.S. Sausalito (PF4)
Re: ComCortRon FIVE ltr 1/10/51;
Subject: PF5 Administrative Inspection
The Type Commander understands the hardships
that have accompanied the PF reactivation
program and has observed closely the obstacles
that have had to be overcome to keep this type of
vessel fully operational.

The Hoquiam rolled sluggishly at anchor in the lee of O Jima—a small jungle-infested island near where the U.S. Navy and her Allies held underway-training drills. This week, Hoquiam and Tilefish, a submarine, were to conduct tracking and depth charge attacks, using concussion grenades to make a loud banging noise. SRF had completed an outstanding task on the sonar equipment. The Sonar Shop really had rebuilt the BQF system from the ground up and the Captain was pleased.

Stewart leaned against the starboard 40mm gun tub, foul weather jacket zipped up tight in the cold breeze, enjoying the view of Fujiyama in the moonlight. His quiet thoughts were shattered by the sudden appearance of Chief Billons and two of his Mates bearing down on him.

Now what? Not good, he's trying to smile!

"What do you say, Stewart? Nice night, isn't it?"

Now I know I'm in deep shit.

"Just great, Chief, just great," he smiled back weakly.

Was just great.

"Stewart, do you suppose you could do us a favor?"

Just wait 'till I find a helmet to cover my ass.

"Maybe," he replied cautiously, as he flicked his eyes from one Boatswain's Mate to another.
"First of all, I gotta different opinion of you after we talked the other night.

Uh oh.

I told these guys," thumbing to Hays and Barnes, "about your skill at piping and they just don't believe it Would you be willing to pipe a few calls to prove I'm not a liar?"

I wonder if the mouthpiece is poisoned?

"Sure Chief," he replied, holding out his hand to the chief for his pipe.
But Barnes had a smirk on his face as he handed Stewart his own Bosun's Pipe instead.

Wow! Would you look at this beat up and dented pipe?

He looked at Barnes. "Been using this as a hammer?" Barnes glared back at Stewart and Hays, as Hays turned away and snickered quietly.

Stewart wiped off the mouthpiece and gave a tentative hiss through the pipe while blocking the bowl. The passage was clear. He looked at the chief for direction, wondering what he wanted.

"Give us some of the same you gave me, Stew."

Stew? Chummy now, isn't he? What's he up to?

Stewart began the various pipes again. This time he included the triple long call, Chow. As he kept working the pipe, he noticed Barnes began glaring at everyone there. When he finished, he tapped the pipe to clear it, and wiped the mouthpiece.

"Now see, Barnes. This candy ass punk Seaman Deuce, a Radioman Striker of all things, with just about two years in this man's Navy, can pipe a better tune on your own pipe, than you ever thought of," Billons said.

Oh shit, Barnes is the wheezer. Candy ass? Punk Seaman Deuce? Well, crap!

"Hey Chief, I do you a favor and for thanks, you burn my ass? Thanks a bunch, Boats." Stewart turned and stalked away.

I don't need this shit.

"Stewart." The Chief's voice cracked, "I ain't done. Getcher ass back here!"

Resentfully, Stewart slouched back, hooking his thumbs in his dungaree pockets, looking back and forth at the three Boatswain's Mates.

"Let's talk about the Practical Factors exam you got coming up shortly."

He looks serious. Maybe it's just I don't trust that little fucker as far as I could toss him.

"Okay, Chief, whatcha got?"

"How rusty are you with the knots, Stew?"

"Hmm!"

Stewart pulled out the wadded up piece of line he had gotten from Hays and shook it out. Slowly, Lee began going through the knots he had remastered. Billy boy, Barnes, and Hays watched closely. All three shook their heads when he tried a barrel hitch.

"No no, Stewart. Do it this way," corrected Hays.

He pulled out his own section of line and slowly explained each move as he did it, with Stewart following through.

My, my, my. Who'da thought this would ever happen?

He went through all the knots he could remember and they recalled several more he should know, that might be asked on the Practical Factors exam.

"Okay, that's enough for tonight, fellas. Stew, after knock off ship's work on most nights, these two will help you refresh your memory. Hays will take you through the ground tackle and the full anchoring detail. Barnes will cover line handing for underway fueling and replenishing, and the davit. I'm still working on a Gunner's Mate. Okay?"

Stewart stared dumbly at Chief Billons and nodded his head.

Why would he want to help me?

He held up his finger like 'number one' for a question. "Go ahead."

"I don't get it, Chief. Why are you going out of the way to help me? You certainly don't owe me any favors and we sure haven't gotten along too well."

"Fair enough, Stewart. You got a bum deal twice. Some people think you'll make a good sailor. You don't want the help? My Mates won't come chasing after you. Nothing is being given to you on test day. You got to cut it on your own. Don't disappoint those people."

"What people, Chief?"

Chief Billons shook his head slowly at Stewart and motioned to his Mates. They glanced at him and strode away.

Well, well, well.

"Hey, Chief," Stewart called out.

They stopped and looked back at him.

"Thanks, Chief, I really do appreciate it. Just didn't expect it, that's all."

They nodded again. He stared after them as they faded into the darkness. The temperature was chilling down but this night Stewart didn't feel it.

*   *   *

The U.S. Navy's Air Armada, from the very beginning of Naval Aviation, had designated several types of squadrons with specific names by code letters and numbers. First letter of the designator was always a V to differentiate from the U.S. Army Air Corps, later U.S. Air Force. A US Navy Fighter Squadron (VF) consisted of a number of fighter planes and pilots, supported by their own ground crews and administrative personnel. Attack or Bomber Squadrons were designated VA, Torpedo Squadrons as VT, and Patrol Squadrons as VP. The U.S. Marines' designators included an 'M', as in VMF for Marine Fighter Squadron.

There were many squadrons of each kind, so numbers follow the designators, like VT1 for Torpedo Squadron One. Very early in Naval Aviation, squadrons were attached to aircraft carriers and were identified by using the carrier's hull number. For instance the old Saratoga CV-3, carried VT3, VF3, and VA3. Before World War Two developed, more squadrons than the aircraft carriers could handle were commissioned. Modern aircraft carriers could handle more squadrons, and for security, matching squadron numbers with ship hull numbers was dropped in favor of arbitrary numbering.

A number of important tasks just didn't fit into those simple descriptive names. The Navy developed a name to cover the catchall situation—Utility Squadron, or VU. Members of Utility Squadrons, also known as UtRons (pronounced you-trons), had to be highly skilled in several lines of work. Mail, spare parts, fresh fruit and vegetables and new personnel were often transported via UtRons. All levels of air training were accomplished with UtRons.

Radio controlled drone aircraft, for example, were the responsibility of Utility Squadron KD units.

January 14, 1951
VU5, Radio Control Drones,
Detachment Able
U.S. Naval Air Station, Atsugi, Japan

Utility Squadron Five was attached to U.S. Naval Air Station Atsugi, Japan, for support. The Utility Squadron personnel were busy imparting their special services far and wide. So much so, the squadron had several detachments scattered around the Western Pacific area while its main headquarters remained at the U.S. Naval Air Station in Atsugi, Japan.

KD Detachment Able, VU5, (KD-Det. A) had been waiting patiently for Hoquiam to become available for anti-aircraft gunnery. KD-Det. A, had been about to board her in late October when Hoquiam abruptly departed for Wonsan. The catapult that replaced the 3 inch, fifty caliber gun—Mount 32—belonged to Det A. Four drone aircraft, crated and stored in pieces, regular tools, aircraft tools, and spare parts were transported by flatbed truck from NAS Atsugi to SRF Yokosuka.

The Officer-in-Charge, Lt. Austen Warren, Naval Aviator, USN, stood five feet, six and a half inches tall in his stocking feet. Lately, he had begun to put on a little more weight, now at one hundred thirty-six pounds.

Sixteen months ago, accompanied by his Commanding Officer of VA-162, Lieutenant Commander Jack C.

Knowles, Lieutenant Warren came before a Medical Review Board.

"As a result of a refueling accident in which Lieutenant Warren breathed a sufficient amount of jet fuel fumes to be rendered unconscious, he had suffered twenty to twenty-five percent permanent damage to his lungs. Therefore, with regret, Lieutenant Warren is hereby permanently grounded."

The blond, brown-eyed flyer stood rigid and then sagged in despair. His voice was ragged as he responded. "Yes sir. Am I to be retired from active duty or will I receive an assignment to another branch of the Navy?"

The Commanding Officer did not have any idea how Warren would receive his new orders. They were almost a studied insult—or a saving grace, depending upon his state of mind.

"Lieutenant Warren, you have been ordered to Utility Squadron Five at Naval Air Station Atsugi, Japan, as Officer-in-Charge of the KD Unit, Detachment Able. Report to North Island Operations for transportation to Atsugi." He paused, looking at a lost soul. "This hearing is closed."

He stood and came around the desk to where Lt. Warren still stood at attention, staring at the wall, a tear trickling down his right cheek. "Austen, try to think of this assignment as a chance to sort things out and decide what you want to do. Keep in touch and good luck."

Lt. Warren, still staring at the wall, saluted his Commanding Officer, about-faced, and marched out of the hearing room.

*　*　*

Lt. Warren arranged to have the drone equipment lifted aboard the ship and prepared for sea. Curtis, Aviation Boatswain's Mate First Class, or AB1, the Leading Petty Officer (L.P.O.), directed the actual move of his babies and oversaw the on-deck stowage of drones and spare parts.

Mere seamen wouldn't have understood the airdales' special requirements. Besides, if the Hoquiam crew had been tasked with the job, the equipment might have been set down about ten inches to the right of the starboard side into the water.

The detachment boarded, bag and baggage, just before the Hoquiam got underway for Sasebo. The ship's crew resentfully ignored their presence, almost to the point of rudeness. Lt. Warren was politely received in the Wardroom and soon learned the reason for his chilly reception. These were warriors and didn't take kindly to this service-to-the-fleet bullshit.

Lt. Warren decided to inspect his men's open area quarters to make sure it was adequate and their needs were being met. The Personnel Office directed him to the overflow berthing area just forward of the Galley, open to the Mess Deck. When he stepped off the ladder onto the Mess Deck, he removed his hat out of respect to the Mess, even though it was not yet noon, and stepped across to the port side where he could observe his detachment forward on the starboard side.

Looking at his men getting settled in, he didn't think they were too happy. Lt. Warren casually walked forward until the Leading Petty Officer noticed him. He motioned to Curtis to join him at a mess table. Curtis drew two cups of black coffee and sat down with his officer-in-charge.

Lt. Warren smiled at Curtis and asked, "The men don't look too happy, Curtis. Anything I ought to know about?"

Curtis handed him a cup of coffee and settled down with him, facing their berthing area.

"Nothing I can't handle," he said, "This crew is pissed off that we've taken them away from Korea, Mr. Warren. They don't want anything to do with our little birds, so we are getting the cold shoulder but good. At least, there's no discussion of throwing us over the side, yet!"

Lt. Warren smiled wryly and nodded agreement.

"I wouldn't tell this to just anyone, Curtis, but I also seem to be a pariah." He took a sip of his coffee and set the cup on the mess table. "It's going to be a while before I get invited to join in an Acey Deucy game, or even bullshit before the evening movie. We're just going to have to bear up. They'll soften after a couple of weeks, I'm sure. Just tell the men to play it square. Okay?"

Curtis got up with his coffee, as Mr. Warren stood. Curtis understood the game. They had gone through it before.

But what I don't understand is why these guys don't want to just relax and enjoy life in Sasebo for a while.

He nodded to Lt. Warren. "I'll take care of it, Mr. Warren. We won't have any trouble." They had been working together with their drone detachment for over a year. Their job was to help antiaircraft gunners learn to shoot down fast moving aircraft. Small drones gave a 'scaled down' effect of larger, faster moving attack aircraft. Curtis knew he and his crew had a lot of work to do before they could begin launching drones. Someone didn't have much confidence in today's naval gunnery. Only four drones had been assigned to their detachment.

U.S.S. HOQUIAM (PF-5)
Plan of the Day

Yokosuka, Japan   **January 15, 1951**

In-port Uniform of the Day: Enlisted, Undress Blue Baker; Officers & CPO's, Dress Blue Able

0600	Reveille
0615	Breakfast; Muster Prisoners-at-large and Restricted Men
0645	Sweepers
0745	Quarters for Muster
0800	Morning Colors
0815	Turn to; commence ship's work
0830	Set the Special Sea & Anchor Detail for getting underway; secure ship for sea
0900	Underway for Sasebo, Japan
0930	Commence three section steaming watches
1000	Shipboard drills by Department
1130	Watchstanders Lunch
1145	Lunch; Knock off Ship's work; Muster PALs and Restricted Men
1300	Turn to; continue ship's work
1330	Commence shipboard emergency drills
1630	Knock off ship's work
1645	Watchstanders Dinner
1700	Dinner; Muster PALs and Restricted Men
1800	Extra duty men muster at the Master-At-Arms office
2000	Eight O'Clock Reports
2000	Movie Call: Mess Deck, Abbot & Costello Meet Frankenstein; Wardroom, James Cagney, Ann Sheridan, Pat O'Brien in Torrid Zone
2100	Muster PALs and Restricted Men
2145	Tattoo
2200	Taps; maintain silence about the decks. The smoking lamp is out.

0830, January 15, 1950
USS Hoquiam PF-5
Underway for Sasebo, Japan

Jerrald Jones, a Jamaican SD3 steward, trailed Captain Brown to his Sea Cabin. He carried the Captain's immediate needs when he slept next to the Bridge: hand towel, wash cloth, soap container with a red Lifebuoy soap bar the Captain liked, Pepsodent tooth powder and blue tooth brush, comb and silver-backed hair brush, extra set of skivvies and socks, and a set of wash khaki pants and shirt. Jones finished setting the toiletries in their places and turned to the Captain. "Would you like a cup of coffee now, Captain?"

"Yes Jones, in a cup and saucer, please," responded the Captain.

Jones moved quietly about his business without disturbing Captain Brown. Meanwhile, the Captain quietly undogged the voice tube covers to the Bridge and Wheelhouse so he could keep track of conversations. Most of the Bridge crew were unaware their voices carried down here. This intelligence gave him an interesting perspective on his own performance. He was also able to gage the crew's morale by listening to the idle conversation that strikes up while the officers were absent.

He glanced at the 21MC to make sure it was powered ON and the switches set the way he wanted. He laid his Journal on the tiny desk. Glancing out the hatch at the weather, he decided to wear his Bridge Coat and White scarf. Captain Brown struggled to slip his arms into the sleeves.

"Here, Captain, turn around and let me help you," said Jones. The Captain held his jacket cuffs and shrugged the heavy coat up onto his shoulders. He turned smiling.

"Thank you, Jones," he said as he took the scarf from Jones's outstretched hand. He sipped at his coffee for a moment and placed his combination hat with black cover on his head. He slipped his binoculars from their case, hung them around his neck and stepped out onto the weather deck below and behind the Bridge.

The 1MC clicked on and 'All Hands' sounded on the Bosun's Pipe. "All hands not actually on watch, quarters for leaving port. Uniform of the day is undress Blue Baker with peacoats for enlisted men, Dress Blue Able with Bridge Coats for officers and chiefs. Quarters, Quarters for leaving port." The 1MC clicked off.

Glancing behind him to make sure that was the Captain he heard stepping up, Lt. Dixon, the special sea detail officer of the deck, saluted the Captain and turned to the voice tube. "Quartermaster, Captain on the Bridge."

"Captain on the Bridge, Quartermaster, aye aye, sir."

"Good morning, Captain. All lines are singled up, SC radar is active, Engine Room is ready to answer bells, Special Sea Detail is manned and ready, and the crew is mustering at fair weather parade for quarters, sir."

"Very well," he responded as he glanced up to confirm the SC bedspring radar antenna was rotating and the Bridge crew was ready.

International signal flags NAN, ZEBRA, CHARLIE, and YOKE, representing Hoquiam's call letters were at the dip from both outer halyards. The international signal flag PETER had a special function. When raised alone,

PETER was called PREP, and as PREP, it was flying two-blocked on the first inner halyard on the Port yardarm, signifying the ship, moored port side to the pier, would soon get underway. Further, it was an indicator that a Harbor Pilot was on board.

PREP had another use. The Senior Officer Present, Afloat (SOPA) Signalmen two-blocked PREP as First Call To Colors at 0755 in the morning and five minutes before sunset in the evening. Promptly at 0800 and at sunset, SOPA Signalmen would execute PREP by hauling PREP rapidly to the Signal Bridge deck. All other ships in port followed suit, and Colors would be rendered — raised or lowered as the case may be. Commanding Officers mainly avoided getting underway at those two times.

The Captain, trailed by Lt. Dixon, stepped to the port wing and inspected the pier and ship's side to make sure everything was clear. Then he looked aft toward the channel and the Yokosuka waterfront in the background.

He walked back to the flag bags, returning Chief Swenson's salute, "Good morning, Chief," and crossed over to the starboard side. On the starboard side, he looked in all directions making sure of the ship's clearance. He nodded satisfaction, and cleared his throat.

"Phone Talker, pass the word to take in all lines except the bow spring line."

The Phone Talker repeated the Captain's order, pressed his mike button and passed the order. "All stations except the bow spring line, acknowledge the order to take in all lines, Captain."

"Very well." The Captain stepped to the port wing and watched as the lines came in. He rubbed his hands together.

Okay, time to go.

"Port engine ahead slow, Left rudder five degrees, Dix." The litany began.

Lt. Dixon leaned over the voice tube, repeated the Captain's order, and listened to the repeat back from the wheelhouse crew. The Captain was watching the water near the fantail, looking for telltale swirls. The fantail began to edge away from the pier. He looked straight at the pier to watch forward motion. Held fast by the forward spring line, the ship began moving slightly forward and in toward the pier.

"Stop engine." He listened to the repeats as he concentrated on the ship's geometry.   There, the ship was pointed in to the pier.

"Rudder amidships."

"Rudder amidships, aye aye, Captain. The rudder is answering the helm."

"Very well." The Captain stepped to the opposite side and checked for shipping again.

"All back slow," he called out.

"All back slow, aye aye, Captain. Engine Room answers all back slow, Captain."

Lt. Dixon turned aft to the Sonar shack bulkhead and pulled on the ship's horn lever with three long blasts on the ship's whistle, letting all ships beware, the Hoquiam was backing down.

The Captain watched as tension eased on the bow Spring line. "Take in the bow spring line."

The pier line handlers lifted the big eye splice from the cleat and let it splash in the water.

"Shiftcolors—shiftcolors."

We're free!

Simultaneously, the National Ensign came down at the fantail, as another National Ensign broke at the Foremast truck, and the Field of Blue with forty-eight Stars — the Union Jack, came down at the bow.

On the Signal Bridge, Prep zoomed back to the deck as the two outer halyards with the Hoquiam call letters bent on, were two-blocked. Hoquiam PF-5 was once again underway.

"All stop," the Captain barked as the ship continued to slide backwards from its berth at the pier.

"All stop, aye aye, Captain. Engine Room answers all stop, Captain."

"Left rudder two degrees."

"Left rudder two degrees, aye aye, sir, rudder answers the helm, sir." came back up the tube to Lt. Dixon.

He and the Captain kept swapping positions automatically. If the Captain decided he wanted to look back on the starboard side, then Lt. Dixon moved toward the port side. Right now, the Captain was on the port side concerned about the bow clearing the pier without scraping the fresh paint.

She's moving back nicely. Good maneuvering without a hard wind to blow you about.

The Captain smiled to himself, pleased with the ship this morning. As the bow neared the end of the pier, he turned to Lt. Dixon.

"Starboard, back slow. Left rudder five degrees."

"Starboard, back slow, aye aye, sir."

"Left rudder five degrees, aye aye, sir. Rudder answers the helm, sir," came the other voice.

"Engine room answers starboard back slow, Mr. Dixon," said the first voice.

"Very well."

The Hoquiam began swinging around as it cleared the pier.

"Stop engine."

"Stop engine, aye aye, sir. Engine room answers stop engine, sir."

"Very well."

As soon as the ship was half way into the channel but clear of the pier's end, the Captain was ready to apply both engines.

"All ahead slow."

"All ahead slow, aye aye, Captain. Engine room answers all ahead slow, sir."

"Very well."

The ship continued to swing as the port propeller applied pressure to the rudder.

"Rudder is still left rudder five degrees, Captain."

"Very well."

He watched the bow swinging around to straighten into the channel proper.

"Rudder amidships."

"Rudder amidships, aye aye, Captain. Rudder answers the helm, sir."

"Very well."

Hoquiam began to pick up speed slowly. An icy breeze fluttered the length of the ship. The crew hunched into their peacoats a little tighter as the wind dashed down the back of their necks as steam trailed from their mouths and noses. The signal flags rustled, flapped, and snapped above the Bridge. The group of submarine piers where they normally moored faded into the background.

It was time to turn eastward toward the Outer Harbor and the channel to Tokyo Bay. The Captain leaned over the voice tube and gave the new course commands that were written into memory.

"Right rudder ten degrees. Steady up on new course zero eight six true."

"Right rudder ten degrees. Steady up on new course zero eight six true, aye aye Captain."

"Very well."

Captain Brown swung away from the voice tube to watch as the ship began its turn. As they turned, a flashing light from SOPA on the U.S.S. Ticonderoga Signal Bridge began calling. Hoquiam Signalmen were manning both of the twelve-inch flashing lights. Similar queries were coming in from all ships. They wanted to know where this vessel, the FIVE, the PF5, the U.S.S. Hoquiam PF5, was bound.

5 5 5 5

Barney aimed his light at the Ticonderoga Signal Bridge and flashed the letter 'K' in Morse code—like picking up your phone and saying 'Hello?'—in Navy communications parlance: responding with 'Over'.

WHERE BOUND?

asked the Ticonderoga.

SASEBO X ETA 01/17

responded Barney with his twelve-inch signal light.

The Ticonderoga Signalman acknowledged the response, snapped off his light, and noted that the USS Hoquiam PF5 was outbound for Sasebo, Japan and their estimated time of arrival in Sasebo Harbor, Japan, was January 17, 1951.

Barney, Red, Curry, and Smitty were busy responding to that question from the fifteen or so Navy ships in port. With only two signal lights, Curry and Smitty were semaphoring their answers to nearby ships.

"Steady on course zero eight six True, Captain."

"Very well."

The Bridge crew looked off to the port side at the sad PF hulks still moored in the Inner Harbor. They didn't look any better today than the Hoquiam looked five months ago.

Lt. Dixon and Chief Swenson were constantly feeding bearings to the Navigator, Lt. Marston, from their alidades mounted on the port and starboard gyro compass repeaters. Channel positioning was vitally important.

The 21MC blared to life.

"Captain, Navigator — recommend coming left three degrees to new course zero eight three true."

"Very well, Mr. Marston."

The Captain leaned over the voice tube. "Helmsman, come left to new course zero eight three true."

"Come left to new course zero eight three true, aye aye, Captain."

The Helmsman turned his wheel a full turn counter clockwise, watching the gyro repeater. Then he turned it back a full turn clockwise. Continuing to watch the gyro, he adjusted the wheel a little bit until he was satisfied and looked up to the voice tube.

"Steady on new course zero eight three true, Captain."

"Very well."

The ship's crew at quarters on the starboard side looked across to the Piedmont Pier where a brightly painted but not yet commissioned PF with all three 3-inch mounts was tied up. Its PF Detail crew and Jap yard workers were busy getting the ship ready.

"All ahead one-third."

"All ahead one-third, Captain. Engine room answers all ahead one-third, sir."

"Very well."

A small wake, barely more than a ripple, began to build as the Hoquiam picked up speed. The channel ahead was clear to the anti-submarine nets. Both the Captain and Lt. Dixon turned around and watched the stack. Sure enough, the smoke turned black.

Lt. Dixon grinned at the annoyed Captain and beckoned to the phone talker.

Gotcha Jim. That's five easy bucks I just won. I wonder whom he's going to chew?

"Tell the Engine room they are making smoke." He turned to the bulkhead and pulled on the horn lever. One long blast alerted the net-tender to open the gate; Hoquiam was leaving port.

The talker nodded and passed the word.

The Net Tender began to pull back as the ship approached the Nets, dragging open the gate.

"Bridge Sonar — Request permission to extend the sonar dome and commence standard sweep patterns," came over the 21MC.

Lt. Dixon raised his eyebrows at the Captain who nodded in return.

"Permission granted. We are two hundred yards inside the nets, closing."

"Clickclick," as the transmitter lever was snapped twice.

Sonarman First Class, or SOG1, Bertowski turned away from the 21MC and reached over to the new RAISE-LOWER push buttons and pressed LOWER. A red lamp flashed for a few seconds, then glowed steadily. The dome was now extended.

He reached over and flipped the BQF power button and watched as the filaments glowed hotly. The meter needles came up showing correct voltage and current readings.

"Okay Rosy, go to Listen Mode first."

Rosas, SO3, nodded and pulled his headphones up onto his ears and clicked a lever from STANDBY to PASSIVE.

I'll raise the gain just enough to hear the fish talking.

He turned a knob until he was satisfied with the level, then snapped a toggle switch.

A falling water sound came out of the speaker. Bertowski fiddled with the filters until the sound quieted. Now, they could hear the fish. "Give me a single ping, Rosy, and let's see what returns."

Rosas moved the lever to ACTIVE MANUAL and touched his Morse key once. A loud PING filled the compartment as the pulse moved outward from the dome.

They watched the CRT monitor for returns. They could faintly make out the Anti-submarine net in an arc in front of them.

The Sonar Officer, quietly observing Bertowski and Rosas until now, leaned over and pulled the 21MC lever down.

"Bridge, Combat this is Sonar — we make the submarine nets four hundred seventy feet ahead of us," called Ensign Hitchcock.

"Sonar, Combat — Confirm four hundred seventy feet."

"Sonar, Bridge — Roger."

The Captain watched as they cleared the Anti-submarine nets.

"You have the Conn, Dix."

"Aye aye, Captain. Simon says. May I go to Standard speed at this time?"

"Permission granted."

Lt. Dixon leaned over the 21MC and checked to make sure WHEELHOUSE, CIC and SONAR switches were active for steaming. He held down the mike switch as he leaned over the voice tube.

"All ahead standard. Make one four zero turns."

"All ahead standard, aye aye, Mr. Dixon. Engine room answers all ahead standard, answers one four zero turns, sir."

"Very well, thank you. Quartermaster, I have the Conn and the Captain is still on the Bridge."

"Quartermaster, aye aye, sir."

Lt. Dixon took a turn around the Bridge sniffing the air, then settled in the port corner as the Captain settled in the starboard corner.

In Sonar, Rosas moved the lever to ACTIVE AUTO and listened while the QBF began pinging every thirty seconds on a new bearing as he moved the cursor ten degrees after each ping, slowly from port beam to starboard beam and back.

The Boatswain's Mate of the Watch, opened the 1MC and piped 'Secure'.

"Secure from Special Sea and Anchor Detail. Secure from quarters for leaving port. On deck Section Three, relieve the watch. Underway uniform of the day, dungarees, watchcap or white hat optional, for enlisted; khakis with ties for Chiefs and Officers. On deck, relieve the watch."

"Stew, is it really your birthday today?" asked James.

"Yepper, Jimmy Bob, but just barely. My mother says I was born at 12:55AM. If she had pushed a little harder, I woulda been born a few minutes before midnight on January 14th."

Masters, the oldest of their gang, peered around the others at him. "So, how old are you now, Stew?"

"Twenty!"

"No shit? You're just a young, fucking punk, Stew," laughed James.

"Well, I'll buy young and a punk. But there just ain't no fuckin' justice. Tonight's the night I wanted to go over and howl at the moon. At least, I've got first liberty in Sasebo."

They all filed in the thwartship passageway heading to the Radio Shack. Much work to accomplish as the underway routine began again. Two weeks getting scraped and repainted had spruced up the ship quite a bit.

* * *

At the very last moment, a pleased Billy Boy had watched as the Jap workers moved their completely refurbished Motor Whaleboat by overhead crane and dropped it gently into the cradle under the davits. Chief Dortas joined him as the yardbirds finished buckling the safety straps.

"You get next to that snipe that was gundecking the lube log, Dortas?"

Chief Dortas looked sheepishly at Chief Billons. "We had so damn much work to do, Boats, it plumb slipped my mind. As soon as those guys get clear, I'll have the Lifeboat Engineer on watch get everything."

Billy Boy just stared at him balefully, shaking his head. Chief Dortas realized that Chief Billons was mightily pissed. He left the boat, as much to get away from Billons' glare as to find the culprit and get the duty Lifeboat Engineer to help him get the job done right.

0615, January 16, 1951
USS Hoquiam PF-5
Sea of Japan
Underway to Sasebo, Japan

Lt.(jg) Trapp pulled the handset from its clip and buzzed the Wardroom. He needed to talk to the Captain. "Captain, there's a small Jap trawler ahead of us about five thousand yards. I think they're broken down and asking for help because they're waving flags and blankets at us." He listened intently. "Thank you, sir," he replied and pushed the handset back into its clip.

Lt.(jg) Trapp continued to scan the trawler as they approached. Under Captain's orders, there would be no change in speed unless needed to control an emergency situation. He waited.

In about four minutes, the Captain appeared at his side in his zipped up leather jacket over khakis and pisscutter. Glancing at the trawler, he leaned over the voice tube:
"All stop."
"All stop, aye aye, Captain. Engine Room answers all stop, sir."
"Very well."

Should have come up directly, dammit. Going to overshoot.

"All back one-third."
"All back one-third, aye aye, Captain. Engine Room answers all back one-third, Captain."
"Very well."
The ship, steaming at fourteen knots, began shuddering and bucking as the screws cavitated, trying to bite some water. The Captain watched in disgust as they slowly passed the trawler, trying to stop. After the ship began to back down its track, he leaned over the voice tube again.
"All stop."
"All stop, aye aye, Captain. Engine Room answers all stop, sir."
"Very well."

He turned to his newest underway watch officer who stood chagrined and red-faced. "Mr. Trapp, I apologize for not getting up here faster, and for not giving you orders to stop. It wasn't your lack of skill that caused the extra engine room bells," he said with a strained smile.

Lt.(jg) Trapp stammered a thank you and waited for further orders. None came forth, so he turned to the trawler to see what the matter was. He picked up the megaphone and yelled to them. "Do you need help?"

Then he put his ear to the megaphone to listen. The words came faintly.

"In jun no go — in jun no go."

"Where you go?"

"Sasebo!"

"Did you understand that, Captain? He's heading for Sasebo, too. We could tow him," suggested Lt.(jg) Trapp.

The Captain considered it a moment and nodded. "That will make our arrival at the submarine nets after dark. However, the experience will be good for the ship. How would you handle this detail, Art?"

If Lieutenant (Junior Grade) Arthur Trapp was surprised at the familiarity of the Captain, he didn't show it. He rapidly outlined his plan and waited expectantly. Captain Brown thought, nodded, and said, "Just make sure the Engineering watch knows what we are doing."

"Aye aye, Captain."

The Captain leaned over the voice tube.

"Messenger, find Mr. Dixon and request he come to the bridge. I believe he is still eating breakfast."

"Messenger, aye aye, sir."

"Art," said the Captain, "you're not acquainted with Chief Boatswain's Mate Billons yet, are you?"

"No sir, I'm not. Why?"

"Look up in the Foc'sl and you'll see him looking directly at the bridge. He's already figured out what we're up to, and he's just waiting to be called. Why don't you wave him up?"

Lt.(jg) Trapp looked to the Foc'sl and saw a short, wiry Chief staring back at him. He pointed very obviously to the Chief and beckoned him to the bridge. Chief Billons acknowledged and swiftly headed aft for the ladder. Lt. Dixon and Chief Billons arrived on the bridge from opposite sides and met in front of Sonar with Lt.(jg) Trapp and the Captain.

"Chief, I don't think you've formally met our new Personnel Officer and qualified underway officer of the deck. Chief Billons, this is Mr. Trapp. Mr. Trapp, this is Chief Boatswain's Mate Billons who's forgotten more about deck seamanship than I'll ever know."

Lt.(jg) Trapp extended his hand in greeting about the time Chief Billons saluted. They hesitated, grinned, and completed the salute before shaking hands.

"Glad to have you aboard, Mr. Trapp."

The Chief was obviously pleased by the Captain's flattery.

With the Captain looking on, Art Trapp began to lay out his plan. Looking at the two arrivals and the Captain, he said, "Here's what I plan to do. This vessel is in need of rescue on the high seas. As her destination is the same as ours, we'll tow her to the Sub Nets outside of Sasebo Harbor and let their security take over. Chief, I'd like to rig a six inch hawser to tow at five hundred feet," he paused to look at the Captain for affirmation and he nodded.

"Those Japs ought to be able to run a bridle through both bow chocks and tie to our line. What do you think, Chief?"

"Only thing I'd do different, Mr. Trapp, is to take their line to our stern bitts, and tow with that. We can always double up later if we feel the need."

"What towing speed, Art?" asked Lt. Dixon.

"After we're fully underway again?" Lt. Trapp removed his hat and scratched his head. Replacing his hat, he said, "I'd say somewhere around five to eight knots."

The Captain, who had let this discussion travel its natural course cleared his throat and conversation stopped. "Take him under tow with his bridle and towing line about five hundred feet. At that short a distance, we want a slow pace. Start out with five knots, Art, until we know how both ships are handling, in the tow. We can always build up speed later. Make sure the Quartermaster logs this."

"Aye aye, Captain."

Lt. Dixon and Chief Billons hurriedly departed for the fantail.

A moment later, a pipe sounded 'Attention'. "Now hear this. The Line Throwing detail report to Lt. Dixon on the fantail."

Gunner's Mate Third Class Bailey looked up from his workbench in the Armory and hurriedly put away his tools. Christ, the way she's rocking right now, I'd find all my tools on the deck when I get back. He unclipped his keys from a belt loop, selected a Masters key and fitted it into the slide bar's brass lock. Removing the lock and slide bar, Bailey pulled out a strange looking rifle, a reel of

1/8-inch nylon woven line, three of the brass rods—just in case—and the cartridge case. He re-locked the slide bar, put on his red helmet liner, stepped through the Armory Hatch, dogged and locked it, and headed up the ladder.

Bailey eased alongside Chief Billons and inspected the Jap trawler off their port quarter.

"Whatcha got, Chief?"

"Bailey, put a line across their foredeck. We're going to take those fuckers under tow all the way to Sasebo. Just a little more underway training for us, understand."

Bailey nodded and laid the nylon line carefully on the deck where it would not catch or tangle. Watching the line, Bailey climbed on top of the port depth charge rack, stood facing the trawler, and flexed his knees as the ship rolled side to side. He shouted and waved his line-throwing gun so the Jap crew could see what he was doing.

He needn't have worried. They could see what he was doing. Waving them aft, he pointed the line throwing gun toward their boat to show he was going to fire across their foredeck. Their skipper shouted commands to his crew. The Jap crew scurried out of the way.

Then Billy Boy turned to Lt. Dixon and raised his white eyebrows in question. Lt. Dixon nodded without saying a word. The Chief looked at his telephone talker.

"Tell the Bridge we are ready to fire."

The talker nodded, pressed his mike button, and started talking. He turned back to Lt. Dixon and the Chief.

"Captain says anytime you're ready, Chief."

"Okay Bailey, let 'er rip!"

Bailey, swaying with bent knees, checked his footing and the line, aimed the gun, released the safety and fired.

The brass rod, manufactured by the Machine Shop below decks, arced through the air toward the fishing trawler, nylon line whipping out behind it. Bailey watched with satisfaction as the rod fell into the water just beyond the foredeck. A Jap seaman leaped up and grabbed the nylon line floating down from above.

A four-inch line was taken aboard from the Jap trawler after some sign language and body English. Seamen the world over know there are only certain choices that can be made under the circumstances.

The Captain and Lt.(jg) Trapp had been watching the tow bridle being set up and attached by Chief Billons and his crew. As they watched, Chief Billons turned to his talker.

"Bridge aye," responded the Bridge phone talker. He listened a moment, nodding his head.

"Captain, Chief Billons requests you take up the slack slowly. He is not terribly happy with the Jap towing line. He thinks it might part."

"Very well." He leaned over the voice tube. "All ahead slow, make ten turns."

"All ahead slow, make ten turns, aye aye, Captain. Engine room responds ahead slow at ten turns, Captain."

"Very well."

Hoquiam crept ahead and the towing hawser lifted out of the water, vibrating and stretching, squeezing dripping water from the hemp as it was drawn out. As the trawler began to move through the water behind Hoquiam, the hawser bounced in and out of the water.

Gradually, she built up speed until they were towing at 5 knots. After a while, Lt. Trapp slowly increased towing speed to 9 knots. The Jap crew never said a word.

The Captain learned later the trawler's bow managed to work enough to develop a leak during the last hour before arriving at the Submarine Net Gate. ComFltActs Sasebo's tug hadn't arrived yet, annoying the Captain who wanted to get to their Mooring Buoy.

Hoquiam passed through the nets and eased its way toward their assigned Buoy, X4, still towing the Jap trawler. In the darkness, red truck lights—meaning "I am at anchor or moored"—of many ships around this large harbor glowed from the top of ship's masts like so many red stars.

Captain Brown did not want to release his tow until the trawler had been searched. To the Hoquiam crew's inexperienced eyes, most oriental people looked the same. The trawler crew could have been North Koreans bent on sabotage as far as they knew. The ComFltActs Sasebo harbor tug met them at the mooring buoy and took over with instructions to search the Jap vessel before releasing it.

"Shift colors—shift colors!"

It was 2012, well after sunset. The underway Colors were removed from the Foremast Truck; the red "at anchor or moored" truck lights were snapped on. By taking the Jap under tow, Hoquiam had reduced its standard speed of fourteen knots almost in half and arrived too late for the crew to go on Cinderella liberty in a new town.

**"THIS IS A F R S TOKYO WITH
THE MORNING NEWS JANUARY
SEVENTEENTH, SERGEANT
RON ROTHCHILD REPORTING.
UNITED NATIONS NEW YORK
CITY. THE UNITED NATIONS
GENERAL ASSEMBLY VOTED ON
A RESOLUTION OFFERING THE
PEOPLES REPUBLIC OF CHINA
A PEACE PLAN. CHINA HAS
REJECTED THE PLAN OUT OF
HAND."**

**1630, January 18, 1951
USS Hoquiam PF-5
Moored Buoy X-4
Sasebo Harbor, Japan**

Red, Barney, and Stewart stood aft between the Depth
Charge racks and waited their turn, huddled shivering in
the breeze. As nonrated men, Barney and Stewart would
be last to go ashore; Red stuck with his friends, even
though he was a Signalman Third Class, or SM3. The
Motor Whaleboat only held thirty passengers plus a crew
of four.

On its first run into the Sasebo Fleet Landing, the
Motor Whaleboat acted as the Captain's Gig with the
National Ensign flying. Captain Brown graciously took
the officers and chiefs going on liberty. It would be at least
a half an hour before the boat returned for its next run.

The three shipmates took a look at the size of the liberty party. The next liberty boat run would be by seniority. That is, the First Class would board first, the Second Class would board second, the Third Class third, if there was any space left. Seamen and Firemen were next, followed by the Seamen Apprentices and Firemen Apprentices. This was the first time since Lee had left the Chilton that he had seen liberty call by seniority.

"You know what, fellas?" said Barney thoughtfully, "let's go have some coffee on the bridge and wait for chow call. We ain't getting off here for a while."

They agreed. It would be dark by the time they got on the beach.

It was a new experience, going on liberty in their Motor Whaleboat. Lee peered over the gunwhale (pronounced gunnel), frowning at 5 inches of freeboard. "Hey Red, isn't this just a little close to the water?"

Red looked it over and grinned. "So long as everyone doesn't lean over the side to check freeboard, we're not going to take on water, so keep quiet about it or the Officer of the Deck is liable to pull some of us out."

Lee thought about it and shrugged. The Coxswain isn't worried, so why should I?

The Officer of the Deck leaned over, calling down to the Coxswain. "Coxswain, after you complete your run to the Fleet Landing, run by the Officer's Landing to see if any of our officers are waiting for a ride back to the ship."

"Aye aye, sir," he responded with a salute. He was standing with the tiller between his legs. Picking up the bell lanyard, he gave it one yank and waved at his bow and stern hooks. They pulled in their boat hooks and sat down as the engineer engaged the engine in forward gear. The coxswain leaned with the tiller just a bit to the right as the boat pulled away from the hull. As soon as they were clear, he yanked the lanyard rapidly four times for full speed. The bow picked up and as Lee watched, the freeboard didn't change a bit.

While they were still inside the Fleet Landing enclosure, they discovered something new. Sailors returning to their ship were being searched. So were Chiefs! A bottle of Tory's 45, a real rotgut Japanese whiskey, was pulled from a sailor's waistband while they watched. A Shore Patrolman, without a word to the sailor, dropped the bottle into an ash can with a sieve bottom where another Shore Patrolman smashed it with a long metal pole. Whiskey odor floated in the air as the whiskey itself dripped into the harbor below. The first Shore Patrolman motioned the sailor onward toward his liberty launch.

The three shipmates had watched this in surprise. No search procedures were conducted in Yokosuka.

Wonder why here and not at Yokosuka? thought Barney.

Outside, Charles stopped a sailor.
"We're new to Sasebo. Where's the action?"
The sailor looked them over for a moment.
"You guys must be off that funny looking little ship. Do you guys think you'll ever see any action around Korea?"
Barney stepped a little closer to the other sailor and stared at him grimly.

"No, asshole, we make the action. Are you on that repair ship that goes up every other month to collect combat pay you don't earn? Wanna answer our question?"

"Hey, I just make a joke, okay?" he protested holding up his hands and smiling. "Grab a forty yen taxi and go that way," he said pointing down the boulevard, "until you get to the Jap traffic control. That's where you want to get out. Just go to the right and have a ball anywhere. Most good bars are on the second deck, okay?"

"Thanks a lot, guy. Keep outa trouble," said Charles.

The three shipmates walked to the Taxi Stand and stared at the little cars. Pedi-cabs were further down the street. They saw that the green and white cabs had 40 Yen painted on them.

"Can we all fit in those little bitty cars?" asked Charles in a hushed voice.

"I'm not sure there's enough room for my legs, Charles, but I'm willing to try it on for size," chuckled Lee. Barney just snorted and headed for the back seat. After considerable grunting, puffing, and laughter, they were in and the doors shut.

"Where you go, sa'rors?" asked the cabbie grinning. "You lika puss now?"

"Nah, boy-san, just go down the street. We tell you where to stop," pointed Lee. The driver bobbed his head and pulled into traffic. "I think my head is pretty well protected, guys. My knees are above my hat!"

The sailors enjoyed the new sights and sounds along the cobblestone boulevard. After a couple of minutes, the little green and white taxi turned the corner and pulled into the curb. The metered fare was ninety-Yen. Lee handed him a hundred-Yen note and waved off the ten Yen.

"Arigato, nei," spoke the driver. Lee nodded.

The driver bobbed his head and mumbled something Lee couldn't hear, and drove off before the Jap traffic cop could get to the taxi. The three looked both ways trying to decide what to do.

"It's your call, Lee. We are buying your birthday drink and that's all we're buying," grinned Charles.

Lee nodded and leaned over the edge of the steep curb away from the metal awning, which seemed to extend way down the street, trying to get a feel for Sasebo. This was not the same as Yokosuka at all.

"Get a load of all the Navies here," he spoke.

"French, English, Australian, New Zealanders, Canadians, and some others I don't recognize." Barney and Charles were impatiently waiting his choice.

"Come on, Lee, where we going?" growled Barney.

"Ah, let's just choose a joint and walk in," Lee said. He looked at several joints and pointed to one. "There, that one."

The three trooped across the busy street, dodging cars, trucks, and a streetcar. Up the stairs they clattered. The place was jammed. Girls stood along the walls in evening dresses—American evening dresses—waiting for a serviceman to pick them out for dancing and other forms of entertainment. The first thing they noticed was that girls could not sit down until invited to do so. The tables were for the sailors and marines and their "guests".

The "Maitre d'" saw the three sailors approaching and scanned his drawing for a table for six. He was sure they would invite some of the girls to their table. He looked up at them.

"Yo lika gur?"

The guys looked at each other. They had eaten and just wanted to sit and enjoy a couple of beers before getting down to the fun business of selecting girls.

"Nahh, we just want . . . " began Lee.

Charles interrupted, holding up his hand like a traffic cop, and began speaking with the headman. The Maitre d' eyes widened with surprise as he listened to Charles order exactly what they wanted in near perfect Japanese. About the only words that Lee recognized were 'hai', and 'somethingsan', as the Jap waiter bowed and hurried away to take care of the order.

Another man walked up and spoke to Charles, sweeping his arm toward the girls. There followed another exchange with Charles. The man laughed, bowed, and left. Charles had a shiteating grin on his face.

"Okay, Charles. What the hell was that all about?" asked Barney.

"I told the Maitre d' we wanted some peace and quiet in this loud place but would settle for some cold Asahi. Since their Asahi wasn't cold, we would accept any Asahi that wasn't still hot from being brewed. Then, please seat us at a comfortable table. Since they don't have comfortable tables and chairs, I allowed that just about anything would do. He wasn't used to American humor, so he just left."

Lee and Barney snickered in appreciation of Charles' put-down.

"The second guy offered us some nice choices of girls, but I explained we were holding out for American-type girls: blondes and redheads. He thought that was funny."

They looked around and settled at the usual eighteen-inch round table. Apparently the art of making chairs was still new to Japan. None of the chairs that Stewart had used in Japan had scooped out areas where cheeks of your butt could rest. They were hard, like sitting on a flat stool. The backs were absolutely straight up and down, forming a ninety-degree angle to the seat, not curved or arched for back comfort.

The Maitre d' appeared and talked with Charles again. This time, Charles looked at him in surprise and what looked like pleasure.

"Come on, guys, let's follow the man."

He led them threading their way across the crowded dance floor and through a door

"Well, I'll be damned," said Lee, "this looks like a USO reading room. Get a load of this: stuffed chairs and reading lamps and larger tables. How about that!"

Charles and Barney nodded in agreement and flopped into the chairs, joined by Lee. The second guy appeared, carrying a tray with Asahi and glasses. Both Japs looked expectantly at Charles. He did not disappoint them.

He spoke at length, sometimes waving his arms at Barney and Lee, and them. He stood and gave a slight bow, which was returned. Then he sat down as the two Japs left.

"They called my bluff, guys. This is going to cost us a little more than those saps out there. Also," he grinned, "The second guy is a comedian. He said their American type girls had decided it was embarrassing to be so different from the rest of the girls, so they dyed their hair and skin dark. So I ordered up tall with big tits. Wonder what we'll get?"

"THIS IS A F R S TOKYO WITH A NEWS BULLETIN, JANUARY EIGHTEENTH, SPECIALIST FIFTH CLASS GEORGE HUMACHER REPORTING. UNITED NATIONS COMMAND IN KOREA REPORTS COMMUNIST FORCES HAVE TAKEN SEOUL, SOUTH KOREA. CHINESE FORCES, NUMBERING OVER FIVE HUNDRED THOUSAND MEN, HAVE PUSHED UNITED NATIONS FORCES FIFTY MILES SOUTH OF THE THIRTY EIGHTH PARALLEL. MORE NEWS AS THIS STORY DEVELOPS."

January 20, 1951
USS Hoquiam PF-5
Moored Buoy X-4
Sasebo Harbor, Japan

"Stewart", called James.

"Stewart, aye," looking up from filing messages with a question in his eyes.

"The Tender has some unclassified changes for our manuals. Take the next Guard Mail boat run and pick them up. Got it?"

Stewart nodded and closed the filing cabinet, grabbed his white hat, canvas pouch, put on the web belt that meant he was on official business, and left to see when the next boat run was due to pass by the ship. LCM's were used as a floating bus service for "Guard Mail Runs", going from nest to nest as flagged down with a MIKE flag hoisted to the yardarm by a Signalman.

He saluted the Officer of the Deck, Mr. Unsenger.

"Mr. Unsenger, I have to go to the Tender to pick up some changes for our manuals. Will you have the LCM flagged down for me, sir?"

"Very well. Where will you be?"

"Right here, sir, unless it will be awhile."

The Boatswain's Mate of the Watch turned, pulled the phone out of its bulkhead clip and pressed the Signal Bridge buzzer. He waited for a Signalman to answer.

"Hoist Mike. We want the Guard Mail boat to stop here." He put the phone back in its clip and turned back to Stewart. "He said it's heading out now. Be about five minutes or so."

Stewart nodded and stepped back into the shadow against the bulkhead to await the LCM.

Stewart climbed the Accommodation Ladder to the Quarterdeck, saluted the Colors and the Officer of the Deck.

"Request permission to come aboard, sir. I'm here to pick up some changes to our manuals."

"Permission granted, sailor. Go forward on this deck to the second thwartship passageway. First office door on the right should help you."

"Thank you, sir."

Stewart saluted again and headed forward. He excused himself as he sidestepped around several Chiefs sitting in the shade. As he continued forward, it hit him that one of those Chiefs looked familiar. He glanced over his shoulder and stopped, very surprised. Backtracking, he stopped in front of one Chief who was looking at the deck while stoking his pipe.

"Mr. Wetter, I mean Chief Wetter," he stammered. "Is that you, Chief?"

The Chief glanced up, then looked up sharply, drawing in a deep breath, and stood.

"Oh, fer Chrissakes! Stewart, what the hell are you doing here? We heard your LST took a hit in the Radio Shack killing or wounding everyone in it the during Inchon invasion."

"Don't know nothing 'bout that, Chief. I missed the LST by two days and got reassigned to the Hoquiam PF5."

He looked out and back in toward the Fleet Landing. Stewart pointed to his ship.

"That's us, right there. I am in the Radio Shack and copying fox solid now. Go up for Seaman in a couple of weeks."

Chief Ned Wetter looked Stewart up and down as he talked. He approved of what he saw.

He is not the snot-nosed kid that was back at Tongue Point!

"Been seeing any action, Stewart?" he asked.

"Yeah. Steamed seventy-three days up and down the North Korean coast and took part at the Hungnam redeployment. We're going back out in a couple of weeks,

I think. But Mr.—I mean Chief, what are you doing here? You were retired."

Mr. Wetter looks different in a Chief's uniform.

"Got recalled, Stew, just like everybody else. I'm running the CW school here on the Dixie, for a bunch of undesignated strikers. Every other month we go out to the War Zone for six days to qualify for Combat Pay. Your ship do any shooting out there?"

"Some, Chief, mostly we've been escorting and passing mine channel overlays for ships entering the Korean ports. But we have seen some action. Hey, gotta go. Can we get together sometime to catch up?"

"Sure, Stew. I almost never go ashore. We can get a beer somewhere, okay?"

"Right, Chief. I'll send a flashing light message when I can get away."

Stewart looked at Chief Wetter one more time, smiled, and went on his way but came back.

"Chief, you ever write to anyone at Tongue Point?" he asked.

Wetter looked at him. "Once in a while. You want to say hello?"

"Stewart's eyes flashed fire as he responded.

"Not to the asshole but howdy to everyone else. See ya, Chief," and strode away.

Chief Wetter watched as Stewart walked away. One of the other Chief's sitting there spoke up. "I gather you know that seaman deuce."

"Yes. He was fairly well fucked at Tongue Point, got into trouble several times because of a misunderstanding and he didn't like shore duty. When the Comm Boss decided he wasn't seaman material, Stewart asked for sea duty just before this war started. He was glad to leave."

When Stewart came back a few minutes later, the Chief had gone back to his classroom.

1015, January 21, 1951
USS Hoquiam PF-5
Moored Buoy X-4
Sasebo Harbor, Japan

Stewart pulled the flashing light message from the typewriter and looked at his typing critically.

So this is what that Service Force shit is all about, huh? We gotta escort a little ship around. Big fucking deal!

This was a hot message. The Signalmen had not routed it to anyone yet.

Stewart clipped it on the message board and looked at James. "Don't plan on liberty for the next few days, James. We're going back to sea this afternoon."

James held out his hand for the board and Stewart handed it to him. James read it and tossed the board back to him. "Fucking service shit," he grumbled.

Stewart went forward to the Captain's stateroom and scratched on the doorframe to attract the Captain's attention. His door was open and the green door curtain moved in a gentle breeze caused by his fan. Heavy rain made him keep his porthole closed.

He looked up at Stewart and smiled politely. "Good morning Stewart. What do you have for me this morning?" as he reached for the board.

"Well, Captain . . . "

But by this time, Captain Brown was studying the message. He glanced at his wristwatch and reread the message.

P 22 JANUARY 1951
FM CTF 95
TO USS HOQUIAM
INFO USS LSU 677
COMFLTACT SASEBO
BT
WHEN RFS AFTERNOON 22 JANUARY LEAVE FOR HAMAKURO ARRIVING AM 23RD IN COMPANY WITH LSU 677 X TAKE SHELTER IF REQUIRED TO AVOID DAMAGE BY WEATHER X RETURN SASEBO WHEN ROAD GRADER LOADED AND WHEN RFS X INSURE PRECAUTION AGAINST MINES X CHART HO 5314 APPLIES X SPECIAL WEATHER REPORT TO BE PROVIDED BY CTF95 EVERY 4 HOURS X OTC IN HOQUIAM X MAKE MOVEMENT REPORTS BT

The Captain picked up his pencil and scribbled his initials in the C.O. box.

"Get this message around to everyone as rapidly as you can, Stewart. Mr. Hansen first."

"Aye aye, Captain."

Chief Billons took the Motor Whaleboat forward to the mooring buoy. He wanted to observe his mooring crew up close. From the Foc'sl, they looked a little sloppy when they came in the other day. He beamed with pleasure at how well the Motor Whaleboat was running. Just purring like a pussycat.

When they got to the buoy, he had the coxswain stop the engine so he could watch and listen as the two men worked on top of the mooring buoy with the mooring chain. The bow and stern hooks held the boat against the buoy.

He frowned as the BM3 and SN made a couple of 'nearly' dangerous moves but he didn't say anything. After they got back aboard, these details could be worked out. He watched Mr. Dixon next to the 1JV phone talker, peering down at the unmooring detail. He watched as the shackle pin was unthreaded and pulled with a flourish from the mooring ring. The mooring chain hung free.

"Shift colors—shift colors."

Retrieving their shackle and pin, the two climbed into the Motor Whaleboat. Billy Boy looked over his shoulder at the Coxswain and lifted his finger to give a wind it up signal.

"Okay Bill, start 'er up," called the Coxswain.

Bill reached forward, made sure the forward-reverse lever was in neutral and the throttle moved to the start location, and pushed the starter button. The engine turned and turned but did not catch.

Bill stopped pushing the starter and checked things as he waited. How the fuck did I flood the damned thing? Started on the second or third cylinder a half-hour ago.

Chief Billon's face was tightening up.

Are we going to have to put up with this shit again?

Bill began to sweat a little in the chill afternoon air. He punched the button again and pushed the throttle wide open to wait for it to catch. The Chief noticed the ship was moving alongside their boat. Lt. Dixon and the Captain had had enough.

Lieutenant Dixon leaned over the rail to say something to Chief Billons. "Captain says to break out the paddles, Chief. We'll take you aboard as soon as you get her turned around and lined up below the davit falls," called Lt. Dixon.

"Aye aye, sir." He looked at the Bow and Stern Hooks. "Well, you heard the man, get this fucking piece of junk lined up under the falls."

"Right, Chief." They answered, as they scrambled for two paddles.

Chief Billons sat upright, looking neither left nor right. He was pissed. They still couldn't trust their Motor Whaleboat.

Stewart was making up the Message Board when Mr. Forsythe came in and tapped him on the shoulder.

"Mr. Marston wants to see you for a moment, Stewart."

"Aye aye, sir," Stewart responded automatically. He took the board with him as he walked up the passageway to Mr. Marston's stateroom and scratched at the door. The door opened and the Executive Officer looked up at Stewart from his desk next to the door.

"Come in, Stewart. Got a Speedletter back from Tongue Point already. The letter doesn't really say anything: just acknowledging receipt of everything by the Station Legal Office. So they are on the job." He looked up at Stewart for a reaction. Stewart smiled and nodded.

"I'm your messenger this trip, Stewart. Just initial the Speedletter here and then I'll look at your Board.

NAVAL SPEEDLETTER
Serial 5110078, January 10, 1951
U.S. Naval Station Tongue Point, Astoria, Oregon
Commanding Officer, U.S.S. Hoquiam (PF5)
Copy to: Commander, Naval Forces, Far Eastern Command (Legal)
Re: ComNavFE Speedletter Serial 51-23A75 of January 4, 1951

Subject: Stewart, Lee H., and deposition regarding felony charges

The Legal Department is in receipt of the deposition and enclosures. The Clatsop County District Attorney's office has agreed to see our Counsel on January 12, 1951, regarding this information. Will keep you advised.

The LSU—Landing Ship, Utility (originally LCT for Landing Craft, Tank)—was directed to make best speed, practicable with existing sea conditions. The Hoquiam set the course and maintained a distance of 1,000 yards ahead of the landing craft. The pair steamed along at eight knots until about a mile past the Anti-Submarine Nets.

Normal seas of four to six feet were present. LSU 677 slowed to six knots and remained at that speed until they arrived off Hamakuro at 0945 the next morning. The LSU came alongside and took Lt. Marston along to observe the loading operation in port. After a great deal of difficulty because the grader didn't want to start, both ships were underway for Sasebo by quarter of five in the evening.

During the day, the weather had worsened until winds, coming out of the northwest, had attained a force of 25-30 knots with attending seas of 8 feet. Because of the weather, the Captain decided to return around the underside of Fukaye Jima.

The initial progress around the end of the island was exceedingly slow, about 2 knots. The LSU made pretty rough weather of it, despite the Hoquiam closing distance and attempting to provide a lee for the landing craft.

Red, Barney, and Lee were on the 02 deck, port side, leaning against CIC's bulkhead and watching the LSU. Even barely moving, heavy spray slammed against its bow and completely back over the ship. Being flat-bottomed, the LSU rolled and bucked through the 3 axes. Barney shook his head slowly. "Man, I thought we rocked and rolled around. Just look at that Those poor bastards can't possibly get any sleep when they are underway at night."

Lee looked at his buddies. "Any idea how big a crew it has?"

"No idea. Have no idea where crews quarters are located, either."

Red said nothing just stared at it.

However, when the LSU was on a southerly course, conditions improved and when on the easterly course, along the underside of Fukaye Jima, very good steaming conditions were encountered and lost time was regained.

As the night wore on the weather abated, and by morning the two ships were making a speedy 7 knots.

They entered the Submarine Net gate about 0900 the next morning and went their separate ways, the Hoquiam heading toward Buoy X1, closest to the Fleet Landing and liberty.

0920, January 24, 1951
USS Hoquiam PF-5
Inbound, Sasebo Harbor Channel

Barney, on special sea detail, was scanning for small boats and shipping as the Hoquiam moved deeper into the long harbor. Looking around, Barney automatically checked all ships' flag hoists for signals. Glancing idly at the Aussie destroyer, he straightened, looking for Chief Swenson. Not seeing him, Barney went to the high-powered bridge binoculars on its pedestal and swung it around to look at the Aussie. Refocusing, he studied a flag hoist on HMAS Duchess D154.

"Hey Chief!" Barney looked around again for his Chief. Chief Swenson appeared from the port side with raised eyebrows.

"Chief, I can't make out that Aussie hoist."

The Chief squinted for a minute at the Duchess, then motioned Barney aside so he could look through the big binoculars. "Well, I'll be damned. So that's where it is."

"Where what is, Chief?"

Ignoring Barney's question, Chief stepped around and caught the Captain's attention. "Captain, the Duchess is flying the Esther Williams pennant."

The Captain and Lt. Dixon twisted to look at the Duchess. As though on command, both raised their binoculars to study the flag hoist.

The Quartermaster hastily thumbed through the List of Allied Warships and ran his finger down the page until he came to HMAS Duchess. Then he read the line.

"Mr. Dixon. HMAS Duchess, Commander Hywaite Bottomsley, is senior to the Captain."

"Very well, thank you." Lieutenant Dixon leaned over the Wheelhouse voice tube.

"Boats, the Duchess is senior to us. We render Honors."

"Aye aye, sir."

The Boatswain's Mate of the Watch stepped to the back of the Wheelhouse next to the 1MC. He watched as they approached the moored HMAS Duchess. Juniors salute seniors, the same applies to all warships. Rendering Honors is another tradition of the sea that had its beginnings in antiquity. Small ship captains would bow to large ship captains. Large ship captains would acknowledge the small ship captain. And merchantmen always bowed to a warship of any size.

The Boatswain's Mate of the Watch pressed the microphone lever just before the Hoquiam bow came even with the leading point of the Duchess.

"Attention to starboard." All personnel on the Hoquiam's weather decks came to attention facing the starboard side as the Duchess slid into view. Immediately after the Hoquiam's call to attention, a bugle call floated across from the Duchess, calling her crew to attention.

"Right hand salute." Everyone saluted.

Another bugle call. A man standing on top of the Duchess's Gun Director, clearly an officer returned the Hoquiam crew's salute.

Now, that's class, thought Barney. *Only one officer from a very high and visible spot is returning our salute.*

"To." All hands completed their salute, arms coming down smartly.

Another bugle call.

"Carry on." The crew continued about their business as the Duchess was left behind. The Captain continued to look back at the Duchess with a slight smile on his face.

The next morning, the Hoquiam nested alongside other ships tied up with the U.S.S. JASON (ARH1) — a heavy repair ship — for a ten day availability granted by ComNavFE. Engineering was still not happy with the main engine shaft bearings. They also agreed to hoist the Motor Whaleboat aboard to tear the engine down for repairs.

FEBRUARY

"THIS IS A F R S TOKYO WITH THE
MORNING NEWS FEBRUARY SECOND
NINETEEN FIFTY-ONE, AIRMAN MIKE
DILL REPORTING. UNITED NATIONS
COMMAND IN KOREA REPORTS THAT
ELEMENTS OF THE TWENTY THIRD
INFANTRY REGIMENT, THE SECOND
INDEPENDENT FRENCH BATTALION,
AND THE THREE FORTY SEVENTH
FIELD ARTILLERY BATTALION
CONFRONTED SEVERAL CHINESE
COMMUNIST REGIMENTS, KILLING
AT LEAST THIRTEEN HUNDRED
CHINESE. UNITED NATIONS
CASUALTIES WERE REPORTED
LIGHT. IN OTHER NEWS . . ."

February 3, 1951
Radio Shack
USS Hoquiam PF-5
Moored Buoy X-1,
Sasebo, Japan

Stewart stared in puzzlement at the message that
Red had brought down from the Signal Bridge: copied in
semaphore, no less. Was this a legal message? Stewart was
very doubtful and decided to let James pass on it before
he typed it up.

He called, "Hey James." James looked up from his
filing cabinet desk. "Is this a legal message we want to

route around. Looks like an unofficial bit of silly shit to me."

He looked up at James who had his hand stretched out. James studied it a minute and laughed. He nodded his head and handed it back.

"Yeah, that's a wardroom game all the ships are involved in. I heard about it at the P.O. club in Yokosuka. Sometime during World War Two a signed pinup picture of Esther Williams was given to an officer on an Australian cruiser. Officers from other wardrooms admired the pinup photo and wrote for their own copies. Regrettably, Hollywood wasn't able to furnish any more copies of that photograph of Esther.

"The cruiser with the picture began rubbing it in. In a little while, another wardroom decided enough was enough. They promptly stole it, installed it in their own wardroom, and messaged, in limerick, other ships of their prowess and the original cruiser's lack of watchfulness. The challenge was on. Later, some officer on another Australian ship decided that their own wardroom should have it." James paused for breath.

Mr. Forsythe who had been sitting and listening at his desk across the passage, got up and stepped into the Radio Shack, and joined in to add a few words with laughter in his voice.

"The first rule is this is officer shit! All enlisted pukes stay clear out of it even though their beloved officers are getting their ass beat and tossed over the side." The radiomen just stared at him in disbelief.

Coyle finally got his wits about him.

"Lemme get this straight, Mr. Forsythe. You mean you officers can walk aboard a ship that has this picture, take it away from them, and nail it to your bulkhead?"

"Essentially true. But what you miss is the spy work, frog man stuff, real fights, and the harsh reality of broken bones and blood." He paused and looked around at his Radiomen. "But we love an opportunity to have fun, just like you." All the Radiomen laughed at the last comment.

"Mr. Forsythe, should I type this up for routing to all officers?" asked Stewart holding out the semaphore message. Mr. Forsythe accepted the handprinted message form and read its contents.

TO ALL SHIPS SASEBO HARBOR
FM HMAS DUCHESS D154
BT
BLOODIED BUT UNBOWED CMA
DUCHESS HELD OFF SUPERIOR
FORCES OF THE USS THOMPSON
AND STILL RETAINS POSSESSION
OF PRECIOUS ESTHER X AFTER
THE THIRD ATTACK CMA WE
ARE STILL HER CHAMPIONS X
ALL OFFICERS ARE INVITED
TO ADMIRE BUT NOT TOUCH
ESTHER
BT

"Don't bother to write it up Stewart. I'll handle it myself." Still reading it, Lt.(jg) Forsythe disappeared down the passageway, last seen heading toward the wardroom.

February 4, 1951
Radio Shack
USS Hoquiam PF-5
Moored Buoy X-1
Sasebo, Japan

The Radio Shack door burst open as James walked in followed by Parks. Stewart glanced at one, then the other. He could see they were up to something from their expressions.

I don't know what but somehow I just know it's going to involve me.

He decided to ignore them and continued to file signed off messages as he waited. He even backed away from the filing cabinet long enough for the pair to draw some coffee.

Parks leaned against the TBM transmitter while James draped his arm over the top of the TDE. James's head was bobbing around as he smiled and chuckled to himself.

"Stew, we just failed the Seaman's written examination. It's a fifty-question exam. It's real mixed up with multiple choice, true or false, mix and match, and fill in. I didn't even come close. There are no trick questions, either. All straight forward shit."

Parks just stood there staring at the deck, shaking his head; didn't say a word. Stewart stood there looking from one to the other, trying to figure out if they were messing with his mind or this was the straight skinny.

"You shittin' me, boss?"

"Nosiree, bob. That's one toughass test you're facing tomorrow. You take the Practical Factors at 0830 and

Written Exam at 1330. The results will be posted before tomorrow night's movie. You better hit the sack, Stew."

Stewart nodded soberly and closed the filing cabinet. He poured a last cup of coffee and lit up a Camel before heading down to his bunk. As he passed through the Mess Deck, Hays waved to him from one of the tables where he was watching an Acey Deucy game in progress.

"Good luck tomorrow, Stewart."

"Thanks, Boats."

0815, February 5, 1951
Secondary Conn
USS Hoquiam PF-5
Buoy X-1
Sasebo Harbor, Japan

The 1MC opened and a pipe called 'Attention' "All Seamen Apprentice being examined for Seaman, report to Chief Billons at Secondary Conn. All Firemen Apprentice being examined for Fireman, report to Chief Dortas in the Engine Room."

With the eyes of the other Radiomen on him, Stewart stood up, took a deep breath, and headed out the door. His armpits began trickling water as good as Niagara Falls ever got, and his belly was thumping.

I am ready for this fucking test. I will pass the son of a bitch! I'm really ready.

He marched out and back to Secondary Conn saying that to himself over and over.

"Hi, Chief, here I am," he said casually. Stewart took a moment to count the number of men being examined. Looks like twelve of us.

"Stewart, are you ready for this test, or do you need a few minutes to think it over?" asked Chief Billons.

Stewart stared at the Chief in surprise.

That's a silly ass question if I ever heard one.

"Sure, Chief, I'm as ready as I can be."

Chief Billons squinted at him balefully for a moment, then looked down at his clipboard. He turned to Hays and pointed to a couple of places on the sheet. Hays nodded, took the Chief's pencil, and initialed those spots.

What the fuck are these guys doing? Stewart wondered.

Next, Barnes took the pencil and initialed where the Chief pointed.

"Okay Barnes, move the rest of these Seaman Apprentices up to Mount 31, so they don't go to school on each other."

Barnes nodded and looked at the other eleven Apprentices waiting to be tested.

"Okay, sailors," Barnes grinned. "You heard the man. Move it." Barnes made shooing motions with both hands, to move them forward, and followed them to make sure they weren't peeking.

The Chief looked at the Gunner's Mate Second Class Harper, and nodded.

"Okay Stewart, come with me to Mount 29," ordered Harper.

A 20mm? Christ, I didn't study that one. Been a while. Oh shit!

When they got back there, Stewart found the protective canvas cover had been removed and the 20mm magazine ready ammunition locker was unlocked.

"Stewart, listen carefully. Here are your instructions. Open the Ready Locker and take out the top magazine. Locate the spring tension key and insert it properly into the magazine. However, assume the spring tension is correct. Replace the spring tension key and load that magazine onto the breech casing. Unlock the cradle and mount. I will help you cock it. Then get into the shoulder bars. Got it?"

"Is this timed?" asked Stewart, somewhat timidly.

"No. Just do it right." He looked around to make sure the other Apprentices were not watching. "One moment, assume the magazine spring is completely unwound. How many turns for proper pressure?"

Stewart thought for a second, and said, "Twenty five full turns, Harper."

Harper grunted but didn't indicate whether that was the right or wrong answer.

Stewart leaned over the breech casing to inspect it and made sure it was clear. He unfastened the Ready Locker eight latching clips and lifted the hatch up all the way.

He saw what Harper had done.

No question which magazine to use.

A canvas sheet lay on top of the rest of the fully loaded magazines.

He reached for the key clipped inside the Ready Locker cover. Stewart picked up the magazine, which was very light and slipped the key into its hole of the clock spring at the center of the magazine. Surprised at the weight, he checked and found it empty.

Shoulda figured on that.

Stewart looked at Harper who nodded. He snapped the key back into its clip, pivoted, stepped to the gun barrel behind the splinter shield and raised the circular magazine with both hands.

Fitting it on to the casing and jiggling it just once, he slammed the magazine home and tested with another jiggle. In the order he was told, he unlocked carriage lock lever, and stepped back as the twenty began to swing free.

Harper stepped alongside him to steady the gun while Stewart unfastened the cocking bar, pulled down the barrel and slipped the cocking bar over its gun-cocking stud on the barrel housing. They both pushed down on the shoulder bars until they heard the bolt snap into cock. Stewart made sure the empty brass shell bag was free and stepped into the shoulder harness. Harper pulled the straps tight and Stewart, with his left hand resting around the trigger, depressed the gun to release the spring-loaded cocking bar, swung the gun left and right, and rocked it up and down.

Harper nodded in appreciation and smiled. "Okay, let's uncock this twenty, unload the magazine, and get you out of here, Stewart. Eleven other guys have to try, also."

Try? I wonder if that means I didn't pass?

The rest of this effort passed quickly. He returned to the Chief while Harper set up Mount 29 for the next victim.

"What's next, Chief?"

Stewart looked around and saw that a lot of sailors were watching the Practical Factors test in progress, including Apprentices who weren't taking the exam this time.

"You're done, Stewart. Clear the test area!"

Stewart was stunned. He knew there were more elements than just the Twenty.

"What? That's all, Chief?"

"That's all for you, Stewart. Clear the area."

What'd I do wrong?

His shoulders slumped dejectedly. Somehow he had fucked up. He turned to head for the Shack.

Chief Billons whispered hoarsely behind him. Stewart!" he cracked.

Stewart looked over his shoulder at the Chief.

"Getcher pecker up, Stewart. You're a sailor. Walk like one."

Bewildered, Stewart straightened up, made sure his hat was square and strode off to the Shack, not quite sure what was going on. What ever it was, he had an idea it wasn't bad. Chief Billons watched him out of the corner of his eye. He smiled thinly and turned to glare at Hays.

"Tell Barnes to send the next Seaman Apprentice being tested down."

Hays nodded and went forward to where he could see Barnes, and motioned for one apprentice to come aft.

"How'd it go, Stew?" asked Coyle.

"I just don't know, Coyle. The Chief had me do one thing I hadn't expected, and then he chased me off. But I'm sure the test was supposed to be more than just that little bit."

Stewart poured himself a cup and lit up. Then he stared out the porthole as he thought back through the last thirty minutes.

Just didn't make sense.

His thoughts were interrupted as James came in.

"Stew, you passed the Practical Factors. Those guys been checking everyone off on things on the q t, and had one more for each to take care of this morning. Feel better now?"

Stewart nodded and smiled. He did—really did—feel better. Time to grab the board and get going again.

1330, February 5, 1951
Mess Deck
USS Hoquiam PF-5
Moored Buoy X-1
Sasebo Harbor, Japan

The 1MC opened and Barnes wheezed his way through Attention. "All Apprentices being examined this afternoon for Seaman or Fireman, report to the Mess Deck."

Stewart clattered down the ladder into the Mess Deck. Lt.(jg) Forsythe and James were waiting for him. He took a deep breath, smiled and walked over to them.

"Stewart, make a head run, get extra cigarettes, and your coffee. Then sit down at the far end of this table where the ash tray and pencils are," said Mr. Forsythe.

Stewart discovered that indeed he did have to go. He trotted in to the urinal trough for nervous pee, clattered down into his compartment for an extra pack of cigarettes out of his locker. Then back up to Mr. Forsythe and James. James pointed at the mess table where his test laid turned over. That was where he was supposed to sit.

Stewart looked around. A snipe was sitting just opposite him, sharing his ashtray, grinning back at him nervously. They had different tests so it wouldn't matter.

Someone tapped on a stanchion for attention. Stewart turned toward the stanchion. Lt.(jg) Trapp was tapping with a spoon. When he had everyone's attention, he spoke.

"Okay gentlemen, here's the story. It's now 1330. You have two hours until 1530 to complete this examination. You may not talk. If you have a question, raise your hand. Your Chief or Leading P.O. will assist you.

Shit, James failed this fucker! Fat chance of getting good dope outa him.

"Answer the questions in any order you wish. All unanswered questions and wrong answers will be discarded. Correct answers will be added at the rate of two points per question. A passing grade is seventy, that is, thirty-five correct answers. Once you leave the test, you cannot go back, you are finished. Leave the Mess Deck immediately. Any questions?" He looked around the Mess Deck at each of the expectant Apprentices.

"No questions? Then, good luck."

Stewart lit up, took a sip of coffee, and turned over his test. He glanced at the first question, then looked again, sharply.

Wow! Are the rest of the questions like this?

He looked up at James and Mr. Forsythe, who looked back at him stonily. He looked down again and began looking at the questions.

This was no joke. Those are the questions. What the hell do they think we are? And James and Parks said they couldn't pass this? Wow!

He picked up his pencil and began answering the questions. In less than fifteen minutes, he had answered all of them. Lighting another cigarette and sipping on his coffee, he started at the beginning to check his answers very carefully just to be sure. There were two he still wasn't sure of but he was damn well sure of the rest. He counted to make sure he had answered all fifty questions.

Yep, that's it. I don't believe how simple this test is.

Stewart put his cigarettes and lighter into his pockets and stood up to stretch. James and Mr. Forsythe looked at him in alarm. He smiled at them, picked up his test, and walked over to Mr. Forsythe.

"Who do I give this to, sir?"

Mr. Forsythe numbly took the test and looked at Stewart's work.

"Aren't you going to finish the test, Stewart?" whispered James.

"All done, boss'" he whispered, "a fucking snap!" With that, he quietly left for the shack.

The gang all looked up in surprise as he entered.

"Christ, Stew, that was fast. What happened: give up?" asked Lloyd.

"It was a snap. There were only two questions I wasn't sure of."

"Well, if you're so fuckin smart, Stewart, take the board around," James growled.

He grabbed the board and saw the Captain hadn't seen the latest weather. Going forward in the passageway, he stopped to let Lt. Marston go by who stopped in front of him in surprise.

"Stewart. Aren't you supposed to be taking the Seaman's examination right now?"

"I finished it, Mr. Marston."

Stewart glanced down at the board and handed it to Mr. Marston for his signature. He was still studying Stewart's face.

"You finished it? You answered all fifty questions?" he asked looking at his watch. "How do you think you did?"

"I don't think I aced it. There were two questions I wasn't sure of. But yes, I did answer all fifty, and I am sure I passed."

Lt. Marston smiled at Stewart, scribbled his initials on a couple of messages, and walked down the passageway to the Wardroom.

Stewart scratched on the Captain's doorway next to his green curtain. A green curtain doesn't have much of a sound when you knock on it and knocking on the bulkheads was too noisy. The Captain pushed the curtain out of the way and looked at Stewart.

"Did I hear correctly, Stewart? You already finished the examination?"

"Yes, Captain."

"And you are sure you passed the test?"

"Yes, Captain. I thought the test was pretty easy."

"Is that right?"

The tone of his voice changed somehow.

Oh shit, now what have I done? That test was as simple as pie.

However, the Captain leaned over the message board and signed off the rest of the messages.

"Well, good luck, Stewart."

"Thank you, Captain."

Lt.(jg) Trapp came down the ladder onto the Mess Deck and marched to the Bulletin Board. He fastened two lists to the Board and departed without a word. A bunch of Apprentices looked at each other and ran to the Board. The names were arranged from highest grade down. On the Seaman's List, Stewart's name was at the top with a 98% grade, way above all the rest. He let out a screech and headed for the Radio Shack.

He was trembling with excitement when he opened the door. James and Parks stood expressionless, sipping their coffee, as Stewart bragged about his score. The rest of the gang congratulated him on his fine showing. Mr. Forsythe popped in for a moment and back out without comment. Stewart wondered when he would actually put on the SN stripes, now or the fifteenth, or the first of the month.

"Stewart," called James softly.

Uh oh I know that sound.

"You will be advanced on Mar 16th."

"That long? What is there, some kind of quota or something?" asked Stewart, frowning as he tried to puzzle it out.

"Well sorta. It has been decided on the basis of priorities who will be advanced first."

"Wait a minute. I had the best score in both categories. The next best score was a guy in Deck with an 86%. Some of Chief Billon's crew has to get advanced ahead of me? That's horseshit and you both know it."

Parks looked up and glared at Stewart.

"You don't make the rules, asshole. You live by them."

Stewart looked at him in amazement, and then at James, waiting for him to stick up for him. James didn't want to meet Stewart's eyes. So Stewart countered Parks comment.

"Parks, you mind explaining why you just jumped on me? I sure as hell didn't say anything to you," complained Stewart.

James held up his hand.

"Wait, Stewart. It was decided higher up that it was more important to advance the SA's in Combat, Sonar, and the Signal Bridge, than in Radio. Therefore, Drew is an RDSN as of February 10th, Davis is an SOSN as of February 16th, Smith is a QMSN as of March 1st, and you are RMSN as of March 16th."

Stewart turned white, then red in a rage. The rest of the Radio Gang just sat listening in disbelief. Glaring at Parks, he said slowly and very low,

"None of those guys even made 80%. That's bullshit. And if you don't like them apples, Parks, put me on report. Now back off and let me get the hell out of here."

Parks didn't respond, just moved out of his way as Stewart brushed by Parks and James, heading for the Weather Decks. He shut the door just short of slamming it.

Any place was better than this.

"Stewart. Did I hear you make insolent remarks to a senior petty officer?" grated Lt. Porter.

Stewart stood at attention in the passageway trembling with rage, holding his arms stiffly at his side.

"Sir, if someone says I did, then I must have. Is that all, sir?"

Lt. Porter, who knew what was causing the commotion, did not want to stir the pot. He wanted it over.

Why hadn't James put up a better argument for his man?

"Carry on, Stewart."

Stewart left and dashed out on deck. Looking around, he walked slowly forward in the driving rain, all the way to the Jackstaff in the bow. Tears of rage that streamed down his face were soon covered by the cold rain. Once again, the purple shaft had been inserted harshly, twisted, and pulled out.

What the fuck did I do this time?

"Did you think Stewart could pull a ninety-eight on that test, Jimmy Bob?" asked Parks, slowly.

James shook his head, flipped the hair out of his eyes and glared at his buddy. "Shit no, and I hate it when someone shows they are smarter than me," he said. Then he looked around with a big grin on his face. "He sure showed everyone else up, didn't he? Damn, no one else even in the nineties!"

"THIS IS A F R S TOKYO WITH THE MORNING NEWS FEBRUARY NINTH, NINETEEN FIFTY-ONE, AIRMAN MIKE DILL REPORTING. UNITED NATIONS COMMAND IN KOREA REPORTS THAT A TASK FORCE OF THE TWENTY FIFTH INFANTRY DIVISION DECIMATED THE ATTACKING CHINESE UNITS IN THE BATTLE OF HILL FOUR FORTY."

February 11, 1951
USS Hoquiam PF-5
Moored in nest,
U.S.S. Jason ARH-1
Sasebo Harbor, Japan

The 1MC whistled its usual song of attention. "Stand clear of ship's propellers during dock trials."

Lt. Hansen and Chief Dortas shook their heads in disbelief. The Jason had not corrected their problems. Actually, the High-Pressure cranks on both engines were knocking worse than before. They watched as the Jason engineers twiddled around the first cylinders' cranks without improvement. After three hours, Lt. Hansen left the Engine Room, heading for the Captain's Cabin.

"Come," the Captain responded to the knock at his door.

Hansen swept aside the green curtain and entered with a disgusted look on his face. LCDR Brown leaned back, watching his Chief Engineer's face.

"All is not well, I gather. I've been listening to those cranks getting worse by the hour. What the hell did they do?"

"I don't know, Captain. They did not want us snooping around while they accomplished their magic art. But I do have a suggestion on how to get them off their dead asses."

The Captain leaned forward, elbows on his chair arms, waiting for Hansen's brainchild to hatch.

"We tell them cease and desist, Captain. Cancel the sea trials. Let us take one engine and let them take the other engine. Using their funds instead of ours, of course."

The Captain studied the idea momentarily. It would make them as popular as lepers if Ship's Company did better than the Repair Ship's crew.

"All right, Mr. Hansen. You take the Starboard engine and let the Jason handle the Port engine. Work around the clock until the work is completed. Questions?"

"No sir. Thank you, sir."

"THIS IS A F R S TOKYO WITH THE MORNING NEWS FEBRUARY THIRTEEN NINETEEN FIFTY-ONE, AIRMAN MIKE DILL REPORTING. UNITED NATIONS COMMAND IN KOREA REPORTS SEVERE CASUALTIES IN THE BATTLE OF HOENGSONG. FIVE

HUNDRED THIRTY MEN OF THE FIVE O THIRD AND FIFTEENTH FIELD ARTILLERY BATTALIONS WERE KILLED IN AN AMBUSH: ANOTHER FIFTEEN HUNDRED CASUALTIES WERE SUFFERED BY THE SECOND AND SEVENTH INFANTRY DIVISIONS AND THE ONE EIGHTY SEVENTH REGIMENTAL COMBAT TEAM."

**2000, February 14, 1951
Signal Bridge
USS Hoquiam PF-5
Moored Buoy X-2
Sasebo, Japan**

Stewart, huddled in his foul weather jacket, stepped onto the Signal Bridge and joined Red at the Cubby.

Red glanced at him, "I thought you were at the movies."

"Saw it before and didn't feel like sitting through it again."

"Well, why the hell are you up here, chowderhead? Doncha know it's freezing?"

"Yeah, I know, but the crisp air will clear my head." He stopped to read a yardarm blinker way across the harbor. "Some guy sure sending the blinkers fast on a private talk. You guys allowed to do that?"

Red looked around to where Stewart was looking.

"Oh him" he said scornfully. "That's the New Zealand cruiser. A signalman there is always looking for someone to talk to. Not too many people can read him, though. He sends way too fast for most guys."

"He's not that fast, Red. I can read him easy."

Red turned and looked at Stewart. "You shitting me? You can read him now?"

"Sure, he's talking about some bar in Kobe that's a great place to pick up government civilians."

"You are reading that!"

Stewart looked at him in surprise. "Of course I am. What the fuck is so difficult about that?"

"For starters, I can't, at least not all of it. The Chief can though. You want to talk to the Zealander?"

"Would that be all right, Red?"

"So, who's to know? Just hit him with 135 after he signs with this guy." Red reached over and snapped on the yardarm blinkers and touched the key. There was a momentary flash on the yardarms. "Okay, whenever you're ready, go to it."

"Thanks, Red."

Stewart watched and waited for the cruiser to sign off. About the time he finished with the other ship, Red spoke softly. "Get him, Stew! I wanna see this."

Stewart began sending 135 over and over. By the fourth time, the cruiser responded.

Red watched the exchange between Stewart and the New Zealand Signalman. After a few minutes, Red piped up, "hold the key down solid as long as you can read him. If you miss a character or word, just let up and he'll repeat the last word you missed.

When Stewart began sending on the third exchange, the distant Signalman held his key down, also, allowing Stewart to speed up.

Finally, they both had enough and signed off. Stewart poured a cup of coffee and joined Red against the forward windscreen.

Red was shaking his head. "Did you really read all of that or were you bluffing it out?"

Stewart looked at him in surprise. "That was easy, Red. It's kinda like copying CW except it is light instead of sound."

They heard someone coming up the ladder and turned to see Chief Swenson walking to them.

"Kee-rist, Red, I never knew you could send so fast.

Oh shit, am I in trouble again?

"Wasn't me, Chief." Red's thumb was rocking back and forth pointing at Stewart. "He's the whiz."

"You, Stewart? Where the hell did you pick up that ability?"

"Hey Chief, it's like I was saying, just like copying fox in the Radio Shack. No big deal."

"Well, Stewart, tell you what. I'm going to have you transferred to my division."

Alarmed, Stewart almost shouted at the Chief. "No fuckin' way, Chief. I'm happy in the Radio Gang. I don't know the rest of the shit you guys do, anyway."

Stewart looked back and forth between Casey and the Chief with worry written all over his face. "I'll see you guys later."

He hurried into the Radio Shack and was relieved to find Jimmy Bob there.

"Ah, James? I think I have a problem."

James turned around and lifted his eyebrows. "Whatcha do this time, Stew?"

"Well, I was playing around on the yardarm blinkers and the Chief caught me at it. Now, he wants to transfer me into the Signal Gang."

"What the fuck were you doing on the lights, shitbird?"

"Was talking to the New Zealand cruiser for something to do. We sure can't do that here. I'm worried about the Chief. He sure had a strange look on his face."

"Well, lemme check it out. Meanwhile, don't go near the yardarm blinkers or flashing lights anymore. Got it?"

"Yowser boss."

0830, February 15, 1951
USS Hoquiam PF-5
Underway to test main bearings

"Shift Colors—shift colors!"

The Hoquiam eased forward, away from the USS Collett, fourth outboard ship alongside the Jason. The Captain and Lt. Dixon watched carefully as their fantail cleared the Collett's bow. Lt. Dixon held his binoculars to his chest as he leaned over the Voice Tube to the Wheel House.

"All ahead one-third, come right five degrees"

"All ahead one-third, come right five degrees, aye aye sir"

The ship trembled and increased speed slightly, turning as it did, to move out into the harbor channel toward the anti-submarine nets. Faint, light gray smoke pushed strongly from the stack.

"Meet your rudder."

"Meet your rudder, aye aye sir. New course is 264 degrees true, Mr. Dixon."

"Very well."

Fresh out of Yokosuka and a few days in Sasebo alongside the Jason for extended repairs, the ship appeared ready to go. In less than half an hour, she cleared the nets and began building up speed toward 165 RPMs on both shafts—about 20 miles per hour—BuShips maximum allowed speed for this type engine.

Lt. Jim Hansen sat on the Engineering Watch Officer's stool next to the Bell Log, at the forward end of the Engine Room. Chief Dortas, standing next to him, countered the buck and roll of the ship as he studied the Port Engine.

There was just something about the sound of the pistons and knuckles that was off. The natural rhythm was just not there. He couldn't put his finger on it yet and that bothered him.

He glanced at the RPM indicators to make sure they were still showing 135 and turned to his Engineman First Class.

"Red, check those bearings again. This time go both directions. Start with Starboard to Port and then reverse it. Okay? Meanwhile, I'll compare the cylinders opposite to you."

Red nodded and approached the first cylinder on the Starboard engine. The lubricating oil gleamed on the silvery surfaces as the rods pushed up and down, with no sign of burning or streaking. He reached in—very slowly—

his hand bobbing up and down as the knuckle moved up and down, and touched the bearing cover. Moving to the second of three cylinders, he repeated his inspection, and then to the third cylinder. Everything felt okay.

The temperatures seemed to be the same as near as the sensitivity of the palm of his hand could tell, anyway.

As Red turned to cross to the Port Engine, Chief Dortas left the Port first cylinder and crossed to the Starboard Engine's first cylinder. Okay, like he said, he's going to check by comparing high pressure to low pressure cylinders. We ought to have a damn good feel for these temperatures.

Red waited for the Chief to finish the first, or high-pressure, cylinder and move away so he could check.

Was it warmer or was that my imagination? He backed off and looked at the oil on the slide arms, intently. Doesn't seem to be streaking.

Looking over at the Starboard Engine for comparison, Red was satisfied the lubricating oil on both engines was the same color. He walked over to Lt. Hansen and waited for the Chief to finish.

"What do you think, Red?" asked Chief Dortas, his brow creased in worry.

"Well, I think the Port HP crank knuckle is just a tad warmer than the others, but the lube oil looks okay on the surfaces."

The Chief nodded and looked at Lt. Hansen who had been listening to their exchange.

"What's your verdict, Chief?" he asked.

"Red and I got the same thing, sir. That Port HP knuckle is slightly warmer, but I think we could go up to 140 now without any trouble."

Jim Hansen nodded and pressed his headset mike button.

"Bridge Engineroom—Pass to the Captain—request permission to increase RPM's to one four zero."

"Bridge aye aye—standby."

"Engineroom Bridge—Captain says permission granted, Mr. Hansen."

"Roger"

"Okay Chief, one forty it is."

The Engineroom RPM indicators changed to 140 and Lt. Hansen pointed to the Throttlemen. With hand signals in a very noisy environment he used both hands to say both engines to go up to 140— two thumbs up, one finger, four fingers and a zero, the Throttlemen nodded and cranked their throttle wheels open just a little more watching their RPM gauges.

The Chief stood back where he could observe both sets of gauges and watched them settle at 140 indicated. They would wait five minutes and test temperatures again. They still had to get up to 165 turns. Be at least another hour before they went to a full power run.

Red moved next to his ear and pointed at the Port High Pressure Crank knuckle. "Hey, Chief, that fucking lube oil is beginning to streak. Think I'd better check it now?"

"Do it!" Christ, it's only been three minutes.

Lt. Hansen moved to the Chief, then leaned over the bearing on the Starboard engine and went through the very careful process of hand heat testing. Chief Dortas followed.

Red nodded soberly. "Port HP definitely hotter, sir."

"I agree, Mr. Hansen."

"So do I but let's wait another couple minutes to see if it stabilizes or continues to climb."

As one, they turned to watch the lube oil on that crank. After another minute or so, Mr. Hansen sighed and put both thumbs out downward and indicated one three five with his fingers. The Throttlemen reached for their throttle wheels as the Chief moved the RPM indicators to the Bridge back to 135 and pressed the bell button. Lt. Hansen pressed his mike button again.

"Bridge Engineroom—Pass to the Captain that Port High Pressure crank is hot and I have reduced speed to 135 RPM's."

"Bridge, aye, aye sir."

The Captain pursed his lips and studied their position in the shipping lanes.

"Come about smartly, Mr. Porter. Have the Messenger send Mr. Hansen to my cabin. Call me when we are 4,000 yards from the nets."

"Aye, aye, Captain."

Before noon, the Hoquiam was back alongside the Jason where a repair team was ready and waiting to board. By this time, relations between the Jason and Hoquiam were tense and deteriorating. Extended dock trials were conducted at 1800 to allay the Captain's suspicions. Even though the dock trials were successfully completed, Captain Brown arranged with the Jason's Captain to have observers ride the Hoquiam on its engineering shakedown for the next three days. The Hoquiam would get underway the next morning for Area George.

"THIS IS A F R S TOKYO WITH THE MORNING NEWS FEBRUARY FIFTEENTH, NINETEEN FIFTY-ONE, AIRMAN MIKE DILL REPORTING. UNITED NATIONS COMMAND IN KOREA REPORTS ON THE BATTLE OF CHIPYONGNI. THE CHINESE CHARGE CONTAINED EIGHTEEN THOUSAND CHINESE COMMUNIST TROOPS IN THE FIRST MASS ASSAULT. UNITED NATIONS FORCES INVOLVED INCLUDED THE TWENTY-THIRD R C T OF THE SECOND INFANTRY DIVISION, THE FRENCH BATTALION, THE FIRST RANGER COMPANY, THE THIRTY-SEVENTH FIELD ARTILLERY BATTALION, AND 'B' BATTERY OF THE EIGHTY SECOND ANTI-AIRCRAFT BATTALION. UN FORCES SUFFERED THREE HUNDRED FIFTY-THREE CASUALTIES."

February 16, 1951
USS Hoquiam PF-5
Moored in nest alongside U.S.S. Jason ARH-1
Sasebo Harbor, Japan

Life on the Hoquiam in the other departments, continued as before while Engineering suffered through its series of trials.

Mr. Forsythe popped his head through the Radio Shack open door.

"Stewart, Mr. Marston wants to see you right away. He has a letter from Astoria."

Stewart nodded, put out his cigarette and followed Mr. Forsythe forward to Mr. Marston's stateroom. He pushed aside the green curtain, then stepped aside to let Stewart in.

"Well Stewart, it's a very interesting letter from the District Attorney. Before I let you read this letter, you need to know that Tongue Point and the Navy Department haven't responded yet."

As Lt. Marston talked, Stewart's eyes got bigger and rounder.

I don't like the sounds of this.

January 15, 1951
Office of the District Attorney
Clatsop County, The State of Oregon
Commanding Officer, U.S.S. HOQUIAM (PF-5)
c/o Fleet Post Office,
San Francisco, California
Re: Lee Stewart, SA

) The State of Oregon
)   vs.
) Lee H. Stewart, a Seaman Apprentice,
United States Navy
) currently stationed at U.S.S. HOQUIAM PF-5

A felony warrant remains in effect for Lee Harrison Stewart's immediate arrest. The minor child, Betty Echols, has read the accused's deposition. She states Stewart's deposition is incomplete, that they copulated, and her unborn child is the result. She declares, under oath, her alleged letter is a forgery and she has no idea how Stewart obtained a copy of the Alpha Delta Epsilon Sorority initiation picture. Miss Echols no longer desires to see or marry Stewart.

The Clatsop County Office of Oregon Children's Protective Service has issued funds to Miss Echols' family doctor to pay for her pre-natal care. Further funds will be paid for the child's birth in March, and post-natal childcare.

The State of Oregon is asking the Department of the U.S. Navy to withhold these funds from Stewart's pay until his issue reaches the age of maturity.

We consider Lee Harrison Stewart a flight risk and request you return him to Clatsop County, Oregon, under arrest, to answer these charges.

A.J. Crowlane,
District Attorney

Stewart shut his eyes tightly and thought bitterly.

What a hell of a birthday present!

He looked in despair first at Mr. Forsythe and then Mr. Marston, who were watching his reaction. "What do I do now, Mr. Marston? This is a lie. We never made love. How can they believe her?"

"Well, first of all Stewart, you are not being returned to Oregon in irons. Second, we have to be patient and wait for other replies. When we get back to Yokosuka or Sasebo, we'll take this up with Legal again to see what can be done. Do not attempt to contact her. The Captain has no intention of taking any action on this."

"Yes sir."

"Stewart!"

"Sir?"

"I don't recommend liberty in Astoria for the next few weeks— okay?"

"THIS IS A F R S TOKYO WITH THE MORNING NEWS FEBRUARY SEVENTEENTH NINETEEN FIFTY-ONE, AIRMAN MIKE DILL REPORTING. UNITED NATIONS COMMAND IN KOREA REPORTS THE UNITED NATIONS BLOCKADE AND ESCORT FORCE, TASK FORCE NINETY-FIVE, BEGAN A NAVAL SIEGE OF WONSAN. NOTHING BY AIR, LAND, OR SEA WILL BE ALLOWED TO PASS THROUGH THE PORT AND CITY OF WONSAN."

0945, February 17, 1951
USS Hoquiam PF-5
Testing Main Bearings
Underway to Area George

"The net is abeam, Captain," announced Lt. Dixon.

"Very well, Dix. All ahead two-thirds. Make one three five turns."

"Aye aye, Captain." Lt. Dixon leaned over the voice tube and passed the instructions.

"Set the regular steaming watch, sir?"

The Captain appeared to hesitate for a moment, and then he nodded yes. Jim will stay in the Engine Room, anyway.

The 1MC opened and a Bosun's Pipe piped 'Turn To'. "Secure from Special Sea and Anchor Detail. Relieve the watch. On deck, Section 1 relieve the watch. Turn to, commence ship's work."

All appeared to be going the way it was supposed to go in the Engine Room. The Jason JayGee and his two Chiefs stood with their arms folded across their chests, staring stubbornly at the Port engine, daring it to burp or wheeze or anything else untoward. All three were in clean but stained dungaree uniforms. They were prepared to tear the engine apart if need be. The old Chief looked scornfully at the engine as the other looked doubtful.

The JayGee, recently promoted to the Officer ranks from Chief was timing the run at 135 RPM. He was just about to ask the Hoquiam's Chief Engineer to bump it up five when one of the ship's crew swayed up the Port engine's first piston. He watched in horror as the sailor casually moved his hand in over the knuckle and laid the palm of his hand on it. He poked his Chiefs.

"What the hell is that guy doing?" he asked.

One of the Chiefs glanced over and did a double take.

"My god, he'll get mangled."

The second Chief looked stonily at the operation.

"Piece of shit, it is. No temperature sensors. That's the only way they can find out how hot the bearings are. Watch what they do."

All three watched in fascination as a Chief, a White Hat, and the Chief Engineer felt all six knuckles and compared notes. The Chief Engineer beckoned to the JayGee who went to Lt. Hansen.

"Okay. All six bearings seem pretty equal in temperature and the lube oil isn't streaking. Now, we're going to increase RPMs to 140 and hold for fifteen minutes. If all goes well, as you believe it will, we'll increase by another five every fifteen minutes until we top out at 165. You'll pardon me if we have some doubts."

The Lt.(jg) had nothing to say—merely nodded. He watched them continue to crudely measure bearing temperatures as the speed increased.

"Bridge Engineroom—tell the Captain bearing temperatures are normal, request permission to increase to 140."

"Bridge—standby—Captain says permission granted, Mr. Hansen."

The RPM bell rang and the indicators changed to 140. He matched them as response. Chief Dortas pointed to the Throttlemen and signaled one four zero with his fingers.

The Captain was in his favorite spot in the forward corner on the Port side of the Bridge looking aft at the stack and ship's clean, straight wake. The Hoquiam was fairly flying now at 160 turns; no sign of any problem or vibration. Mr. Morgan had the Conn and approached the Captain. "Jim wants to go to 165 now, Captain. Shall I turn him loose?"

"Yes, but tell him to hold at 165 for at least 30 minutes. Then I want Jim to tell us whether it would be safe to go to higher RPMs—no forget the last. I'll discuss it after thirty minutes if she holds together that long."

"Aye aye, Captain."

Mike Morgan turned to his telephone talker and gave instructions, then leaned over the voice tube.

"All ahead flank, make one six five turns."

"All ahead flank, make one six five turns, aye, aye sir. Engine room answers all ahead flank and one six five turns, sir"

"Very well."

Lt. Morgan joined Chief Swenson at the Starboard flag bag and watched their foaming wake. The stack gases turned black and immediately eased off to gray smoke.

Captain Brown motioned to the telephone talker and took his headset. He had some questions to ask his Chief Engineering Officer. The Hoquiam was still responding superbly after thirty minutes.

Lt. Hansen pressed his mike button

"Yes, Captain?" and listened.

"How's it going, Jim? Do you have an opinion?" asked the Captain.

"Captain, we just checked the temperature. All six bearings feel the same and in good range. The lube oil is not streaking anywhere."

The Captain closed his eyes and thought for a second. He pushed the mike button. "I want to push the engines. Let's go for five more turns and see if this bucket of rust will hold together."

Lt. Hansen's eyes widened and a tight grin formed on his face. "Captain, the Jason force is watching. Do you want to exceed BuShips while they're here?"

"Fuck em. It's our life and ship. Let's see how loud they squeal. As long as the engines seem to be holding together, stay at 170 turns. At the first sign of trouble, back off the turns first, then let me know."

"Aye, aye, Captain."

Hansen's face broke into a broad grin as he replayed the Captain's response in his mind. He didn't think the Jason-ites would care to hear it. It would be interesting to determine at what point the valves began to float, destroying the engines if left that high. However, that would not happen at 170 RPMs.

He leaned next to Chief Dortas's ear.

"We gotta play this real cozy, Chief. Crank up 170. We'll practically live on the bearings to see if anything goes wrong. Captain says to hold 170 all the rest of the way to Area George as long as temperature stays in bounds and the lube oil doesn't streak."

"What about these guys, boss? They're gonna shit a brick."

"To quote the Captain—fuck 'em. If they don't like it, let them leave!'"

Chief Dortas laughed and reached up to the RPM indicators, matching 170 just rung up.

The Jason trio were standing in the middle of the Engine room now, listening to the engines bellow and idly watching the ship's company Chief Engineer and Engineering Chief. The older chief's eyes narrowed as he watched the Chief move the RPM knob. He knew that was an increase. As he nudged his Division Officer, the chief and big white hat opened the throttles some more.

Lt. Hansen smiled as he watched the JayGee almost run to him.

"Sir," he stammered, "you're exceeding Buships specification by going above 165 turns. You must reduce your speed."

"Nope. You said you fixed it. We'll be going back up to Korea pretty soon and those extra turns might save our ass. One seventy or bust for about two more hours."

"Sir, I shall have to write you up for this. It's against regulations to exceed BuShips restrictions."

"You do that, fella. You'll be our witness that the Hoquiam can do better than nineteen knots." With that, Lt. Hansen joined the other two in testing temperatures.

The older Jason Chief walked over to Chief Dortas. "I hope you make it, Chief. Do you mind if I try to take temperature readings, too?"

Dortas looked at him and smiled. "Be my guest but be mighty fucking careful, Chief. Those damn knuckles got big teeth!"

The Hoquiam proceeded to the Allied Navy test area, Area George, trembling as she moved faster than she had ever moved. The Captain exercised the crew at various drills on the way to Area George. When he was satisfied with shipboard drills, the crew stood down for noon chow. The Plan of the Day clearly stated the Hoquiam was going to test the drones all afternoon.

"Engineroom Bridge—all ahead two-thirds. Make 135 turns both shafts."

"Engineroom—aye aye sir."

1330, February 20, 1951
USS Hoquiam PF-5
Underway
Area George for Drone exercise

"General Quarters General Quarters All hands man your battle Stations."

BONG BONG   BONG...

Everyone was already at their GQ station except those still on regular steaming watch, waiting to be relieved.

The Captain looked over his shoulder at Chief Swenson. "Chief."

The Chief hurried three steps to his side.

"Aye, Captain?"

"We're about to launch aircraft. Fox to the dip for flight quarters, please."

"Aye aye, sir." Chief Swenson turned to his Signalmen who immediately became attentive.

"Flag Hoist. Fox to the dip on port outer halyard. Two block after we launch the drone."

Smith got there first, clipped on the 'F', a red pennant with horizontal white diamond in the middle, and hoisted it to the dip. Then he stood by, waiting for the command to launch aircraft. This action might puzzle ships in the near vicinity because they knew the Hoquiam was not an aircraft carrier.

Lt. Austen Warren had arrived on the bridge several minutes before with his radio control transmitter. It was about the size of one of those cigar and cigarette cases pretty girls carried around in fancy night clubs. Removing it from its protective suitcase, he flipped the neck strap around his neck and clipped that strap to the farthest corners of the RC transmitter. Then he wrapped the leather waistband around his middle and fastened it to the near corners. This way both hands were free to control the birds on a stable platform.

He rolled his shoulders and pivoted from side to side letting the straps and case settle into his back. Looking around at the Bridge Watch, he stepped up to the port forward corner of the bridge and peered down at Curtis AB1 and his crew assembled around the drone clamped to the catapult.

Around the corner on deck on the starboard side, the rest of the drone crew had put the second drone together, except for the wings. They would attach the wings after that drone was clamped to the catapult.

Curtis looked up at Lt. Warren and wound up his index finger. Curtis wanted to start the drone's engine. Lt. Warren nodded his head and called down to him, "Okay, Curtis, wind up the rubber band."

The Captain looked amused, Chief Swenson laughed out loud, and others smiled or chuckled—just as Lt. Warren had intended.

Curtis nudged his engine specialist, Dennis, Aviation Machinist Mate Third Class, or AMM3, who fiddled with the drone's carburetor, pulled the eighteen-inch propeller through three turns, connected the battery, adjusted the carburetor some more, and yanked the propeller once. The little engine sneezed and snarled into life.

Dennis fussed with the carburetor until he was satisfied with the sound of the engine and disconnected the battery. He stepped back next to Curtis and leaned over his ear to tell him the engine was fine. It was time to test out the radio control circuits. Curtis nodded and waved at Lt. Warren, pointing to the tail surfaces wanting Lt. Warren to test the control surfaces.

Lt. Warren nodded, put on his headphones, and reached out to his radio control transmitter with several switches and knobs on it. He twisted a knob counter clockwise and looked down at the drone. The elevators moved smoothly downward. He let loose, allowing the knob to return to its center position. The elevators moved to the level position. He twisted the knob clockwise and watched the elevators move up, then he let loose and watched the elevators return to a level position.

Satisfied with the elevators, he moved his fingers to another knob and twisted it. Ailerons and rudder moved together showing a banking left turn. The drone quivered throughout the tests, attempting to follow as the prop blast flowed over the control surfaces.

Curtis threw a four-oh at Lt. Warren, who turned, nodded at the Captain and looked back to his red drone aircraft. He shifted his position, hands poised over his control panel. UtRon Five Det A was ready for action.

"Standby to launch drone aircraft. All hands forward of the Bridge take cover."

Mr. Dixon straightened from the 1MC, his eyes darting between the Captain and Lt. Warren.

"We're ready, Captain," shouted Lt. Warren above the snarling engine.

Now he let both hands rest lightly on the controls and got ready to fly the drone. The Captain looked down at the drone on the catapult, seeing Curtis holding his hand high, finger on the trigger to fire the catapult, with a long cable stretching back to the base of the ram. He looked back at Lt. Dixon and nodded.

"Launch drone Launch drone," came from the 1MC.

Curtis squeezed the trigger, releasing the hydraulic ram shoving the drone up the rails at high speed. Lt. Warren began his flight by continuing the drone's direction away from the port bow. He began twisting the elevator knob to gain some altitude just as the drone's engine sputtered and quit. Nosing over, the drone splashed in the ocean before Lt. Warren could flip the parachute switch on the control panel.

"All stop," called the Captain with a slight smile on his face.

"All stop, aye aye, Captain. Engine room answers all stop, Captain." A suggestion of a snicker floated up from the Wheelhouse voice tube.

"Very well."

The Captain looked where the drone was 'tilted nose down in the choppy water.

He turned to Lt. Warren who was red-faced and appeared to be talking to himself.

"Too bad your bird doesn't have pontoons, Mr. Warren," he said with a straight face, "you could drive it back to the ship." He leaned over the voice tube to the Wheelhouse.

"All back one-third."

"All back one-third, aye aye, Captain. Engine Room answers all back one-third."

"Very well."

"Boatswain's Mate of the Watch, pass the word for the recovery crew to lay to the portside of the fantail to recover the drone."

"Aye aye, Captain."

"Hey Chief, should I leave Fox two blocked or execute?" Smitty called.

Chief Swenson smiled and turned to the Captain.

"I heard that. Cancel Fox for now."

"Aye aye, Captain." Turning to Smith, he said "Cancel Fox."

Smith nodded, yanked the pennant back to the deck, stored the 'F' pennant in its slot in the flag bag and secured the halyard.

Recovery operations lasted nearly an hour because the ship's company recovery crew and UtRon personnel had to get their signals straight on how things were done. The Detachment didn't want their bird bent anymore than it was.

Lieutenant Warren and his detachment were ready to try again.

"Standby to launch drone aircraft. All hands forward of the Bridge take cover."

Mr. Dixon straightened from the 1MC, watching the Captain and Lt. Warren. The Captain looked over his shoulder at the Chief. "Two-block Fox, Chief."

Smitty who had expected this had Fox clipped on and ready to haul up.

"Do it, Smitty."

He hauled it up rapidly, with the Captain watching.

"We're ready to try again, Captain," yelled Lt. Warren above the snarling engine. Once again, he let both hands rest lightly on the controls and got ready to fly the drone. The Captain looked down at the drone on the catapult, saw that Curtis was holding his hand high, ready to squeeze his trigger finger to fire the catapult. He looked back at Lt. Dixon and nodded.

"Launch drone Launch drone," came from the 1MC.

Curtis squeezed the trigger and watched the drone zoom up the rails at high speed. Lt. Warren began his flight by continuing the drone's direction away from the port bow. He began twisting the elevator knob to gain some altitude, leaning back as though he were in the cockpit of the drone.

Mr. Warren flew the drone far forward and turned it 180 degrees to race along the port side about 1,000 yards out. As he flew the drone, he moved with the plane by swaying from side to side and leaning forward and back. And while he was manipulating the elevator and rudder rotating knobs, everyone could see he was inside that plane holding the joystick. Mr. Warren made the drone move up and down and side-to-side—jinking—in an effort to spoil the gunners' aim.

The port 40mm blasted it out of the sky with the third shot of the first clip. The drone broke apart in the air, bursting into flames near the engine just before it hit the water and sank.

Drone Number three was launched successfully. Mr. Warren flew it far forward of the ship, turned it about and sent it jinking its way back, out from the starboard side. Before the starboard 40mm could fire, the bird turned toward the ship. Mr. Warren determined he could not control the drone and flipped a toggle switch. The engine stopped and the drone nosed over. A parachute popped from the top and slowed its descent. This time the drone was nearly flat in the water. Deck and UtRon crews recovered this drone in less than a half-hour.

"Mr. Dixon, secure from General Quarters and head for Sasebo. Set Standard Speed at 140 turns. Steer 057 degrees true. Bring it slowly up to 165 RPM as we did before. Let's see if we can shake those HP bearings apart again. I'll be in my stateroom if you need me."

"Aye, aye, Captain."

"Captain to his Stateroom, Quartermaster."

"Quartermaster, aye, aye, sir."

Lt. Bob Dixon leaned back from the voice tube as the Captain's steps faded on the ladder. He stepped to the port side to watch his deck crew and UtRon finish with drone recovery. When the recovery operation was complete and the lifelines secured, he walked to the voice tubes. "All ahead standard. Make one four zero turns."

"All ahead standard. Make one four zero turns, aye aye, sir. Engine room answers all ahead standard and one four zero turns, sir."

"Very well. Left standard rudder. Come about to new course zero five seven true."

"Left standard rudder. New course zero five seven true, aye aye, sir. Rudder answers the helm, sir."

"Very well, all ahead flank. Make one six five turns."

"Make one six five turns, aye aye, sir. Engine room answers all ahead flank and one six five turns, sir."

"Very well."

Lt. Dixon raised his binoculars and began a slow look around, out to the horizon. Ending up looking aft, he took simple pleasure in the clean arc of the foaming wake as the ship came around to their new course for the high speed run to Sasebo.

"Steady on new course zero five seven true, Mr. Dixon."

"Very well, thank you."

1800, February 23, 1951
Wardroom
USS Hoquiam PF-5
Moored Buoy X-2
Sasebo Harbor, Japan

It was a miserable night. The Captain held the cup of coffee and saucer with both hands as he stared out of his closed glass porthole at the heavy rain coming down. Small craft warnings were up.

No liberty tonight. As restless as they are, I think they're ripe now. I'll bring it up at dinner and see who wants to bite Esther.

Captain Brown smiled as he thought about it, then sat down at his tiny desk, and continued writing in his journal. Finally, the Steward's Mate chimed for dinner. He deliberately waited a moment until he knew they were waiting for him. Then he rose and headed down the passageway to the Wardroom.

Thirteen officers rose to attention as he entered.

"Thank you. Be seated, please," he said and sat down at the head of the long table.

He pulled his napkin from its sterling silver ring and placed it in his lap as he glanced around the table.

Lettuce looks as bad as it did last week. A little more dressing ought to cover that.

He lifted a fork full of salad to his mouth and sat munching the salad. He reached for the pepper and added a significant amount to his salad.

Now's the time, I think.

He deliberately began searching the bulkheads for something. As he finished his salad, a Steward's Mate removed the small plate and slipped a bowl of Cream of Mushroom soup before him.

Plain military brown can or red and white label, Campbell's Soup is still Campbell's Soup.

He sipped quietly on the soup. For added flavor, he buttered humidity-laden squares of saltine crackers with not quite rancid butter. He continued to frown and look quizzically at various places on the Wardroom bulkheads. Some of his officers had noticed and were also looking at the bulkheads where he was looking without any idea of what he was doing.

He waited patiently.

Now, who is the most curious cat in this group?

Another Steward's Mate removed his soup bowl and laid a warmed dinner plate before him. Tonight's offering was roast pork, dehydrated mashed potatoes and powdered gravy, canned corn, and dinner rolls fresh from the Wardroom Galley. He looked at the slices of roast pork. He pointed to a particularly juicy looking slice and looked at Santos. "I'll have that slice, Santos, please," which Santos served with a large spoon and fork.

A large bowl of mashed potatoes appeared at his elbow and he took a generous portion, waving off the gravy in favor of butter, then accepted a healthy spoonful of corn and two rolls.

Damn, out of applesauce!

He continued his search, munching on a bite of pork. Finally, the natives were getting restless.

"Excuse me Captain, but you seem to be looking for something on the bulkheads. Is something missing?" asked Jim Hansen.

Oh thank you, Jim!

"Yes, I was wondering where the safest, most secure place for Esther might be."

Deafening silence. The fans roared like a fighter's propeller at high speed. Forks seemed to crash as they struck plates in search of food.

Eyes shot back and forth as each officer chewed as much on the comment as on their food. A few sat up straighter as they considered the Captain's strange comment.

Was it possible? Did the Captain want to play?

Lt. Robert Dixon laid his fork and knife across his plate and patted his mouth with a napkin. He studied his Captain's face for a moment, then grinned across the table at Lt.(jg) George Unsenger whose eyes got larger. Ensigns George Alice and Don Hitchcock stared across the table at each other and shrugged.

Lieutenant Marston cleared his throat. "Captain, I believe the best place is directly on the centerline where everyone entering our Wardroom through its only door will have a chance to admire it from afar." Lt. John Marston paused for a sip of water, his brow wrinkled in concentration, then continued. "This calls for one hell of a war plan, you realize that, Captain?"

"I do not believe this venture will be a cakewalk, John. Have you intelligence to share with us or is this idle chatter?" asked the Captain with a smile and dancing eyes filled with mischief.

"Well, I do know they are a rather prideful bunch over there who needs their noses tweaked. It seems to me we could visit the Thompson and sympathize with them. Might be able to gain some useful knowledge."

"Captain?" called Mr. Alice, hand waving in the air. The Captain nodded to him.

"My classmate from Gunnery school in San Diego is on the Thompson. I've been meaning to look him up anyway. This might be a way to find out something without obvious action."

"Okay, that's a great source. Why don't you see if you can talk one of the Signalmen into a P V T (private message) with the Thompson? See if you can invite yourself over there, or him over here, for a dinner visit—or meet at the O Club on your next shore leave? Bring up the subject and see what happens."

Ensign Alice smiled and nodded eagerly.

Lt.(jg) William Barris slouched back in his chair and looked at his buddy, Lt.(jg) Roger Forsythe.

"Rog, you're the one that showed me that message. Why don't we reconnoiter the Duchess Wardroom? I understand they have a fine bar and are eager to teach Americans a gentlemen's game of cards known as Whist. What do you say we take their money? Look how much we've taken from these guys at Bridge," he said waving around the Wardroom.

Lt. Porter snorted.

"I think I just heard a challenge, Art. Should we throw our money at them now or make them work for it," asked Bob Porter.

"As long as they're not working with 53-card decks, we ought to clean their clocks this time," commented Art Trapp.

Bill and Roger smiled in great delight. Their next shore leave would be on that pair.

The gentlemen of the Hoquiam Wardroom looked at each other with different eyes and relaxed in their chairs. They were going to have an adventure for a change.

Lieutenant Commander Maxfield J. Brown watched and smiled back at Lt. John Marston at the other end of the table. Then he bent to continue eating his cooling dinner.

Ensign George Alice had the 2000 to 2400 In-port Officer of the Deck Watch. Standing by the port quarterdeck with the Petty Officer and Messenger of the Watch, George thought this might be a good time to pay an inspection visit to the Signal Bridge to make sure the Bridge Watch was on their toes. He pulled a folded piece of paper from his pocket and looked at the message again.

TO THOMPSON DMS-38
FOR ENS PETER WILLIAMS X HOW
ABOUT DINNER YOUR PLACE OR
MINE X TIME TO SWAP SHOOTING
STORIES X REGARDS
ENS GEORGE ALICE

"Boats, I'm going to make the rounds, inspecting the weather decks. Be back in ten or fifteen minutes."

"Aye aye, sir. Need a flashlight?"

Ens. Alice held out his hand, then clattered up the ladder to the oh-one deck. Taking the complete tour, he walked quietly up to the bow on the port side, but didn't catch the anchor watch asleep.

After a couple of minutes of friendly talk and inspecting the mooring tackle, he walked down the starboard side to the ladder and climbed to the Signal Bridge. Curry had the watch. They both wandered around the Bridge a few minutes as Curry kept a weather eye cocked for flashing light signals from SOPA—a ship carrying the Senior Officer Present, Afloat.

"Curry, would you do me a favor please and send this to the Thompson? I'd like to get hold of an old buddy on there."

"Sure Mr. Alice, no sweat."

Curry took a minute to read it under the light.

"Tell you what, sir. I'm going to hit the yardarm blinkers with number 38 until I get an answer. She's somewhere out there in all those red anchor lights. Help me watch for someone to answer on their yardarm blinkers with a 'K'—okay?"

"Sure thing." Ensign Alice headed to the front of the Bridge to look in that direction.

Curry stepped back to the taffrail between both flag bags, snapped the switch and uncovered the key. Then he began sending 38 over and over, waiting for the Thompson to answer.

A blinding white light swept by and settled on the water in front of him. The Thompson's Signalman had decided to answer with a white 12-inch light from a five hundred yards away. Curry gave an AS1 — wait a minute, snapped off the yardarm blinker, and covered the key.

Stepping to the starboard 12-inch flashing light, he twisted the amber four-inch cover on, and snapped the light on. He pointed in the general direction of the Thompson, with the beam directed down toward the water.

No sense in blinding that Signalman.

Then he sent the message. Instead of an R for roger to acknowledge receipt of the note, the Thompson Signalman flashed back

HE OOD X BE RIGHT UP

Curry translated for Ensign Alice who didn't read code that well yet. The Thompson hit them with a light again. Curry was ready.

GEORGE X YOU SLY DOG X MOOCHING DINNER ALREADY X COME TOMORROW NIGHT 1800 X GOTTA GO X PETER

Thanking Curry, Ens. Alice continued his rounds before returning to the Quarterdeck. He was pleased. Their Wardroom would have some good dope about the Duchess Wardroom pretty fast.

1745, February 24, 1951
Wardroom, U.S.S. Thompson DMS-38
Sasebo Harbor, Japan

Lt.(jg) Barris, the 1600 to 1800 In-port Officer of the Deck, long glass tucked under his left arm, leaned outward and addressed the coxswain below in the motor whaleboat.

"Coxswain, deliver Mr. Alice to the quarterdeck of the Thompson DMS-38, then proceed to the Fleet Landing with the liberty party. Do you understand your orders?"

"Yes sir," came his reply.

"The Thompson is about five hundred yards off our starboard side. Carry out your orders," he said, returning the coxswain's salute.

"Aye, aye, sir."

The coxswain flipped the bell lanyard once.

Ding

The Motor Whaleboat eased away from the Jacobs Ladder at the Quarterdeck, controlling the tiller with his knees. Reaching down, he pulled the bell lanyard smartly four times.

Ding Ding Ding Ding

Ding Ding

The motor Whaleboat with a 5 on its bow bubbled along in neutral as it approached the Quarterdeck of the U.S.S. Thompson.

Ding Ding Ding

The engineer pushed the gearshift into reverse and stopped the Motor Whaleboat's forward motion.

Ding

The Thompson's Officer of the Deck put his hand to his mouth and called out, "Coxswain — state your business."

"Ensign Alice, U.S.S. Hoquiam, is invited to dinner on board the Thompson."

"Very well — come alongside."

Ding

The coxswain brought the Motor Whaleboat alongside the short accommodation ladder smartly.

Ding Ding

Ding Ding Ding

Ding Ding

A momentary surge of reverse and the Motor Whaleboat stopped where Mr. Alice stood ready to board.

"Sir, Ensign George Alice requests permission to come aboard for a visit with Ensign Peter Williams."

"Permission granted, Mr. Alice. Come aboard."

Mr. Alice trotted up the ladder, stepped aboard, and saluted the fantail, then the Officer of the Deck.

"Welcome aboard, Mr. Alice. The Messenger is rustling up Peter now."

"Thank you, sir." He turned, looked down at his coxswain, and raised his eyebrows in question to the Officer of the Deck. Hastily, the Thompson Officer of the Deck called to the coxswain in the Hoquiam Motor Whaleboat.

"Carry out your orders, Coxswain."

"Aye aye, sir." They exchanged salutes.

Ding

Ding Ding Ding Ding

Formalities over, the Motor Whaleboat raced away for the fleet landing with the liberty party. Mr. Alice studied the Officer of the Deck's face. He appeared to have some scratches and a black eye, as though he had been in a fight. Ensign George Alice decided to say nothing and turned away to look over the Thompson's after deck.

"Hey George, welcome aboard." Mr. Alice turned to greet his friend.

"Yea, Pietro, you're looking good," he responded automatically.

They shook hands and sized each other up as Ensign Peter Williams continued to talk. He, too, had a black eye, plus a puffy lower lip, and had seemed to limp as he had approached. His knuckles looked swollen and he winced when they shook hands.

"Dinner is in a few minutes and we'll have a couple of hours to catch up on chasing women." He winced again as he removed his hand from George's paw.

The two young officers walked forward along the warm inside passageway then pivoted and climbed the ladder one deck to enter the Wardroom. George took in the modern equipment as they walked along. Peter explained his gunnery duties with their five-inch mounts.

Several officers were present in the Wardroom and stared at George as he walked in.

"Gentlemen, let me introduce my friend and Gunnery School classmate, George Alice. George, this is the duty section. The rest of the Wardroom is on the beach at the Rest House recovering from various and sundry bruises."

George noticed that about half these officers seemed a little battered. "I see, Peter. If those gentlemen look anything like these gentlemen, I'd suggest less strenuous games."

"I suppose you wonder at our appearance, George," said Peter.

George laughed. "I read the Duchess message. That's how I knew your ship was here, in port. Seemed like looking you up was the thing to do.

One of the other officers spoke up.

"Wouldn't be fishing for a little information on Esther, now would you?" he said with a sly grin.

"Perish the thought. Just looking at you gentlemen gives me the sentiment that approaching Esther might be a little difficult."

"Very difficult is a better statement," growled another inmate.

"I wouldn't say they cheat and use enlisted men but there must have been a dozen officers waiting for us to make our move. Those guys are tough." This latter comment came from an officer who was holding his arm tenderly.

A voice from the door asked "Peter, is this your friend or just a spy from another ship trying to get Esther?"

"Yes sir, right both times, sir. This is Ensign George Alice from the Hoquiam PF-5. I think they have dreams of catching Esther, also. George, this is our Executive Officer, Lieutenant Hugh Owens."

George had an interesting evening on two counts. He heard several stories and different points of view, of their war efforts along both coasts, including the Inchon invasion, mine sweeping, and carrying frogmen to Hungnam to destroy the port. They had seen the Hoquiam and other PF's but were mystified as to their mission and capabilities.

After exploring that and inviting the officers to inspect the modern facilities on the Hoquiam, they told of their repulsed attack on Esther, how they hadn't even gotten to the Duchess Wardroom. Eventually, the Hoquiam Motor Whaleboat came along side and George took leave of his friendly hosts.

Lieutenants (Junior Grade) Barris and Forsythe returned from HMAS Duchess a little richer from a game of chance known as whist and not at all sober. Their thoughts about that Wardroom were fairly sober. Some planning ahead, some real planning was needed if they were to be successful.

They had admired Esther from afar, being blocked from too close an approach. They could see she was attached to the bulkhead with four half-inch bolts and nuts. A ratchet with half-inch socket attached ought to free those nuts.

Now how do we get in there to do this neat trick? asked Bill Barris to himself.

February 25, 1951
Naval Motion Picture Exchange
U.S. Naval Fleet Activities, Sasebo, Japan

The Blue sign with Gold lettering read

Officer-In-Charge

U.S. Navy Motion Picture Exchange

U.S. Naval Fleet Activities, Sasebo, Japan

Edge, YN1, knocked on the Officer-In-Charge's door and waited. Lieutenant Commander Nesworth looked up with a question on his face.

"Mr. Nesworth, there's a Lieutenant Commander out here, the Commanding Officer of U.S.S. Hoquiam. He requests a moment of your time."

Nesworth signed the letter in front of him and returned the ink pen to its holder. He handed the letter to Brown and said, "Send him in. Let's see what his complaint is."

Captain Brown, it seemed, had an admirable, sneaky, underhanded plan. He wanted a new movie, the newest available, in fact. It wasn't for his own wardroom, he claimed, but that of the U.S.S. Eversole. He said he didn't know a soul on that ship. Captain Brown went on to explain the purpose behind this request. Nesworth thought Brown had a fascinating plan.

He scanned his list of movies to see if he could find one that might help out.

"I think this will do it. This is the newest movie I have in stock. Claudette Colbert, George Brent, and Orson Welles in 'Tomorrow Is Forever'. Nineteen Forty-six—that's practically brand new around here, Captain."

Captain Brown was pleased. The movie had Claudette and she ought to attract a lot of viewers from the Duchess. Pretty good-looking bait.

He nodded, "That sounds just fine to me. Now, how can we arrange for the Eversole to get it for tonight?"

Lt. Comdr. Nesworth leaned around Captain Brown.

"Edge, when is the Eversole due to make its next movie run?"

Edge looked up from his desk, pointing to a ledger.

"Due in today, sir, to exchange films. She gets the in-port treatment, comes in every third day. One film for each projector every day."

Captain Brown's eyebrows lifted a notch. "In-port films?"

"Yes. When we get brand new films—this one qualifies—we send it around to all the ships in port. We receive all ships movement reports, and arrange to give those ships leaving port for extended periods a large selection of slightly older movies.

That explain how we get copies of movies from the Thirties, I suppose.

If the movie operator gets suspicious about this generous offer, Edge will tell him this is a sneak preview— got that, Edge?"

"Yes sir, do we get to watch the fireworks from afar, Captain?" he answered from outside the office. Captain Brown smiled back at him.

"Mr. Nesworth, how would you like to join us for a baked ham dinner with all the trimmings day after tomorrow night as appreciation for your help?"

"I accept with thanks," he said eagerly. "Don't get much of a chance to eat in a Wardroom in this assignment. I'm sure you're going to have a hell of an interesting tale."

"My gig will be at the Officers' Landing at 1730 for you day after tomorrow evening."

2130, February 25, 1951
PF-5 Captain's Gig
Sasebo Harbor, Japan

Her Majesty's Australian Ship, Destroyer Duchess, was moored at Buoy 24 nested with two American destroyers on her port side, and a Netherlands destroyer on the starboard side. Mike Morgan's roommate at college was the Executive Officer of the outboard American destroyer, the U.S.S. Walke.

Ding Ding

The Hoquiam motor whaleboat engineer moved the gear knob to Neutral.

Ding Ding Ding

He shoved the gear knob into the Reverse detent and fed just enough throttle to keep the engine from stalling.

Ding Ding

Back to Neutral. He looked up the side of the USS Walke at the Quarterdeck. His Coxswain held the boat about ten yards away, looking at the Walke's Officer of the Deck. The OOD did not disappoint the coxswain.

"State your business, coxswain," called the OOD.

"USS Hoquiam PF-5, Lieutenant Morgan to visit Lieutenant Hastings, sir." Yelled the coxswain.

The Officer of the Deck disappeared for a moment, then returned to the Quarterdeck. "Very well, come along side."

Ding

The engineer engaged forward with just enough throttle to keep the engine from stalling while moving the boat forward.

Ding Ding

Lt. Morgan hopped onto the accommodation ladder and climbed to the brow. Saluting the Officer of the Deck and the Fantail, he asked, "Request permission to come aboard, sir?"

"Permission granted, Mr. Morgan. Mr. Hastings will be here momentarily." Then he leaned over the side and called out to the coxswain. "Coxswain, carry out your orders."

"Aye aye, sir," saluting, as he reached for the bell cord with his left hand.

Ding

As the motor whaleboat cleared the accommodation ladder, he signaled for full speed to return to the Hoquiam.

Ding Ding Ding Ding

Lt. Morgan enjoyed a fine dinner, staying until close to movie call at 2000.

"Ken, it's been a great evening. I'll have you over to our wardroom in a couple of days. You'll get a chance to see our wonderful life."

Lt. Hastings grinned and shook his head. "No need for the soft soap, Mike. I've heard all about your marvelous modern vessels. But I do accept." He started to escort Lt. Morgan from the wardroom.

"No need, Ken. Think I can find my way to the Quarterdeck."

He closed the door to the Wardroom behind him and quietly headed up the ladder to the wheelhouse. From there, Lt. Morgan sneaked rapidly up to the open bridge and climbed across onto the U.S.S. Eversole's open bridge, a rather easy trick. All commanding officers like to line up their ships to present a sharp naval appearance when moored in nests. Mike Morgan hid in a shadow where he could see the Quarterdeck and gangway to the Duchess without being seen by the duty Signalman.

The Eversole's 1MC opened. "Movie call movie call. Tonight's movie on the Mess Deck is the nineteen thirty-eight classic 'The Dawn Patrol' starring Errol Flynn. In the Chiefs' Mess is the nineteen forty-five comedy 'Blythe Spirit' starring Rex Harrison. The Wardroom movie is the nineteen forty-six movie with Claudette Colbert, George Brent, and Orson Welles, in 'Tomorrow is Forever'. Movies start in five minutes."

Four Australian officers left their wardroom and approached their Quarterdeck to the U.S.S. Eversole

Quarterdeck. In the American Navy tradition, they saluted the fantail and the Officer of the Deck.

"Request permission to come aboard and watch your movie, sir?"

The young Ensign smiled with pleasure. He returned their salutes.

"Permission granted, gentlemen. Enjoy the hospitality of our wardroom and the movie. Sorry I can't join you. Maybe after the movie for a few minutes."

The officers smiled back and nodded to him as they went forward to the Americans' Wardroom.

It wasn't often officers of other Navies visited U.S. Navy wardrooms. The American Navy is the only Navy that did not serve intoxicants of any sort since a straitlaced Secretary of Navy banned spirits from U.S. Navy ships one hundred years ago. Spirits on board had to be either in Sickbay for medicinal purposes or held in sealed compartments for delivery to some naval station.

Mike Morgan's smile grew as he watched the Australian Navy officers hurrying forward below him. He crouched and scuttled across to the starboard side of the Eversole Bridge next to his target. Staying in the deep shadows, he watched the Australian Signalman until he knew his walking pattern. Like any other Signalman, he had to keep watch in all directions for signaling ships. The Duchess's open bridge was a little further away but just slightly lower in the water.

At the next opportunity, Lt. Morgan carefully made his way to a dark spot next to where he would board the Duchess. He watched the Aussie stroll around to the other side of his open bridge.

NOW!

He jumped lightly onto the Duchess open bridge and scurried into another dark spot, trying to avoid breathing heavily.

I'm getting too old for this shit.

Lifting his wrist to his eyes, he read the luminous dial on his watch. It was not yet time to head for the Wardroom with his ratchet driver and socket wrench, so he sat down on the cold deck and made himself as small as possible.

The silver number '5' on the Motor Whaleboat faded as clouds pushed over the moon. Since the Hoquiam had only one motor whaleboat, it served as the Captain's Gig when he was aboard it and the American flag was displayed at the stern. At all other times, the American flag was not displayed. This was such a time, even though the Captain was on board.

The boat moved silently through the water toward the nest of destroyers. Eight officers grunted and puffed with each stroke of their paddles. One officer, with gold oak leaves on his collars, sat benignly next to the tiller whispering encouragement to his younger officers.

"I still don't understand why I have to swim in this ugly water," whispered Ensign Don Hitchcock.
"That's because the rest of us" — puff — grunt — "outrank you, Don. Better" — grunt — "save your breath now" — puff — "before you slip into the water," snickered Ensign George Alice.

"All together now," whispered the Captain, "one last pull — stroke!"

The Motor Whaleboat drifted closer to the nest mooring chains and stopped.

"Over you go, Don," the Captain whispered. "Remember to make a stealthy-like racket to attract attention when you grab the Duchess mooring chain. We want you to have a nice, large, friendly reception when you arrive at the edge of the fantail."

Don Hitchcock nodded and slipped quietly over the far side and began breast stroking toward the mooring buoy, trying to breathe through his nose and keep water out of his mouth.

What the hell is that? Aaghhh, it's a turd!

Twirling around in the water, he discovered that garbage and shit—real shit—surrounded him. Grimly, Don stroked his way through the water.

"All together now," Captain Brown whispered, "one hard back stroke before I turn us. Stroke!"

They all dug in and pulled. The Captain pushed the tiller over and they turned.

"Okay, we need to get beyond the Walke and in its shadow before we start the engine.—Stroke stroke stroke . . ."

"That's good enough. Jim, if you can sprinkle holy water on that miserable engine and start it, we'd all be eternally grateful."

Lt. Jim Hansen nodded, puttered in the dark a few moments and pushed the starter. Nothing happened.

No cranking sounds! Not even a solenoid click!

Shit, the friggin' key, I forgot to turn the key!

He located and turned the key, then pushed the starter. The starter ground and the engine caught immediately. Jim hastily throttled back to an idle and put the engine in Forward as the Captain pulled the tiller and pointed the bow away from the Walke. Jim looked around at his friends who were still puffing and rubbing their arms. He was dripping sweat, too, even though it was a very cold night.

The Captain turned toward Hanson, waved at him and made the cavalry signal to move out. Jim advanced the throttle to full speed. Captain Brown had no intention of being close to the nest as he approached Hr.M.S. Evertsen, destroyer of Her Majesty's Netherlands Navy. Circling wide, he approached the Evertsen from the direction of the Fleet Landings.

Lights suddenly illuminated the fantail on the Duchess. There seemed to be activity involving several people. More were running from the main superstructure area.

"Okay, ahead slow, Jim, then neutral about fifty feet off the Quarterdeck," called the Captain in a normal voice. The Captain waited until they were close aboard and the Evertsen Quarterdeck Watch was looking at them through the long glass.

"Ahoy, Evertsen," he called.

"Ahoy, Five. Are you calling on us?" came back the voice of the officer on duty.

"Request permission to cross over to the Duchess, sir. We would like to visit them this evening."

"Permission granted. Come alongside," responded the Dutch Watch Officer with a slight accent. He was now chuckling as he realized their mission. The Hoquiam officers rendered Honors as they came aboard with grins on their faces.

"Good luck, gentlemen. They are a tough bunch."

Captain Brown, leading the way, broke into a run. No Honors this trip. Their plan was to make noise and try to make their way toward the Wardroom. Hopefully, the Aussies would fall for this ruse.

They hit the gangway between the Evertsen and Duchess without slowing down and turned forward, still running. A gong began ringing faintly and loud voices came from the fantail. The intelligence returned by Bill Barris and Roger Forsythe did not prepare them for the kinds and numbers of obstacles placed in their path.

Attacked from the front and rear, Captain Brown realized they would be overpowered in moments.

Come on, Mike. Get that trophy! I hope we bought him enough time. Ooo that hurt!

He lashed out at the body in front of him. As they exchanged blows, the battle moved back and forth along the starboard main deck.

One by one, the Hoquiam officers were lifted into the air above four officers and rushed to the fantail where they were tossed unceremoniously into the harbor, accompanied by cheerful rude noises, laughter, and insults, all intended to humiliate them.

Seven officers treaded water as they waited for the Motor Whaleboat to make its way to them. Bob Porter, who couldn't swim a lick, was handling the boat alone. He managed to get the boat back to their watery spot without running over them.

The boat coasted to a stop very near the group who was looking up at the rowdy Aussies still calling insults and laughing at them. Painfully, each of the officers pulled themselves into the boat, helped by Bob Porter. Art Trapp, never seasick in his life, was heaving his guts out. Something had bumped his face while he waited to board. He sucked in his breath in shock as he recognized the large lump, almost taking it in with his breath.

Shit! Ooo, that smells ugly.

Captain Brown sat miserably with his skin crawling as he remembered all the shit he had to swim through. Ugh! He shivered but not from the cold water.

He counted noses and realized Mike Morgan was still missing.

"Jim," he said in a low voice, "start the engine and let's run out of here, then creep around to the bow mooring buoy. Maybe Mike made it."

They pulled out fast, swept far around, and crept back in with paddles to stop by the forward mooring buoy to look for Mike.

"Gentlemen."

Their heads whipped up to the bow of the Duchess. Eight or ten officers stood there, Lieutenant Mike Morgan held over the heads of six strong Aussie gentlemen. "Are you looking for this piece of garbage? Please check his new haircut."

With that, they heaved him out as far out as they could. Legs and arms flailing, Mike Morgan hit the water in the middle of garbage and other unmentionable material.

"Aaghh, it's crap!"

Mike was pulled aboard the boat. With that, Captain's Gig of the PF-5 beat a quiet retreat to their ship.

Three showers later, the Captain still felt unclean but headed for the Wardroom to see how his gang of thieves was faring. They were waiting for him. He waved them to their seats, drew a cup of coffee from the Silex pot, and leaned back against its sideboard.

Captain Maxfield J. Brown gazed upon his officers. Hmmm, the makings of four black eyes, a split lip, and five fat lips—and look at Mike. He burst out laughing. "A likely bunch of thieving pirates we turned out to be. Mike, what the hell happened to you?"

"Well, Captain, the first thing those sneaky bastards did was set us up. Esther was not in the same place as when a game of Whist was being played the other night."

Roger and Bill looked at each other in shock.

"Then, instead of four half-inch nuts to unfasten from the bolts, there were eight five-eighths-inch nuts on long bolts so regular sockets can't reach down that far. A crescent wrench would have worked on the first two or three before time ran out but that's all."

A general shaking of heads followed over the deceit and trickery of the Duchess officers.

"While I was trying to figure that one out, three of them charged into the wardroom and pounded me into the deck before removing my hat and shirt."

He stood and leaned over until the top of his head was plainly clear. This brought about several strong laughs and chuckles.

"Then, I got a haircut. Although I heard the clippers, I think they pulled out each hair by the roots." He grinned ruefully as he continued. "Those sporting bastards were just as friendly and polite as could be as they did me in. They did compliment us on our cheeky methods though."

"Mike, they shaved a capital 'D' on the top of your head."

"That figures."

"Captain, it looks like you could use some touchup makeup on your right eye. That's going to be a real shiner."

Captain Brown reached up and felt around his face. It did feel a little puffy. After a while, Captain Brown left the Wardroom and returned to his Stateroom for another shower before retiring.

0915, February 28, 1951
Wardroom
USS Hoquiam PF-5
In nest alongside U.S.S. Jason ARH-1
Sasebo Harbor, Japan

Two Chiefs stood with combination hats tucked under their arms outside the Wardroom door, waiting to be invited in by the Captain. Chiefs Billons and Dortas had requested a combined meeting of their respective department heads with the Captain. The engine in the Motor Whaleboat was still giving them fits, and they didn't trust it as far as they could throw the Whaleboat.

Both were aware they would be heading up to the newly established blockade along the Northeast coast of Korea. The Motor Whaleboat needed a new engine. This engine was beyond the combined wisdom of SRF Yokosuka and the U.S.S. Jason.

After hearing the chiefs, the Captain requested representatives from the Jason Repair Office attend this meeting. The representatives, an officer and a chief, had just arrived for the discussions.

Lt. Dixon pushed aside the green curtain and smiled at them. "Come on in and sit down, Chiefs. Grab some coffee. We could use some ideas here."

Billons and Dortas laid their hats on the sideboard with the officers' hats. Chief Billons sat down next to Lt. Dixon. Chief Dortas sat next to Lt. Hansen. They both looked around and focused on two strangers — an officer and chief they recognized from the Jason. Leaning forward, Chief Dortas poured coffee into two cups and pushed one across to Chief Billons.

"Chiefs," said the Captain, "we have been explaining how the Motor Whaleboat is very important and the motor is untrustworthy. We'd like to add your comments to ours.—Chief Billons, what say you?"

Chief Billons placed both hands on the green cloth and rose to lean toward the Jason-ites. His eyes narrowed as he thought what might impress them.

Yeah, this ought to do it.

"Let me tell you about a terrible day in December off Hungnam while the evacuation was going on. It was as cold and stormy, with as high winds and waves, as I've ever seen it. The Hoquiam was on station at the Sea Buoy. Those waves—" he turned to Mr. Marston who rode in it that day and whispered, "twenty foot?"

Mr. Marston barely nodded his head. He really would rather not remember that ride.

The Chief continued. "Well, at least twenty foot waves, anyway. We had to send Mr. Marston in the boat over to a Jap LST which wasn't cooperating with us."

He leaned a little farther toward the Jason people and his voice turned gravelly.

"You shoulda seen that fuckin' little boat. As we lowered the boat, we didn't know if it would start or not. And if it started," he slowly sat, leaned over the table, and pounded his index finger on the table to emphasize each word, "would that piece a shit keep runnin?"

"There were times that boat was on its beam ends or almost straight up and down. The coxswain did one hell of a job of keeping it upright. I really thought they was a goner a couple of times."

He paused for a moment and slowly sank into his seat without taking his eyes off them.

"If the boat had capsized, the only thing we coulda done was maybe recover their bodies. We don't have a second boat, like destroyers do. The first one, the only one, has to work every gawdamned time we take the fucker out. I know we're going to be facing the same kind of situation again, shortly. That's all."

He leaned back and looked down at his lap. Then he leaned forward and held up a finger for attention before anyone could start talking.

"Please give us a new engine."

The assembled group of Hoquiam officers and chiefs remembered that day off Hungnam, soberly. The Captain glanced at the Jason officer and chief who seem shocked by Billon's story and plea. He cleared his throat and pointed to Chief Dortas.

"Chief, you have anything to add?"

"Yes, Captain." He stood and backed around his chair to lean against its back.

"We can't fix it. Lord knows we've tried enough times. The Ship Repair Facility in Yokosuka worked it over three times in their shop. You have worked on it twice before, and have it aboard right now. The Missouri Engineers tried to help once.

"Problem is that old motor needs a chain added to it. It might make a good boat anchor if it doesn't drag."

Several chuckles relieved the tension.

"No one is going to fix that damn thing, it's plumb worn out. Mainly, I can't turn to Chief Billons and his boat crews and say that I trust that motor. We check that boat engine out thoroughly every morning we're underway. It always seems in good shape. But from one lowering to the next, we just don't know if the engine will start. We have to have a new one."

Chief Dortas pulled the pitcher of coffee toward him, poured another cup, and sat sipping.

Hell, this isn't as good as the Mess Deck's coffee!

Captain Brown looked down the table at the Jason representatives. His two Chiefs really put the story out straight, as professionals.

"I think that says it all. Can you tell us anything now? Or will we have to wait for a letter?"

The Jason Engineering Repair Officer and his leading Chief looked at each other for a moment. The Chief looked at his lap and moved his fist—with thumb up—slowly up and down.

The Repair Officer, in complete agreement, looked up, glanced around and began to speak deliberately. "Chief Billons, your tale made quite an impression, and Chief Dortas, we do understand. However, I have to see if the Repair Boss will go along with our recommendation to replace the motor. We should be able to get back to you within an hour."

Everyone stood and shook hands around. The three Chiefs left and disappeared forward into the Chiefs' Quarters for a cup of coffee and talk. After they settled down in chairs with coffee mugs in their hands, the Jason Chief turned to Dortas.

"Do you really think it's worn out?"

"Hell yes, it's worn out. The Russkies had it for three years. No telling what they did to it. We know what they did to the rest of the ship. We just can't fix that fuckin' thing."

"Boats, was it really that bad up there?"

Chief Billons straightened up and looked him square in the eye.

"Worse than the words I know how to use," he growled. "I was scared shitless. My dumbass young crew didn't have enough sense to be really scared but Doc took about three hours to thaw them out when they got back. I'd rather leave port without that fuckin' boat, the way it works now."

The Jason Chief just shook his head.

"I can't swear to it, you understand, but we will probably yank your engine tonight. There's a rebuilt Buda in storage below decks. We can uncrate it in the early morning and start testing it before noon. When you guys due to sail?"

"I hear day after tomorrow. That enough time?" asked Chief Billons.

"Shit yes. We don't go up to the battle lines but we do work around the clock. Your boat's already in a cradle. I'll put a little more pressure on Mr. Stevens. He'll go to bat for you."

**FM HMAS DUCHESS
TO ALL SHIPS SASEBO HARBOR
BT
ALAS ALAS WE RETURN TO OUR HOME DOWN UNDER X WITH TEARS OF PRIDE AND GREAT SADNESS WE MUST LEAVE ESTHER BEHIND X WE CHOOSE A WORTHY WARDROOM TO PROTECT AND ADMIRE ESTHER AFTER WE DEPART X SEVEN SHIPS HAVE GIVEN BATTLE X SEVEN SHIPS RETIRED IN HUMILIATION WITHOUT THE COVETED TROPHY IN THEIR POSSESSION X BY UNAMINOUS VOTE WE PASS ESTHER TO THE USS HOQUIAM PF5 X WE BELIEVE HER CHEEKY ATTACK WAS THE SNEAKIEST AND HER FEW OFFICERS THE BRAVEST TO TAKE ON THREE TIMES THEIR SKIMPY FORCE X WELL TRIED HOQUIAM X GUARD ESTHER WELL
BT**

FM USS HOQUIAM
TO ALL SHIPS SASEBO HARBOR
BT
OUR TRANQUILLITY WAS SHATTERED,
WHEN AN OLD AND RATHER
BATTERED,
HIGHLY THOUGHT OF BIT OF TROPHY
CAME ABOARD,
AND WE PLEDGED OURSELVES
UNENDING,
IN OUR EFFORTS TOWARD DEFENDING,
AND TOWARD KEEP ESTHER HERE
THROUGH FIRE AND SWORD.
THE DUCHESS THOUGHT SHE'D SEND
IT,
AND LET US TRY TO DEFEND IT,
'CAUSE SHE SAYS THAT WE'RE THE
ONE WHO REALLY RATES;
BESIDES ESTHER'S UNDER ORDERS,
TO REMAIN THE FAR EAST WATERS,
AND THE DUCHESS' LEAVING
SHORTLY FOR SYDNEY DOWN UNDER.
THEY'LL COME BY PUNT AND
WHERRY,
AND THEIR PLANS ARE SANGUINARY,
AND THEY'LL TRY BY STEALTH AND
FORCE TO TAKE OUR PRIZE,
THEY'LL THINK THAT THEY CAN DIG
IT,
'CAUSE THEY REALIZE A FRIGATE,
HASN'T MUCH WITH WHICH TO FIGHT
BECAUSE OF SIZE.
IF THE ESTHER FLAG IS SHIFTED,
IF THE TROPHY'S OVER LIFTED,
TO GRACE ANOTHER WARDROOM DAY
AND NIGHT,

THEN THE PEOPLE WHO HAVE DONE IT,
WILL HAVE REALLY TRULY WON IT,
AND BY GOD THEY'LL KNOW THEY HAD A FIGHT.

Thanks to then Lt.(jg) Lawrence Hawkinson, USNR, Damage Control Officer, who helped write the Hoquiam Wardroom reply to the two Duchess messages.

MARCH

March 4, 1951
Executive Officer's Stateroom
U.S.S. Hoquiam PF-5
Underway to Wonsan, North Korea

The ship rolled gently as she picked up speed beyond the harbor anti-submarine nets. Stewart sat in Mr. Marston's stateroom, reading the Red Cross message again. Coyle copied it on the Fox broadcast.

They kept me moving around so I wouldn't see this. James had written it up while I was making rounds, I guess.

> FM AMCROSS WASHDC
> TO USS HOQUIAM PF-5
> BT
> FOR COMMANDING OFFICER X
> ADVISE STEWART L H SA THAT BETTY
> ECHOLS DELIVERED A BOY BABY 6
> LBS 3 OZ MARCH 2 1951 AT 231AM IN
> GENERAL HOSPITAL CMA ASTORIA
> OREGON X BABY NAMED RALPH
> ROGER NO LAST NAME X SHE INSISTS
> STEWART IS FATHER X ASTORIA
> RED CROSS REPRESENTATIVE SAYS
> FAMILY IS DEMANDING STEWART
> BE PLACED ON EMERGENCY LEAVE
> AND RETURNED TO ASTORIA TO

MARRY MISS ECHOLS X REQUEST
ESTIMATED DATE OF ARRIVAL
BT

The Hoquiam creaked and shook as it headed through Tsushima Straits at full speed. The Hoquiam was going to take part in the Wonsan naval blockade and bombardment. Stewart sat numbly, once again in despair. He felt like life was beginning to squeeze the shit out of him. Stewart looked up at Lt. Marston with anguish on his face.

"What do I do now, sir? I never laid her. That's not my baby." He stopped to read it again. He exploded as he discovered something he'd overlooked.

"Holy shit, Mr. Marston, she named the baby after the father—I mean that guy that went into the Air Force. If I'm supposed to be the father of that kid, why'd she name him after that guy?"

Lt. Marston looked steadily at Stewart as he read that message.

"We decided to hold that message until we had more information for you. You will want to look at these, too, Stewart."

He handed him a message flimsy to read.

FM USS HOQUIAM
TO AMCROSS WASHDC
INFO BUPERS
BT
REGRET UNABLE TO SEND STEWART
ON EMERGENCY LEAVE X HIS
PRESENCE IS REQUIRED ON BOARD X
NO OTHER PERSONNEL AVAILABLE

FOR HIS DUTIES X IN RECEIPT FURTHER INFORMATION FROM ASTORIA X SUGGEST YOUR LOCAL RED CROSS REPRESENTATIVE CONTACT CLATSOP COUNTY DISTRICT ATTORNEY SOONEST X COMMANDING OFFICER USS HOQUIAM SENDS HIS SYMPATHY TO THE FAMILY
BT

As soon as Stewart absorbed the Hoquiam message, Lt. Marston held out another flimsy.

NAVAL SPEEDLETTER
MARCH 01, 1951
FROM USNS TONGUE POINT, ASTORIA, OREGON
TO USS HOQUIAM PF5 C/O FLEET POST OFFICE, SAN FRANCISCO, CALIF
SUBJECT: STEWART V. STATE OF OREGON FOR BETTY ECHOLS
ENCLOSURES:
(A)   COPY OF SEARCH WARRANT AND SAMPLES
(B)   COPY OF LETTER TO ONI
(C)   COPY OF ONI LETTER
(D)   COPY OF LETTER TO NAVY DEPT & BUPERS
(E) COPY OF LETTER TO DISTRICT ATTORNEY

1. DISTRICT ATTORNEY, CLATSOP COUNTY, INITIALLY OBJECTED TO OUR REQUEST FOR SEARCH WARRANT, REF (A), OF BETTY ECHOLS

HIGH SCHOOL RECORDS AND ANY HOMEWORK ASSIGNMENTS, REPORTS, OR PAPERS IN WHICH HER HANDWRITING APPEARS. FACT THAT STEWART HAD NO OTHER COPY OF HER HANDWRITING THAN THE ALLEGED LETTER WORKED IN HIS FAVOR.

2. SAMPLES OF PAPERS SEIZED AT ASTORIA HIGH SCHOOL AND PHOTOCOPY OF THE LETTER TO STEWART REFERRED TO ONI LAB, NAVAL AIR STATION SAND POINT, SEATTLE, FOR INVESTIGATION, REF (B). THEIR REPORT TO DISTRICT ATTORNEY AND BUPERS, COPY THIS COMMAND, STATES THERE ARE SUFFICIENT POINTS OF SIMILARITY TO UNEQUIVOCALLY STATE THE LETTER IS GENUINE, WRITTEN BY BETTY ECHOLS. IT IS NOT A FORGERY, REF (C).

3. THIS COMMAND, IN REFERENCE (D), OPINED THERE IS NO BASIS OF CHARGES AND REQUESTED BUPERS AND THE NAVY DEPARTMENT NOT SUPPORT THE ECHOLS FAMILY DEMANDS.

BY SEPARATE LETTER, REF (E), THE DISTRICT ATTORNEY HAS BEEN REQUESTED TO DROP CHARGES AGAINST STEWART. THE NAVY SUPPORTS STEWART'S CONTENTION HE DID NOT HAVE THE OPPORTUNITY TO COPULATE AND FATHER HER CHILD. IT APPEARS STEWART HAS GROUNDS TO FILE CHARGES AGAINST THE ECHOLS FAMILY. THIS COMMAND WILL UNDERTAKE NO FURTHER ACTION IN THIS MATTER.

Stewart looked up with gratitude as he finished the Tongue Point letter. Mr. Marston held out his hand for that letter and gave him another letter to read.

NAVAL SPEEDLETTER
MARCH 03, 1951
FROM U.S. NAVY BUREAU OF NAVAL
PERSONNEL (B-21143)
TO USNS TONGUE POINT, ASTORIA,
OREGON
          AMCROSS WASHDC
          COPY USS HOQUIAM PF5 C/O FPO,
SAN FRANCISCO, CALIF.
          NAVY DEPARTMENT, WASHINGTON,
D.C.
SUBJECT: STEWART V. STATE OF OREGON FOR
BETTY ECHOLS
REFERENCE: (A) YOUR LETTER TO NAVY DEPT
& BUPERS

1. EVIDENCE PROVIDED BY ONI COMMANDANT
THIRTEENTH NAVAL DISTRICT OFFICE SHOWS
MISS ECHOLS IMPROPERLY ACCUSED STEWART
OF PATERNITY.
2. BY SEPARATE COVER, DISTRICT ATTORNEY
IS ADVISED THE U.S. NAVY HAS NO INTEREST
IN THIS MATTER AND WILL NOT SUPPORT
CHARGES AGAINST STEWART. THE NAVY
DEPARTMENT FURTHER SUGGESTS THAT IF
THE DISTRICT ATTORNEY HAD RESEARCHED
THE CHARGES PROPERLY, THIS CASE WOULD
NEVER HAVE DEVELOPED.

Stewart looked up at Lt. Marston with a grin. "Is that it, Mr. Marston?"

"We still have to hear from the District Attorney. However, ONI cleared you of forgery and said it was her letter. But, I still wouldn't ask for liberty in Astoria for a while, Stewart."

"No way, sir, no fucking way. Thank you for everything. I think my ass was really on the chopping block."

"It was, and you are entirely welcome—you got the board with you?" Back to business. Stewart checked the board and handed it to him for reading and initials.

"THIS IS A F R S TOKYO WITH THE MORNING NEWS, MARCH EIGHTH, NINETEEN FIFTY ONE, AIR FORCE SERGEANT RICHARD HENNING REPORTING. DATELINE UNITED NATIONS COMMAND IN KOREA. SUPREME UNITED NATIONS COMMANDER GENERAL DOUGLAS MACARTHUR ANNOUNCED TODAY THE BEGINNING OF OPERATIONS RIPPER. THIS OPERATION WILL DRIVE THE COMMUNISTS BACK TO THE 38TH PARALLEL AND RETAKE SEOUL, HE SAID. SEVEN U.S. DIVISIONS ARE PARTICIPATING. THEY ARE FIRST CAVALRY, FIRST MARINE DIVISION, SECOND, THIRD, SEVENTH, TWENTY-FOURTH ARMY DIVISIONS AND THE NATIONAL GUARD TWENTY-FIFTH INFANTRY DIVISION. . . ."

1730, March 9, 1951
Bridge
USS Hoquiam PF-5
Arriving Wonsan, North Korea

"Phone talker, advise engine room to be ready to answer all bells."

"Aye aye, Captain," answered the phone talker as he pressed his mike button.

"Engine room ready to answer all bells, Captain."

"Very well."

"Mr. Porter, reduce speed to two-thirds, please."

"Aye aye, Captain." He leaned over the voice tube to the wheelhouse.

"All ahead two-thirds."

"All ahead two-thirds, sir. Engine room answers all ahead two-thirds, sir."

"Very well."

The Captain continued to study the ships at anchor behind Yo Do with his binoculars. They were guarding the mouth of Wonsan Harbor as the ship slipped into the shadow at dusk. Let's see, Saint Paul is hiding back there somewhere—ah there it is. He glanced down at the gyro repeater and lined up on the Saint Paul's mast.

"Come to course one zero three true, Mr. Porter."

"Helmsman, right standard rudder. Steady up on course one zero three true."

"Right standard rudder, aye aye, sir. New course one zero three true, sir. Rudder answers the helm, sir."

"Very well."

The ship heeled over as the ship bit into the turn to starboard to head for the Saint Paul with twenty-three bags of mail. She also had mail for the destroyers and ComMinRon Three to pass to her squadron of minesweepers.

"Steady on new course one zero three true, Mr. Porter."

"Very well."

"Saint Paul is challenging us, Captain," called Chief Swenson as he ran to the Signal Shack for the codebook. In a moment, he popped back out.

"I have the reply ready, Captain."

"Use the long form, Chief, I want him to look for the counter sign."

The Chief chuckled, as he looked it up.

"Red—reply is baker william zero able.—Let's see how long it takes for him to respond with charlie niner xray four."

Red's light clattered as he sent the four characters and waited. Finally, the Saint Paul came back with an answer.

"Charlie niner xray four is his reply, Chief."

"Okay, now he knows we know he knows how to use the challenge pubs."

"Chief, message to Saint Paul about the mail bags. Ask him if he wants us to come alongside or anchor and use our rebuilt Motor Whaleboat?"

The Chief nodded and walked over to Red. "Did you get all that, Red?"

"Yeah, wait one, Chief."

Red switched his flashing light back on and swung the light, aiming it at the Saint Paul, and sent:

3 3 3 3

the U.S.S. Saint Paul CA-73, Heavy Cruiser, hull number 73, responded with

K

BT
MAIL CALL 23 BAGS X MY PLACE
OR YOURS
BT

WAIT

"You better hope he really understood that, asshole. There he goes, get him!"

Red gave him a K and read the incoming message.

BT
COME ALONGSIDE STARBOARD
QUARTER LIL FELLER
BT

R TKS

Red rogered for the friendly message. The Chief went back to the Captain.

"He said . . .

"I know what he said, Chief." His voice was low pitched, angry and tight. "I also know what Red sent. Advise Red I have just conducted Captain's Mast. That cost him four hours extra duty. We will maintain proper communications procedure regardless of what other ships do. Is that clear?"

"Aye aye, Captain." He pivoted, smarting from the Captain's angry words, and marched stiff leggedly back to where Red was lounging against the flashing light stand.

"Wipe that shiteating grin off your face, idiot. The Captain reads light. That little piece of fun just cost you a Captain's Mast and four hours of extra duty. We will maintain proper communications procedures at all times. Got it?"

Red looked at him with wide eyes and just nodded. Then he sneaked a hurt look at the Captain who had other things to do at the moment.

"Mr. Porter, station the Special Sea and Anchor Detail, please. I have the conn."

"Aye, aye, Captain." Leaning over, he spoke, "Boatswains Mate, station the Special Sea and Anchor Detail, port side to. Quartermaster, the Captain has the conn."

"Captain has the conn, aye aye, sir."

The 1MC popped on and out wheezed 'All Hands'.

"Station the Special Sea and Anchor Detail — port side to. Station the Special Sea and Anchor Detail."

"All ahead one-third."

"All ahead one-third, Captain. Engine room answers all ahead one-third, sir."

"Very well."

"Come left five degrees to new course zero niner eight true.

"Come left five degrees to new course zero niner eight true, aye aye, Captain."

"Rudder answers the helm, Captain. — Steady on new course zero niner eight true, sir."

"Very well."

"Bridge Combat — range to the Saint Paul is 800 yards, Captain."

"Clickclick"

"All ahead slow."

"All ahead slow, Captain. Engine room answers all ahead slow, sir."

"Very well."

"Bridge Sonar — request permission to retract sonar dome, Captain."

"Permission granted, Sonar."

"Clickclick"

"Bridge Combat — range to Saint Paul 500 yards. Also SOPA in Saint Paul assigns Radar Guard for Air Search to Hoquiam, Captain."

"Bridge aye — permission granted to light SA radar, combat."

"Clickclick"

The Captain looked up to the SA radar antenna to see if it was turning yet. This would be its first use since December in Iwon and Hungnam. There it goes.

Bridge Sonar — sonar equipment is secured, Captain."

"Clickclick"

Lt. Dixon appeared on the Bridge to take over as Special Sea and Anchor Detail Officer of the Deck.

"Good evening, Captain. Do you want to retain the Conn, sir?"

"Yes Dix, we're too close in now to change over."

"Bridge Combat—range to Saint Paul is 250 yards, now at minimum for surface radar. Ready to secure sugar charlie surface radar at this time, Captain."

"Standby Combat"

"Wheelhouse Bridge—stop starboard engine."

"Stop starboard engine. Engine room answers stop starboard engine."

"Right rudder two degrees, helmsman."

"Aye aye, Captain. Right rudder two degrees."

The sky was darkening rapidly now. They needed to get alongside without exposing lights to the enemy. They could see red-lensed flashlights glowing where line handling crews on the St. Paul stood.

"Meet your rudder."

"Meet your rudder, aye aye, Captain."

"Stop port engine."

"Stop port engine, aye aye, Captain. Engine room answers stop port engine, sir."

The Hoquiam bow passed the Saint Paul's stern.

"Bridge aye aye," responded the phone talker. "Captain, the bow line handlers request permission to pass a heaving line to the Saint Paul, sir."

"Permission granted."

"Starboard back slow."

The ship continued to creep forward.

"First line over Captain."

"Shift colors—Shift colors."

"Wheelhouse—do not turn on the truck lights. Maintain darken ship."

"Boatswain's Mate, aye aye Captain. Maintain darken ship. Do not light the truck lights."

"Thank you."

"Starboard engine stop."

"Starboard engine stop, Captain. Engine room answers Starboard engine stop, sir."

"Very well."

"Line handling detail on the fantail has a line over, Captain."

"Very well, thank you. Are all fenders in place? We wouldn't want to scratch their pretty paint."

Lt. Dixon smiled. The Captain has made an impressive landing with a senior officer watching. He is now ready to make jokes.

"Phone talker, advise the engine room we are through with engines for now. But to stay on the line."

"Aye aye, Captain."

"Get our gangway across, Dix, I want to pay a call on the Saint Paul Captain who is also Task Group Commander, to see what he has in mind for us. Maybe we can ignore our little airplanes. I'll be in my stateroom getting cleaned up."

"Aye, aye, Captain. Right away. Talker, find Chief Billons and tell him to get the gangway set up on the oh-one deck between the three inch practice loader and the port thwartship passageway hatch. The Captain's going calling."

"Aye, aye, sir."

"Quartermaster, Captain to his Stateroom."

"Quartermaster, aye aye, sir."

1930, March 9, 1951
Radio Shack
USS Hoquiam PF-5
Moored port side to U.S.S. St. Paul CA-73 Starboard side

Ding ding

"Hoquiam arriving."

Stewart glanced up at the speaker and grabbed the message board. There was one very interesting ALNAV the Captain would want to see right away. Mr. Forsythe was still on the Saint Paul receiving the classified communications operations orders, so I will be the first to see him.

He stepped to the doorway and waited until Lieutenant Commander Maxfield J. Brown passed him with a thoughtful look on his face.

Stewart waited until the Captain had a chance to be alone for a second, then walked up to his stateroom door and scratched on the panel.

"Enter."

Stewart opened the door and smiled.

"Good evening, Captain. How are you this fine evening?"

The Captain studied Stewart suspiciously.

What has he got on his devious mind, I wonder?

"Good evening, Stewart. What's on the board?"

"The usual, sir, plus an ALNAV general message."

The Captain reached for the board and initialed the originals of each message without reading them. Stewart would have mentioned any hot action item. Then he handed the board back to Stewart.

"Pull my flimsies and I'll read them later. I have officers call in a few moments."

Stewart didn't leave. Instead, he pulled the ALNAV and placed it on top.

"Sir, this one is important. I think you better read it."

What's that in Stewart's voice?

He grabbed the board a little sharply because he had already given the necessary instructions. Then he glanced at the message, looked up at Stewart, and started reading it very carefully.

"Well, I'll be damned," he said softly. "How many others know about this, Stewart?"

"Just the Radio Gang, Captain—or can I call you Commander now?" he asked with a big grin.

The Captain grinned back at him. Wheee!

"Commander will do just fine — for the moment." Then he re-read the ALNAV.

FM BUPERS
TO ALL NAVAL COMMANDS
BT
ALNAV 4-51 X THE PROMOTION BOARDS FOR COMMANDERS OF THE LINE CMA SUPPLY CORPS CMA CIVIL ENGINEERS CMA AND MEDICAL OFFICERS HAVE CONVENED AND CONSIDERED THE LIST OF NAMES OF ELIGIBLE OFFICERS FOR PROMOTION TO THE RANK OF COMMANDER X ALL OFFICERS WHOSE NAMES APPEAR ON THIS LIST ARE PROMOTED WITH A DATE OF RANK OF 1 APRIL 1951 SUBJECT TO PASSING THE ANNUAL PHYSICAL X (17th on the list)
BROWN CMA MAXFIELD J X . . .
BT

He looked up at Stewart. "We must be doing something right. I didn't figure this promotion for at least another year — and your promotion to SN comes through in one week, is that right?"

Stewart's smile froze for a second. He still resented how advancement had taken place in Operations Department. Then his smile grew and he nodded.

"Just so long as I stay out of trouble between now and the sixteenth, Captain. Congratulations on your promotion." The Captain nodded and turned to his copy of the ALNAV again.

Stewart took the board back and returned to the Radio Shack. Coyle and Lloyd looked up as he came in.

"I didn't hear any screams of joy from up there. Did he read it?" asked Lloyd.

"Yeah. One happy man up there. He even remembered my promotion coming up."

"Who was happy about what, Stewart?" came the voice of Lt.(jg) Forsythe behind him.

He turned and handed the board to his Division Officer, with the ALNAV still on top. He started to bristle and say something about routing a message before he had a chance to see it. Then he understood why Stewart had taken it up. He initialed and checked the routing on all the messages and handed it back.

"Officers' Call Officers' Call. All officers assemble in the Wardroom in five minutes."

Mr. Forsythe glanced at the speaker and wondered what that was about. Stewart interpreted his quizzical look correctly.

"Just before the Captain saw the ALNAV, sir, he mentioned he had to hurry for an officers meeting, Mr. Forsythe." He nodded and headed for the Wardroom.

Captain Brown entered the Wardroom where everyone was standing waiting for him to arrive. They all had big grins on their faces.

"Wipe those silly grins off your faces. We have some interesting work ahead of us."

Lt. Marston, with impeccable inflection inquired, "Very good, sir. Shall we ignore congratulations so you don't have to buy us drinks at the Club?"

"As a future former Lieutenant Commander," with a big grin on his face, "I accept your congratulations, perhaps a drink or three in a few weeks. Meanwhile, I had an interesting chat with Admiral Smith, Commander Task Force 95, who is visiting the Saint Paul today. He told me his plans for us." He had their attention now.

"A little bit of everything. Anti-submarine patrols, escort duties, little airplanes, goat, and shore bombardment at different places in a mix to make sure we stay on our toes."

He took a sip of the coffee that Jones placed in front of him, and continued.

"Wonsan, Songjin, Chongjin, maybe Hungnam and Iwon for bombardment. Task Force 77 for Submarine Screen and Plane Guard. Anti aircraft training for Task Force 77 ships. Escorting the supply ships to various points. Oh yes, playing goat."

There were a few puzzled looks as he took another cup of coffee.

"Goat, Captain?" inquired Lt. Dixon, suspiciously. "Is sahib in a tree blind waiting for the tiger to strike?"

"Very perceptive, Dix. Substitute the names with the Hoquiam, Saint Paul or Missouri, and the ChiCom's cave railroad guns overlooking Wonsan Harbor."

Uneasiness rolled around the wardroom.

"Here's the problem, gentlemen. Long before the Navy began to blockade Wonsan last week, the ChiComs had managed to roll in some heavy artillery on railcars. There are several caves where we believe they are hiding. They have gotten in some good shots at our ships in the Harbor without getting hit themselves. We need something to tempt them to come out and shoot at us."

By now, the members of the wardroom had a sinking feeling in their bellies.

"We are going in, anchor, and bombard a couple of the little islands where they have troops and spotters. Hopefully, that will get their dander up and they'll roll out one or more of the big guns to swat us. Meanwhile, our spotters upstairs are ready to instantly call a Fire Mission to the Saint Paul, or Missouri when she arrives, and any destroyers within range, to close the cave and get the gun."

The Captain stirred his coffee and sipped a little.

"To make sure we draw their fire, we go one step farther. It should insult them and perhaps tempt them to come out. The enemy isn't stupid but losing face is another thing. We're going to hold personnel inspection, at anchor in Wonsan Harbor."

There was an unexpected murmur and rustle as that shock wave settled over them.

"The ship will be at Condition One going in and out but reduce to Condition Two while at anchor. The anchor watch will be prepared to jettison the anchor and chain if it really gets tight. Jim, you need to be prepared to answer bells immediately."

At least, they aren't screaming.

"We go in tomorrow. Questions?" He looked around.

Some were just staring at him; others soberly shook their heads.

9 Mar 51 Ammo expended on Harassing and Assigned Targets Wonsan Harbor, 3"50cal: 26 rounds AA Common.

10 Mar 51 Ammo expended on Harassing and Assigned Targets Wonsan Harbor, 3"50cal: 2 rounds Star, 11 rounds AA Common.

11 Mar 51 Ammo expended on Harassing and Assigned Targets Wonsan Harbor, 3"50cal: 32 rounds AA Common.

March 12, 1951
USS Hoquiam PF-5
Anchored Wonsan Harbor

The Hoquiam had been at Condition Two for three days firing the two three-inch batteries at Targets of Opportunity in the harbor area. From the looks of the schedule, watch and watch would continue for several more days.

Stewart studied the Plan of the Day carefully, looking for an out. He couldn't find one and sighed in disgust.

The Captain has gone apeshit! He's going to conduct Personnel Inspection, or rather, the Executive Officer, Lt. Marston, will conduct it for him in two days.

Uniform for inspection will be Dress Blue Baker with ribbons, peacoat, watchcap and gloves, at Fair Weather Parade. Woe betides the fellow wearing someone else's peacoat!

The Port Watch would be inspected Saturday morning when the Port Watch was off duty. Then, the Starboard Watch would be inspected. No big deal but in the middle of March, it was windy and colder than a witch's tit.

People were scrambling to prepare for inspection. Would-be barbers, usually happy with a dime a cut, suddenly found a gold mine of shaggy hair at two bits a cut. Three-stripe piping on jumpers got a critical inspection. If the piping wasn't sparkling white, a dash to the Ship's Store for a new toothbrush to scrub the piping with Ivory soap and water took care of that. Small Stores had a run on watch caps and woolen gloves until they were gone.

Masking tape was perfect to remove lint from dress blues. Masking tape rolls were not to be found in the usual storage places; they were in use on uniforms in all living compartments.

Electric irons were in heavy demand as sailors all over the ship put an extra sharp crease on their trousers and jumpers. Damp wash cloths under the hot iron helped to steam out wrinkles. No problem about lining up to use ironing boards—there were no ironing boards aboard. Didn't matter: sailors knew how to get around that.

One removed a blanket from one's bunk and spread it out flat on the deck, which is usually spotless. Then one got down on one's hands and knees and commenced ironing. After nearly a month at sea wearing dungarees and foul weather gear, the Dress Blues appeared momentarily to be prepared for inspection, then folded gently according to the book and stowed away in lockers. Woe betides the sailor who leaves his spotless, freshly pressed blues hanging from his bunk or locker vent. The Masters-At-Arms would be looking for such items as Lucky Bag bait.

The morning of the big day arrived with cold wind and high clouds. The Port section was in their living compartments, preparing for personnel inspection. Stewart kept hearing someone humming and chuckling under his breath.

Now, who the hell is that?

He thought it was coming from the next row of bunks but so far he couldn't identify which of six sailors might be ready for a transfer to happy land. Finally, he spotted Sorenson, the big Radarman Second Class who was fumbling with something on his watch cap. Stewart shook his head.

Nothing goes on the watchcap; the bare watchcap sits on top of your head.

Standing in goose bumps, zoris, and dog tags, fresh from showering and shaving, Stewart began dressing. His clean skivvy shorts were followed by a skivvy shirt and black socks. He removed his folded pants from his bunk and pulled them right side out. Stepping into the two legs, Stewart turned and removed his freshly spit-shined black shoes from his locker and slipped them on his feet. Tugging his pants all the way up, he drew the waist flaps together with two black anchor buttons that formed sort of a belt, and buttoned the main flap side buttons two at a time, finishing off the buttons across the top.

During the midwatch, he'd gone to Fireroom Number Two and had steamed his neckerchief to remove all creases, then tightly rolled and sealed it with scotch tape wrapped around the middle of the roll. Stewart removed it from his locker, gently shaking the neckerchief. His watchcap was still drying in back of the hot receivers in the Radio Shack.

He pulled his folded Dress Blue jumper from the locker and turned it right side out. Stewart frowned as he snapped it to shake out any fold marks.

Would have been much better to let it hang from a hanger, but if the ship took a shell hit or mine in the compartment, the jumper might clog the pump strainer. Anyway, the Master-At-Arms would have loved to have found his Dress Blue jumper hanging on his bunk chains the night before inspection.

He laid the jumper out on his bunk on the clean fart sack and fixed his Navy Occupation Medal (Japan) centered above his jumper pocket.

Stewart slipped the jumper over his head and his arms into the sleeves. He folded the cuffs back for now so there would be no chance of rubbing dirt onto the white stripes of piping. He reached back and flipped his collar up, then tied his neckerchief into place with a neatly presented square knot right at the vee of the jumper. Steamed, stretched, and rolled very tightly, there was plenty of length below the knot to hang slim and be attractive.

Stewart picked up his billfold and wedged it over the top of his pants, covering the billfold with his jumper.

Ready!

Quickly glancing at his bunk to make sure it was squared away, he turned and closed his locker, fastening the combination lock.

He lined up at the peacoat locker with the other sailors. Stewart removed and simultaneously began slipping into the bulky jacket. He would button it as he came onto the weather deck. As he headed for the ladder, more locker doors slammed shut.

Sorenson RD2, still humming and chuckling to himself, carried his watchcap in his hand as he headed up the ladder ahead of Stewart. A stream of Operations personnel was heading for the ladder just aft of the galley. As they hit the 01 deck by the Officers' Galley, the 1MC crackled its usual scratch. A mediocre Bosun's Pipe began to pipe 'All Hands'.

"All hands in the Port Section, Quarters for muster and Personnel Inspection at Fair Weather Parade. Officers' Call Officers' Call."

The 1MC went silent while Stewart retrieved his watchcap from where it had been drying behind the RBA receiver. He rolled the regulation two folds into the cap and placed it carefully, squarely on his head, while he walked out to Quarters for muster, pulling on his woolen knit gloves as he went through the watertight door. As he stood waiting for the call to fall in, he quickly buttoned the peacoat inner button and four of its five large black anchor buttons. Stewart's breath, along with every other man, was steaming in the cold.

The Operations Department usually mustered every day near their working spaces, as Radiomen, Radarmen, Electronics Technicians, Sonarmen, Quartermasters, and Signalmen, with their division officers. However, for Personnel Inspection, the four Officers, two Chiefs and thirty two White Hats mustered outside the Radio Shack as the whole Operations Department—much more military looking.

Chief Swenson, senior to Chief Hathaway, formed the Port Watch of the department, put them at Parade Rest, and waited for two officers to return from Officers' Call. The sixteen men stood there swaying uneasily, as they looked shoreward. Somewhere back there, the ChiComs had a rail car with a big cannon that must be ready to come out and fire a shell at them right now.

They hoped the Saint Paul was ready to fire everything they had at the Chinks' guns. The Chinks were good but it still took nearly three minutes to roll out, stop, prepare and fire. Hopefully, the spotter aircraft way up and off to the side would radio a Fire Mission to the Saint Paul before the Chinks were in position. The Saint Paul could respond to a Fire Mission in less than a minute with their eight-inch guns.

"Operations Department, Aaa Tennnn Shun. Hand Salute!" shouted the Chief, as he saluted the two officers approaching. The department saluted as one and held.

"Good morning Mr. Porter, Port Watch, Operations Department present or accounted for. Ready for inspection, sir."

The officers returned their salutes. Then, over his shoulder, Chief Swensen called, "To."

Hands held stiff in salute, returned crisply to their right leg side crease. Lt. Porter and Lt.(jg) Forsythe nodded and smiled in the crisp air. Already cheeks were beginning to turn white from the cold.

"Have the department open ranks, Chief, and have them remove their watch caps," Lt. Porter ordered.

"Aye aye sir," he answered and turned to the group of men who were beginning to shiver.

"Open ranks for inspection, March." The front rank marched forward two steps; the second rank took one step forward. "Division, Close Interval, Dress Right—Dress." Elbows and heads snapped to the right, and sailors shuffled left and right and front to back in ranks until the three ranks were just so. "Ready—Front." Faces whipped to the front as arms dropped to their sides. "Uncover." Gloved right hands whipped to hats and held position, gripping their watchcaps.

"To!" Hat in hands, the hats whipped down to belly height, where the left hand was waiting to grab the other side, and held. The ship rolled gently, tugging at its anchor chain in the breeze. The men in ranks swayed back and forth, countering the ship's roll.

Lt. Porter and Lt.(jg) Forsythe walked slowly along the front rank checking every inch of their uniform for dirt, wrinkles, lint; faces for beard stubble, the inside of the cap for dirt, and shoes that did not glisten. As they passed Sorenson, they smiled back at his broad smile. When they finished the usual inspection, Lt. Porter turned to the Chief.

"I know it is very cold but have the men open their peacoats for name inspection."

The Chief chose to interpret his orders. "Unbutton your peacoat front buttons. When the inspecting officer comes to you, open the coat panel so he can see the stenciled name."

He looked back and forth at the men.

"Department . . . Coverrrrr." Both hands brought a watchcap up and set it on their heads. The left hand dropped. "To!" The right hand dropped.

"Now, unbutton your peacoats."

Stewart wasn't the only one grinning. It was the strangest order he had heard at inspection.

Still a strange command, but they could handle it. When Lt. Porter approached, Stewart brought his coat panel back to the inner button snappily and waited while cold air whipped icily beneath his peacoat. Lt.(jg) Forsythe nodded as they passed. Stewart closed his peacoat panel to keep the cold breeze out.

"Good lookin' crew, Chief. Keep up the good work. The Executive Officer will be here in just a few minutes."

The Chief saluted as he beamed. Chief Swenson had reason to be proud. In just a few months, these retreads had made the Operations Department really look sharp among other ships, the REAL ships. He cocked his head, frowning.

Who the fuck's humming in ranks?

"Operations Department, Aaa Tennnn Shun." The humming stopped.

"Close ranks, March." The men in the two rear ranks moved forward.

"About Face! Three paces forward, March! About Face. Now cover off. Department, Parade Rest!"

The Operations Department personnel were back in their original position waiting for the Executive Officer, and it was getting colder as the breeze picked up.

The Executive Officer appeared, rounding Mount 31. He broke into a run as the gong clanged and the gun crew began to respond to an order from Fire Control in Combat. They were preparing to fire.

"Operations Department, Aaa Tennnn Shun." Lt. Marston spoke before the Chief could sound off.

"Chief, have your men stand at ease and protect their ears. Mount 31 is about to fire several rounds." Lt. Marston came to stop directly in front of Sorenson and stood facing forward to Mount 31.

"Department, stand at ease. Cover your ears from shot blasts. Keep your mouth open to protect against shock waves."

He took his own advice. Sorenson was standing with his eyes scrunched shut, mouth open, and hands over his ears when Lt. Marston glanced at him and did a double take. He reached out and snatched Sorenson's watchcap off and stared at it. He looked up at Sorenson with wide open eyes and pointed to the cap

"What is that, Sorenson?" he demanded.

From the distance came the command, "Fire!"

CRACK

followed by the clatter of a brass casing hitting the deck. Everyone turned toward the Executive Officer and

Sorenson. Sorenson was smiling broadly as he lowered his hands.

"That, sir, is my watch cap." Lt. Marston began to turn red.

"Fire!"

CRACK

and more clatter of a brass casing.

"What is this thing on your watch cap" he spoke furiously.

"Fire!"

CRACK

And clattering of a brass casing.

"Why, I believe it is—yes, it's a Soviet Navy Petty Officer's hat device, Mr. Marston."

Mr. Marston was doing a slow burn as he realized that Sorenson was playing with him.

"Where did you get that, Sorenson?" he demanded.

"Sir, I found that yesterday under the SA radar console preparing for materiel inspection. Under the circumstances," he waved his arm in a circle, "Wearing it today seemed to put a little humor into this tense situation."

Lt. John Marston continued to glare at Sorenson. He flipped the watchcap over his shoulder into the water. Sorenson's eyes popped out.

"But that's my hat, sir. You can't do that," he protested. Lt. Marston closed the distance between them and spoke furiously.

"There's also a rule about having contraband in your possession. Having truck with the Reds or their equipment is poor judgment on your part. I have just destroyed the contraband. You have any questions?"

Stewart could see Mr. Marston's expression, and it was tough. He never batted an eye. Sorenson slowly shook his head.

"No sir, I have no questions."

"Fire!"

CRACK

and clatter of a brass casing rattling among the others.

Lt. Marston stared at Sorenson for a moment longer and strode off completely forgetting about inspection. When he got as far aft as the ladder to the 02 deck, he stopped and looked back. Speaking to his writer, he strode off to the next division as the Yeoman writer ran back to the Operations Department.

"Mr. Porter, sir. Please advise Sorenson, Radarman Second Class, that the Executive Officer noted he is out of uniform, not having the prescribed hat. Two hours extra instruction is awarded as a result of the Executive Officer's investigation." Then he turned and ran to catch up with the Executive Officer.

1900, March 12, 1951
USS Hoquiam PF-5
Anchored seaward of Yo Do
Outside Wonsan harbor

"Secure from Special Sea and Anchor Detail. Section Three has the watch. All department heads meet in the Wardroom in five minutes."

Lt. Marston looked around at the seven department heads, including Chief Farmer, as they settled in their chairs with coffee. It had been a tough day in Wonsan Harbor. The shadow of this island gave peace and security to their minds.

"Gents, we have a problem each of you has attempted to handle alone. That's the Ship's Allowance List. I want to find out what you have accomplished, and before anyone protests, there is no grade on this. Just," shrugging his shoulders, "what have you been able to do?"
He looked around the table.
"Chief, what do you have?"
Chief Farmer looked at the Executive Officer thoughtfully for a moment.
"Mr. Marston, not a hell of a lot. I do maintain a list of every piece of equipment under my control, including serial numbers and date of acquisition. The key word here is acquisition. But I don't know if there is more equipment needed or if the ship is over allowance on some things I have requisitioned or smuggled on board."

Most of the department heads nodded in agreement and exasperation of the situation. No one really knew what they were supposed to have. Lt. Hansen raised his finger and Lt. Marston nodded.

"Over the last six months, my department has gradually built up a list of equipment like Doc, here. I don't think it's complete, and like Doc, I have no idea of whether we're under or over allowance." He paused for a minute, and continued. "Since we don't have allowance list flip-files, we try to keep things organized in regular filing cabinets; that is a huge, however neat, mess."

There were more murmurs of agreement.

"All right, I drafted a letter for the Captain's signature. Let's throw it in BuShips lap and let them whine and snivel their way out of it. At least, it will get the monkey off our back. Meeting dismissed."

12 Mar 51 Ammo expended on Harassing and Assigned Targets Wonsan Harbor, 3"50cal. 56 rounds AA Common, 1 round VT

March 13, 1951
LtrSer 95
FM C.O. USS HOQUIAM PF5
TO Chief, Bureau of Ships

It is requested that two (2) sets of up-to-date Bureau of Ships Allowance Lists applicable to PF type vessels be sent to this command.
/s/ M.J. Brown
Lieutenant Commander

13 Mar 51 Ammo expended on Harassing and Assigned Targets Wonsan Harbor, 3"50cal: 61 rounds AA Common

2345, March 14, 1951
USS Hoquiam PF-5
Night Patrol,
Wonsan Harbor, North Korea

CTF Ninety-five decided to augment the blockade with something different. He wanted to catch the ChiComs smuggling troops and supplies around the harbor at night in sampans and other craft. The Hoquiam quietly slipped into the harbor two hours after sunset. Visibility was reduced by smoke combined with fog, and lack of a hunter's moon. As usual when moving into and around Wonsan Harbor, the ship was exercising at Condition Two watches, at a very slow speed to surprise any vessels sneaking around.

"Bridge Combat this is Sonar—Contact! Hull and screw noise bearing zero seven four degrees relative. Range nine hundred yards. Standby for course and speed."

The sudden blare of noise on the open bridge was deafening. Lt.(jg) Forsythe leaned over the gyro repeater and aligned the alidade to 074°/254° and laid his binoculars on the repeater. He crouched down and squinted through the eyepieces. Snatching his glasses, he leaned against the windscreen and looked again. The 21MC blared again.

"Bridge Sonar This is Combat—I have a surface contact bearing zero seven five relative—range nine two oh yards."

Lt.(jg) Forsythe reached down and pressed the 21MC lever.

"Sonar Combat Bridge—I have visual on the contact. Combat, start the DRT. Mark this contact SUGAR ONE."

"Roger that Bridge, sugar one. Ahh, Mr. Forsythe, there's no one on watch that's checked out on the Dead Reckoning Table, sir. Our watch lost the DRT operator to the Gloucester last week."

Shit! Roger Forsythe thought furiously.

Oh Christ, the Captain.

He whirled and snatched up the sound powered handset and pressed the Captain's buzzer.

"Yes?"

Fantastic. The Captain's voice changed from sleepy to alert in that brief word.

"Captain, Forsythe, sir. We have a sonar contact, confirmed by radar and visual sighting. Bearing oh seven five relative about nine hundred fifty yards, sir. I've sent for a DRT operator."

"Very well. I'll be right up."

"Aye aye, Captain. Shall I go to general quarters?"

"No."

Lt.(jg) Forsythe hit the 21MC lever and announced,

"Captain to the Bridge. Combat send somebody for the DRT operator. Get him up here, choto!"

"Click click"

"Messenger, coffee for the Captain."

He absorbed their responses as he picked up the target again. In the night darkness, made worse by mist and smoke, he had trouble focusing and resolving the object. He was still trying to make it out when the Captain appeared at his side. The Messenger of the Watch appeared and handed the Captain a fresh mug of coffee.

"Thank you," he responded, glancing at the sailor with a smile.

The Captain placed his coffee on the windscreen ledge in front of him and looked toward the target with his glasses.

"Bridge Sonar—we plot sugar one inbound toward the Wonsan dock facilities."

The Captain reached down to the 21MC and turned the sound level down, as Sonar continued their report.

"Sugar one course is two eight one degrees true. Speed three knots."

The 21MC fell silent.

"Bridge Combat—we concur."

"Click click"

The Captain straightened up from the 21MC and studied the target.

"Mr. Forsythe. Have you evaluated the target and come to any conclusion yet?"

Lt.(jg) Forsythe let his binoculars down to his chest as he quickly considered how to answer the Captain. He noticed the Port Lookout was trying to make out the target instead of checking the port side.

"Smith, you're port lookout. Keep alert to the port side only."

"Aye, aye, sir. Sorry, sir."

Smith began studying the waters to port, looking for any object to report.

"Captain, I can't make out what the target is. It is too blurry in the mist and darkness." The Captain nodded and reached down to the 21MC.

"Sonar Combat this is the Captain—target evaluation?"

There was a pause, then Sonar responded.

"Captain, evaluate possible sub trying to sneak in and watching for mines. That would be consistent with their three knot speed."

Combat, who had been listening commented, "Sir, the target is small. If it is a submarine, the decks are awash. We see no evasive maneuvers. I don't think they have spotted us. No friendly ships or small craft are supposed to be in Wonsan Harbor but us. Course and speed, as before. Extending their track places the target at the port facilities in seventy-five minutes. Therefore, evaluate as unknown and unfriendly, Captain."

That was Lt. Marston, the Executive Officer. Someone must have rousted him out, or he heard the Captain leaving his sea cabin above him, thought Forsythe.

Lt.(jg) Forsythe looked at the Captain, who grunted. Forsythe doubled clicked the 21MC and straightened again.

The Captain took another long look at the target and seemed to come to a decision. He looked at Forsythe.

"Turn all the radio circuit speakers off, Mr. Forsythe. We want to quiet the ship."

Then he squatted in front of the 21MC and began issuing orders quietly, steadily and rapidly. He pressed the Wheelhouse lever, leaving Sonar and Combat on.

"Wheelhouse this is the Captain" (really unnecessary because all hands knew the Captain's voice when they heard it) "Do NOT sound general quarters," accenting 'not' firmly. "Boatswain Mate of the Watch and Messenger of the Watch quietly and as rapidly as you can go to the deck, engineering compartments, and Chiefs' Quarters, turn on the lights and announce General Quarters, Condition One Charlie. Tell everyone to be silent. No noise throughout the ship and weather decks, tiptoe. Maintain darken ship. Do you understand all that?"

Hayes BM2, Boatswains Mate of the Watch had been ready to hit the general alarm when the Captain called. He carefully avoided the red box and pushed the 21MC lever.

"Aye, aye, Captain. We understand wake deck hands, engineers, and Chiefs for GQ One Charlie and tell them to be quiet."

The Captain smiled and double clicked in response, and lifted the Wheelhouse lever. Now he pulled down the 21MC Radio Room lever.

"Radio Bridge—over." The Captain was prepared to wait. First, the two Radiomen on watch probably didn't hear the fact they were called.

"Radio—Aye, Captain?"

"We are going to general quarters on the quiet. Wake all officers. Tell them general quarters Condition One Charlie, to maintain quiet and darken ship. We have an unfriendly less than a thousand yards off our starboard side. Acknowledge, Radio."

"This is Radio—Acknowledged wilco out."

"Combat. Send someone to your compartment and to the Artificers compartment with the same procedure. Also if Chief Billons hasn't left Chiefs' Quarters yet, tell him I want to see him on the Bridge immediately."

The 21MC clicked twice as a hatch on the next deck below opened and shut. He could hear someone from Combat racing down the ladder heading for the compartments.

"Combat I have turned all the radio circuits down on the Bridge. I want silence on the weather decks. You'll have to guard those channels now. We'll turn 'em back up later."

"Click click."

The Captain was beginning to get excited. His normally careful enunciation was slipping.

The Captain turned back to Lt.(jg) Forsythe, and smiled a broad smile.

"Mr. Forsythe, we are going to board and capture that vessel! I believe you are the Boarding Officer?"

Lt.(jg) Forsythe just stared at him, stunned. Then stuttered, "Yes sir, I am."

"Very well, then. Your basic orders are to take the Boarding Party in the Motor Whaleboat and paddle quietly to the vessel. Board stealthily, if possible. Surprise the bridge crew, and take command of the vessel. If they discover you before boarding, we will fire to cover your retreat to the ship. Keep me advised on the Handy Talky. Questions?"

Lt.(jg) Forsythe thought for a moment, came to attention and saluted. "No sir, no questions, Captain. Are you relieving me now, sir?

The Captain returned his salute and formally announced, "I relieve you, sir."

He turned to the 21MC and pressed the lever, "This is the Captain, I have the Conn," and turned back to study the target.

"Sonar—Aye aye Captain."

"Wheelhouse—Aye aye Captain."

"Combat—Aye aye Captain."

"GENERAL QUARTERS GENERAL QUARTERS"

Stewart started to swing out of his bunk, then hesitated. That was someone shouting G.Q. in the compartment, and the G.Q. alarm gong was silent. Then the compartment lights started coming on. A Radarman was standing there, yelling at top of his voice.

Has he flipped his lid?

"Hurry it up. This is really general quarters without any noise. Come on, you guys. There's a sub off our starboard side. Don't make any noise and walk—you hear me?—walk to your G.Q. station. We're at Darken Ship. You guys got all that?"

There were a few curses and mumbles as the Operations Department crew quietly got out of their bunks and began dressing. Stewart checked his watch as he walked through the Mess Deck on his way to the ladder to the Shack.

Well, he thought, *at least I got two hours of sleep. Into the Midwatch. Sunrise G.Q. goes at 0530. This night is shot.*

Stumbling into the Shack, Lee pulled the new 1JV sound-powered headset from its box on the bulkhead and plugged into the receptacle. Glancing around the shack, he saw Lloyd was on Task Group Common, Roney, the new RMSN, was holding the Message board, James was standing in front of the coffeepot stirring sugar into coffee, Masters was copying George Fox, and Coyle was standing in front of the TBM transmitter. Chief Hathaway was in his ET shack. Everyone but Stewart had their life jackets and helmets on.

Where the hell was Corning?

Thump! The door hit Stewart in the back as Corning dashed in.

"Bridge this is Radio—Radio and ET manned and Ready."

"Roger Radio."

"Bridge this is Combat—manned and ready."

"Roger Combat."

"Bridge this is Sonar—manned and ready."

"Roger Sonar.—Uh Sonar? The Captain says under no circumstances are you to ping. You got that?"

"Bridge Sonar—yeah, don't ping. We got it."

"Radio Signal Bridge—Is that you, Stewart?"

"This is Stewart go ahead Signal Bridge."

"Chief Swenson wants to know if you forgot your new GQ station is on the starboard twelve-inch light."

That got Stewart's attention. What the hell is this? I'm JV Talker in the Radio Shack during G.Q.

"The hell you say, Signal Bridge. This is my G.Q. station right here."

"Oh shit," James slammed his cup down and turned to Stewart.

"Stew, I forgot to tell you. Your new G.Q. station is on the Signal Bridge. Ever since you talked on yardarm blinkers with the New Zealander cruiser, the Chief has been after my ass to transfer you up there to strike as Signalman. Getcher ass on up there now. We'll work it out later on."

Stewart wasn't sure whether to be pissed or not. True, the Bridge is surely where the action is, no matter how hot or cold it is. At least tonight in Wonsan Harbor, it was just cold and damp. He moved toward the door, only to be stopped by James.

"Helmet and life jacket, dummy. Captain catch you again, your ass is really going to be grass." James turned and motioned Roney to come over.

"Roney, take the JV circuit headset. Anyone calls Radio you answer 'Radio aye', got it?" James asked impatiently.

Roney had only been aboard for a few days. As Stewart was going out the door, Roney was indignantly explaining why he couldn't be Radio Messenger and 1JV Phone Talker at the same time.

Stewart moved down the Main Passageway, turned right to the Port side hatch and undogged it. As the hatch began to open, the red night-light turned off just like a refrigerator light, and he stepped through, dogging the hatch tightly behind him. He glanced at the sky.

The sky was overcast. No stars or the moon to shine on us.

Stewart climbed the ladder to the top at the 03 level, next to the flag bags. The Chief gripped him by the shoulder and told him to hold on. He turned to the JV Talker:

"Red, tell the Bridge we are now manned and ready."

"Right Chief— Bridge this is Signal Bridge—manned and ready."

Stewart could tell the Chief was upset about something. Otherwise, the situation would have been amusing. Stewart was standing three feet away from two JV Talkers, Bridge on his left and Signal Bridge on his right.

"Stewart, I don't know if I want you in my gang if you can't be where you're supposed to be. I think you'll have a little extra instruction tonight because you were in the wrong place."

Stewart smoldered.

I don't need this shit at all.

He glowered back at the Chief.

"There's two things wrong with that, Chief. First, I'm not in your fuckin' gang. We've already gone through that malarky. Second, until Red called me, I didn't know I was supposed to be up here. We square on that now, Chief?"

He'd had it up to here with some petty bullshit and wasn't taking any more. Suddenly, Stewart was lying on the Flag Bag with the Chief about a half-inch from his nose.

"Listen, shitbird, if I want any shit outta you, I'll squeeze you 'till your ears dribble. You got that?" He whispered hoarsely.

His fists had Lee's life jacket up under his chin. He gulped and nodded.

So much for standing up for my rights.

"Yeah Chief, I got it. Sorry. Just don't like to be given trouble that's none of mine."

He glowered at Stewart for a moment, then relaxed.

Stewart relaxed and thought about it.

Damn Reservists are all alike —mean and too sensitive.

The Chief pulled Stewart off the Bags and helped pull his life jacket straight. As though nothing had ever happened, he said, "You have the starboard twelve-inch light. Take the amber shield off quietly and store it in its clips on the bulkhead. Do not turn the light on at this time. If the Captain calls to illuminate the target be quick to turn it on, open the shutter and grab the target— Understand?"

Stewart nodded and whispered, "Is that all, Chief?"

"No, one other thing. Whoever you light up isn't going to like it at all, and may try to shoot your light out. That includes you. Be ready to drop to the deck behind the bulwark."

Whoops!

Stewart made sure his life jacket was tight. It afforded some protection against small arms fire and shrapnel. And he made sure his helmet chinstrap was tight, too. Then, and only then, did he step over to the twelve-inch flashing light and remove the amber shield. He pointed the light in the general direction of the target and peered down the v-notch sight, trying to figure out what to aim at.

Everyone was talking hoarsely and in whispers. He got the starboard lookout to show him the submarine.

God, it was right THERE! Looked to be less than three hundred yards away.

He heard a noise on deck and saw the Motor Whaleboat being quietly eased over the side into the water.

What the hell is that all about? At least the sheaves weren't squealing.

Stewart found out later that Billy Boy had an engineer give all the zirc fittings a squeeze of lube grease before they started to lift the Whaleboat out of its cradle. Stewart turned to the lookout and whispered: "What's going on? Why are they lowering the Motor Whaleboat?"

"Boarding party to capture the submarine," he whispered back.

When Billy's crew had gotten the Whaleboat quietly into the water, another crew pulled it aft to the starboard quarterdeck on the Main Deck. There, the Boarding Party slipped aboard.

For Chrissake, James is in the Boarding Party!

Lee recognized a couple of the Gunner's Mates and an Engineering Chief.

My god, Mr. Forsythe is in charge!

Mr. Forsythe sat in the stern sheets and manned the tiller as everyone else paddled away. For once, they didn't want the Motor Whaleboat engine to work.

Mounts 31, 33, and 42, 20mm's 20, 22, 24, and 26 were all pointed toward the submarine. The Mark 10 Hedgehog was manned and all twenty-four shafts were loaded with hedgehogs. Fire Controlman Williams had the optical rangefinder pointed toward the sub's conning tower, not that he could make out any detail.

Mr. Forsythe's Handy Talky radio channel was piped into a speaker in Combat and Sonar by Radio. The Captain had the other Handy Talky. He waited until the Motor Whaleboat was about 50 yards out and whispered into the mike:

PETER ONE THIS IS LASHING PETER OVER.

Stewart watched Mr. Forsythe snatch up the Handy Talky.

LASHING PETER THIS IS PETER ONE LOUD AND CLEAR OVER.

Stewart could hear his muted voice since the Captain was standing next to him.

THIS IS LASHING PETER ROGER OUT.

He and Mr. Forsythe had just exchanged a radio check. The Captain put down the Handy Talky and recognized Stewart on the light. He seemed surprised.

"What are you doing here, Stewart? I told you to stay at your general quarters assignment and not race up to the bridge."

He started to answer but the Chief beat him to it. The Captain frowned as the Chief explained. "Captain, I'm desperately short of Signalmen, and Stewart, knowing message procedure, is really good on the lights. I arranged with James for Stewart to be here during G.Q."

Hmmm, the Chief was squirming a little bit.

The Captain is particular about who is on the G.Q. Bridge crew and does not like being bypassed.

"I see, Chief. Leave Stewart up here this time. We'll discuss this later."

"Aye aye, Captain," he said and hustled away to the Signalmen's cubbyhole forward of the Flag Bags.

The Captain turned to Stewart, holding out the Handy Talky.

"Stewart, you act as my personal radio operator tonight. I doubt if we illuminate that target and become a target for incoming, ourselves. If Mr. Forsythe calls, just give me the Handy Talky."

"Aye aye, Captain," Stewart answered, and put the Handy Talky to his ear.

He watched the Motor Whaleboat fading into the mist as it got closer to the submarine. With his bare eyes, he could just barely see the Motor Whaleboat. They didn't seem to be paddling, anymore.

ITSA GAWDAMMED ROCK!

Stewart shoved the Handy Talky to the Captain at the same time he realized what Mr. Forsythe had said.

PETER ONE THIS IS LASHING PETER SAY AGAIN OVER.

Everyone on the bridge could hear shouts of laughter coming from Sonar and Combat.

IT'S A ROCK.

PETER ONE THIS IS LASHING PETER USE CORRECT CIRCUIT DISCIPLINE AND PROCEDURE. MAKE YOUR REPORT OVER

LASHING PETER THIS IS PETER ONE CAPTAIN, THIS IS A SMALL ROCK SHAPED LIKE A CONNING TOWER. IT IS NOT, REPEAT, NOT A VESSEL OF ANY KIND. THERE ARE NO PEOPLE ON IT.

THIS IS LASHING PETER ROGER RETURN TO BASE OUT.

The Captain handed the radio set to Stewart absently as he thought this out. He stepped over to the 21MC on the forward windscreen. Leaning over it, he pressed the lever and began speaking in icy, oh so very angry but controlled tones.

"Sonar Combat this is the Captain—There will be a meeting in the Wardroom immediately after the Motor Whaleboat is taken aboard. Sonar and Combat watchstanders, who were on duty at the beginning of this farce, Sonar and Combat Leading Petty Officers, their Division Officers, and the Executive Officer, will be present. The purpose of this meeting is to determine how fast a rock can move through Wonsan Harbor waters."

"Sonar—Aye aye, sir." You could cut the embarrassment in that voice with a knife.
"This is Combat—Aye aye, Captain."

A rather subdued reply from the Exec, Stewart thought. *Wow, do I want to sneak into the Wardroom Galley and listen to a masterful asschewing, or beat a cowardly retreat to my bunk?*

"Boatswain's Mate of the Watch? Pipe secure from General Quarters, and since it's already 0335, on deck the next watch section. There will be sunrise general quarters at 0530."

The Captain straightened up and walked around the Bridge, inspecting his ship as it stood down from G.Q. Lt.(jg) Unsenger would arrive shortly as next Officer of the Deck.

"THIS IS A F R S TOKYO WITH A LATE BREAKING STORY, MARCH FOURTEENTH, NINETEEN FIFTY-ONE, AIR FORCE SERGEANT RICHARD HENNING REPORTING. THE EIGHTH ARMY HAS ATTACKED AND RETAKEN SEOUL, THE CAPITOL OF THE REPUBLIC OF SOUTH KOREA. MORE ON THIS STORY AS IT DEVELOPS. WE RETURN TO THE PROGRAM IN PROGRESS, FIBBER MAGEE AND MOLLY. . . ."

March 16, 1951
USS Hoquiam PF-5
Anchored Seaward of Yo Do
Wonsan Harbor entrance, North Korea

Glory Hallelujah! Today is the day. I'm finally Seaman, making $75 per month. Stewart stretched in his bunk before dropping to the deck. And since I am designated a radioman striker, I can put the flashes above my seaman stripes—RMSN—even if I can't go to Radio School. In six months, I can take the fleet wide exam for Third Class, if Jimmy Bob will recommend me.

He grabbed his gear and headed for the showers. Standing in the shower, Stewart began to count how many new sets of SN stripes and RM flashes he would need. The laundryman wants fifty cents for each set sewn on.

Crap, that's going to take most of this payday but it's worth it.

He finished showering and shaving and headed back down to the compartment to dress.

3/16/51
DEAR MOM AND DAD,
I FINALLY MADE SEAMAN AS OF THIS MORNING. ANY KIND OF LUCK, OUGHT TO BE ABLE TO GO FOR RM3 IN SIX MONTHS OR NEXT FLEET WIDE EXAMS AFTER THAT. THE CAPTAIN CONGRATULATED ME WHEN I MADE ROUNDS WITH THE MESSAGE BOARD THIS MORNING. HE BECOMES COMMANDER THE FIRST OF THE MONTH.
WE CONTINUE TO CRUISE AROUND WONSAN TRYING TO RAISE SOME INTEREST FROM THE GOOKS OUT THERE. THEY REFUSE TO COME OUT OF THEIR CAVES. WE'VE JOINED SEVERAL DESTROYERS IN GUARDING THE MINESWEEPERS FROM HARASSING FIRE FROM THE DINKY LITTLE ISLANDS IN THE HARBOR OR FROM SHORE. ONCE IN A WHILE WE FIRE OUR "BIG" THREE-INCH RIFLES BUT I DON'T KNOW IF WE EVER HIT ANYTHING.
HEY, GUESS WHAT? YOUR WONDERFUL CHRISTMAS PFEFFERNUSSE COOKIES AND FRUITCAKE ARRIVED DAY BEFORE

YESTERDAY. YOU TRYING TO GET ME IN TROUBLE? MR. FORSYTHE COULD SMELL THE BRANDY IN THE FRUITCAKE CLEAR ACROSS THE PASSAGEWAY IN HIS STATEROOM. HE WAS REALLY UPSET. THOUGHT WE HAD BOOZE IN THE SHACK. ALL OF A SUDDEN, THE RADIO SHACK AND MY FRUITCAKE WERE VERY POPULAR WITH THE OFFICERS. DIDN'T LAST VERY LONG. FORTUNATELY, NOT EVERY ONE LIKES THE COOKIES OR DOESN'T UNDERSTAND YOU NEED TO DUNK THEM IN BLACK COFFEE TO ENJOY.

THE WEATHER UP HERE IS REALLY NASTY. IT'S HARD TO BELIEVE THAT WONSAN IS THE SAME LATITUDE AS SAN FRANCISCO. PEOPLE WON'T BELIEVE HOW COLD IT GETS. DID I TELL YOU ABOUT THE TIME OFF HUNGNAM IT WAS SO COLD WE PUT ON CLOTHES — LOTS OF CLOTHES — WHEN WE HIT THE PAD? THAT WAS THE NIGHT THAT WATER FROZE ON DECK JUST UNDER MY BUNK.

WELL, ALL IS WELL. MY LOVE TO EVERYONE.

Lee

March 18, 1951
USS Hoquiam PF-5
Anti-submarine patrol,
Songjin, North Korea

PING—The shock pulse raced out from the ship every ten seconds, automatically. Kocinski SOSN listened attentively for a return echo, then moved his cursor ten degrees right before the next ping went out.

At least they had an important job, now. Anti-submarine guard for the Songjin bombardment group: not that fucking drone shit. There weren't even many whales around here to track.

He continued his important and so boring duty of moving the cursor ten degrees for the next ping, swinging from beam to beam.

What I want to do is swing around and look inward toward the bombardment group to study the destroyer sounds and the Missouri screw sounds I thought I heard some of her salvos through the water, once.

Lt. Porter had the Conn. He was leaning against the Sonar Shack forward bulkhead watching the Mighty Mo a couple of miles away. Combat was going to let him know as soon as the Missouri had a new fire mission. The other Deck Watch officers had told him they could see those massive sixteen-inch shells as they went overhead. On their next approach to the north end of their sweep, they would be under the Missouri's trajectory again.

"Captain on the Bridge," sang out a Signalman.

Lieutenant Bob Porter turned around and grinned at the Captain.

"I'm waiting for a Missouri fire mission, Captain. Want to find out if I can see one of those 3,100 pound, 6-foot shells zooming overhead."

The Captain nodded absently.

He had come to the Bridge for the clean, crisp air to clear his head. He wanted the Hoquiam to take part in bombardment. He had originally asked the Task Group Commander to treat a PF like a DD, allowing PF's to assume regular DD duties in the Group. The Task Group commander was not sympathetic to his desires, so far. He hadn't quite sneered when Captain Brown requested bombardment assignments, though he suggested that Anti-submarine patrol for the bombardment group would be pressing any PF's limit.

He probably feels that battlewagons are still the first line, that carriers are not quite part of the real Navy.

Captain Brown knew their next assignment was to fly the rest of the little planes off. After that, UtRon Five, Detachment Able personnel would be transferred from the Hoquiam. He dreaded the following assignment.

In denying the Hoquiam the privilege of shore bombardment with other destroyers, the Task Group Commander, with some sort of twisted logic, had requested of CTF 77 that the Hoquiam become part of the Task Force screen and assume regular plane guard duties with the carriers.

After the current bombardment cycle, the Missouri was going to join TF 77 for a few days. The Hoquiam,

as part of her Anti-Submarine patrol would escort the
Missouri—who could run almost twice as fast as the
Hoquiam—out to TF77 and join the screen.

WALTZ KING THIS IS ABLE SEVEN
CHARLIE DO NOT ANSWER
FIRE MISSION
TWO RAILROAD TRESTLES
ITEM JIG FOUR SEVEN THREE
ABLE
GEORGE BAKER FIVE ONE
CHARLIE
FIRE FOR EFFECT
OUT

"Bridge, Combat—Captain. The Missouri just got a
fire mission on two railroad bridges back in the valley.
Gunfire Support is on speaker number three, Captain."
"Click click."

Lt. Porter reached down to turn up speaker three
he and the Captain swung around and brought their
binoculars to bear on the Missouri. Turret One with three
sixteen-inch rifles trained out to the port bow, raising the
barrels as it turned. Both officers dropped their glasses
to avoid the flash on their eyeballs: a sudden expulsion
of yellow-gray smoke as triggers were pulled. The blast
and subsequent recoil of those three guns in one turret
is so powerful, they fire in rapid sequence rather than
simultaneously.

"Son of a bitch, I see 'em. Damn things are really
moving out!" exclaimed Lt. Porter.

A rumble increased in sound to something like a
train passing overhead on a railroad bridge, as the three
shells soared overhead. A heavy thump arrived from the

Missouri about the same time. They watched the shells go out of sight.

"SPLASH"

crackled from the speaker as the Missouri announced salvo arrival on target.

The side of a hill lifted and fell in the distance.

**"CEASE FIRE. MISSION
ACCOMPLISHED. OUT"**

rang hollowly from Speaker #3 from Gunfire Support.

The Missouri had just destroyed two railroad bridges and their approaches with one salvo.

**March 19, 1951
USS Hoquiam PF-5
Task Force 77 Screen**

Navy Radio Guam indicated it was going to repeat a series of earlier messages. Stewart who now copied fox one hundred percent leaned over and looked at their own list of missing messages. He listened to the message numbers and learned he was going to have about a five minute break.

Stewart flipped a switch so the code was coming out of a speaker, stretched, and got up. He had been sitting for nearly two hours copying messages. His butt was numb and his ears were sore and tender. Twisting his torso, he bicycled his legs to loosen up as he took a few steps to the coffeepot by their open porthole. Pouring fresh coffee into his cup, he spooned in some sugar and casually gazed out the porthole.

He frowned for a second as he tried to identify what he was seeing.

"Holy Shit!" He yelled.

Stewart simply didn't know what to do. The Missouri, close aboard, was bearing down on them.

If something didn't happen soon, the Hoquiam was going to be rammed and sent to the bottom in two pieces.

The piercing scream of the Collision Alarm shattered his ears.

"Emergency! Standby for collision starboard side. Set Condition Zebra. Close all watertight doors and hatches. Emergency! Standby for collision starboard side. Set Condition Zebra. Close all watertight doors and hatches. Emergency!"

The ship shuddered as the propellers dug in, all back full. Stewart could hear hatches and doors slamming shut and being dogged down. He grabbed his life jacket knowing full well if the ship was hit, he was dead. But procedures were procedures.

The Missouri began to turn away, passing in front of the Hoquiam by less than one hundred yards. The engines stopped and began all ahead standard again.

Was this just another day in the life of Task Force 77?

The 1MC popped to life.

"Resume normal routine. Set Modified Condition Baker throughout the ship. Resume normal routine."

Stewart couldn't leave because he was on Fox Watch. Lighting up another Camel, he took his fresh coffee back to the George Fox broadcast position and sat down. Pulling the phones onto his head, Stewart listened to catch the current message number of the reruns. Then he relaxed. Roney would tell him what happened.

The door crashed open and Roney walked in shaking his head while tapping an ear.

"Did you see what happened, Roney?" asked Stewart.

"Shit no. I was in the Engineroom with messages for Mr. Hansen when that damn alarm went off. I'm not even sure why we had a collision alarm."

Oh, ignorance is indeed bliss.

"Because the Mighty Mo just tried to ram us. Fuckin' near did, too."

Stewart spotted Barney already eating lunch and joined him. Barney nodded and opened his mouth to speak as he ate.

"Fuckin' Mo put up a flag hoist to change the task force course. Supposed to make a fifteen-degree right turn. They executed and promptly turned left right into us. First time I ever saw a Lieutenant Commander chew out a Captain — senior Captain at that — with one word."

"Yeah? What was that, Barney?" asked Stewart.

"Oops!" smiled Barney.

"You're shittin' me," Stewart laughed.

"No shit, I sent it. Even more, Chief Swenson sent a private remark to the Chief Signalman on the Mo."

"What'd he say?"

"He semaphored E-A-T, then grabbed his balls. — That Chief understood, all right. He disappeared and didn't respond."

Stewart chuckled and continued eating. He thought it would have been something to be on the Bridge and listen to the Captain discussing the parentage of the Missouri's Captain.

"That's not all, Stew. I saw the message the Captain had second thoughts about. He sent that 'oops' instead."

Stewart waited. He knew Barney would say what it was in his own good time. Stew grabbed their coffee cups and went for a refill. When he got back, Barney continued.

"Yeah, he — how was it again? — 'What are you trying to do, ruin your paint job?'" Barney said with a laugh.

"What's nasty is, the Missouri Captain's apology was short, almost like it was our fault. Captain Brown was not thrilled, I can tell you that."

"Got something else for you, Stew. Did you hear what happened when the Boxer flew Fox — Flight Operations — this morning?"

Stewart shook his head because he was chewing on a mouthful of navy beans.

"Well, up came Fox to the dip and Mr. Morgan turned to the Captain. 'Captain,' he says, 'I think we're in a world of hurt!' The Captain laughed and nodded.

Then the new course and speed came up. 'Mr. Morgan, when he executes, go to flank and assume our position on the rear screen.' It was funny. They executed; we all turned and went to flank. New speed was twenty-eight knots. Fifteen minutes later, we were huffing and puffing along at 19 knots and the task force was long gone over the horizon. But Chief Swenson broke them up with his question. He said, 'Do you suppose they'll invite us back?' The Captain cracked up."

Stewart returned his clean tray to the scullery and headed up the ladder.

There might be some traffic to write up.

There was.

FM CTF 95
TO USS HOQUIAM
INFO CTF 77
BT
WHEN DETACHED BY CTF 77 CMA PROCEED SONGJIN X PICK UP PASSENGERS AND MAIL X PROCEED WONSAN FOR MORE PASSENGERS AND MAIL X SAIL RHUMBLINE TO SASEBO X REPORT DEPARTURE EACH POINT
BT

FM CTF 77
TO USS HOQUIAM
INFO CTF 95
BT
DETACHED
BT

"THIS IS A F R S TOKYO WITH A LATE BREAKING STORY, MARCH TWENTIETH, NINETEEN FIFTY-ONE, AIR FORCE SERGEANT RICHARD HENNING REPORTING. THE U S S MISSOURI HAS SHOWN THE AWESOME POWER SHE USED DURING WORLD WAR TWO AS SHE RETURNED TO THE NORTHEAST COAST OF KOREA. THE MISSOURI'S SIXTEEN INCH GUNS HAVE DESTROYED EIGHT RR BRIDGES AND SEVEN HIGHWAY BRIDGES IN THE SONGJIN AREA DURING THE PAST WEEK."

March 22, 1951
USS Hoquiam PF-5
Moored Buoy X-2
Sasebo Harbor, Japan

The Hoquiam had been up on the line for three weeks. The ship came up the Sasebo Harbor channel at slow speed, rendering honors to ships as she passed. Finally, she arrived at Buoy X-2 and moored. The In-port routine and watch was set with Section One. Liberty would commence at 1300 for Sections Two and Three. The Disbursing Officer was already on the way in the Motor Whaleboat to draw funds to hold a delayed payday.

"James," yelled Griffin urgently, "Flash enemy contact report coming in, addressed to this area."

"Stewart, go tell the Captain and Mr. Forsythe, chopchop", shouted James as he leaned over Griffin.

Stewart didn't say a word. He dashed to the Wardroom, knocked and entered after a hesitation. He stepped over to Mr. Forsythe and spoke loud enough for the Captain to hear.

"Sir, Captain, there's a flash enemy contact report message coming in, addressed to this area." he said and hastily stepped out of the way as both dashed to the Radio Shack.

"What do you have, James?" asked the Captain.

"Captain, it's in plain language, a general recall for all military and civilians to report to their ships, stations, and bases, immediately." spoke James, baffled.

They all leaned over Griffin as he continued to copy the message. Guam had slowed its transmission speed for this important message. Finally, it was complete.

**FM CINCFE
TO ALL MILITARY ACTIVITIES FAR EAST COMMAND
BT
ALL LEAVES CMA FURLOUGHS CMA LIBERTY CMA PASSES CANCELLED X RETURN TO BASES AND SHIPS X ALL MILITARY AND CIVILIAN DEPENDENTS REPORT TO NEAREST MILITARY ACTIVITY X INDIVIDUALS ON REST AND RECUPERATION CMA TDY OR TAD AND DETACHMENTS CMA REPORT TO HOST ORGANIZATION X PERSONNEL FAILING TO REPORT WILL BE SUBJECT TO IMMEDIATE ARREST BY MILITARY AUTHORITIES X MORE TO FOLLOW
BT**

"What's it all about, Captain?" asked Lt.(jg) Forsythe. The Captain shook his head. He had no idea what this was about. But he was sure they would find out soon. He contemplated exercising at General Quarters, then discarded the idea. SOPA would decide that.

The door opened and Curry walked in, thrusting a message at the Captain. Mr. Forsythe glared at him momentarily, then wondered if this was more of the same. It was.

> **FM COMFLTACTS SASEBO**
> **TO ALL SHIPS AND COMMANDS SASEBO AREA**
> **BT**
> **ALL OFFICER AND ENLISTED PERSONNEL ARE CONFINED TO THEIR COMMANDS X THE FLEET LANDING IS CLOSED UNTIL FURTHER NOTICE X RECALL YOUR SMALL CRAFT X MAKE FULL ACCOUNT FOR ALL PERSONNEL X REPORT PERSONNEL ABSENT FROM YOUR COMMAND AND CURRENT LOCATION X NEGATIVE REPLIES ARE REQUIRED**
> **BT**

The Captain was mystified why but not about his next decision.

"James, send Stewart to the Quarterdeck and ask Mr. Unsenger to report to me on the double."

"Aye aye, Captain." and he nodded his head at Stewart who was already on the way.

Stewart ran aft to the ladder and down to the Port Quarterdeck. Saluting, he said, "Mr. Unsenger, this is hot. Report to the Captain," he held his fingers up like quote marks, "on the double. No shit, sir. This is really important. He is in the Radio Shack or Wardroom."

Lt.(jg) Unsenger didn't even return Stewart's salute. He jumped up the ladder and ran forward to the Port thwartships watertight door, startling several sailors. The Captain stood there waiting. He grabbed him by the shoulder and spoke urgently in his ear. Mr. Unsenger bobbed his head in understanding and raced back to the Quarterdeck.

The 1MC opened
"All hands not actually on watch, quarters for muster. Officers Call for all officers aft Secondary Conn. All hands not actually on watch, quarters for muster. Officers Call for all officers aft Secondary Conn."
Stewart remained in ranks for fifteen minutes before Mr. Forsythe came. Even then, there was no information except it looked like liberty at 1300 was going to be delayed.

"THIS IS A F R S TOKYO WITH A BULLETIN, MARCH TWENTY SECOND, NINETEEN FIFTY ONE, ARMY SPECIALIST FOURTH CLASS ROMAN NOKOWSKI REPORTING. (The announcer was speaking very slowly and enunciating carefully.) **LISTEN CAREFULLY. ALL MILITARY PERSONNEL, ALL MILITARY DEPENDENTS, ALL CIVILIANS ATTACHED TO THE U S GOVERNMENT ARE REQUIRED IMMEDIATELY TO REPORT TO THEIR SHIPS, BASES, STATIONS, OR HOMES. ALL FACILITIES ARE CLOSED TO JAPANESE NATIONALS AND FOREIGN PERSONNEL NOT ATTACHED TO THE UNITED NATIONS COMMAND OR THE FAR EASTERN COMMAND. ANY PERSON DISCOVERED AWAY FROM THEIR DESIGNATED ASSEMBLY AREA AFTER TWELVE HUNDRED HOURS WILL BE SUBJECT TO ARREST. REPEATING. . ."**

"What the fuck is going on, Jimmy Bob?"

Stewart looked at James quizzically, who looked at the overhead and threw up his hands.

"Route the fuckin' board, dummy. I just work here."

Stewart flipped the pages, grabbed a pen, and took off to make the rounds.

Everyone was certainly aboard. Ought to clear this bunch of messages in no time at all.

Chief Signalman Swenson and the Captain leaned over the windbreak on the Bridge, idly contemplating the harbor. The Chief squinted at the shore signal tower and looked over his shoulder at Casey who was looking at SOPA.

"Red, the Base has a general call up on semaphore and flashing light."

Casey whipped around, grabbed a stubby pencil and his message board. Acknowledging the call, he waited for the remainder of the ships to acknowledge and then copied the message as it came in.

FM COMFLTACT SASEBO
TO ALL SHIPS AND COMMANDS
SASEBO AREA
BT
DISBURSING OFFICERS REPORT
TO FLT ACTIVITIES MOVIE
THEATER CMA BLDG FORTY ONE
CMA AT 1230 X ALL COMMANDS
SHALL BE REPRESENTED
BT

"Oh shit, you know what this is, Captain?" asked the Chief. "Well, you can forget about liberty until later tonight. They are changing our Military Payment Certificates. Yes sir, we're going to get new MPC issued, that's what it is."
"You think so, Chief?" asked the Captain politely.

"Yeah, I do, Captain. There is going to be wailing and gnashing of the teeth tonight all over the Land of Nippon. A lot of mama-sans have old issue MPC and it is totally worthless as of now. I heard they did this shit about a year ago. Really caused problems on the beach. Lot of hari kari, too."
The Captain heard him out, nodding. The only thing that really fits considering the last message.

Chief Swenson leaned back against the windshield and looked at their Motor Whaleboat heading to the Officer's Landing with Lt.(jg) Barris. There were a lot of small boats heading that way.

About an hour later, Chief Swenson sent Smitty scurrying down to the Captain's stateroom. Mr. Barris was on his way back.

"All hands not actually on watch, quarters for muster. Officer's call."

"Division, Attention," called James, saluting Mr. Forsythe.

"At ease, men. Okay, here it is. It's a money change. As you know, letting the Japs change your MPC for Yen is against regulations because that is a black market activity. The MPC you have in your possession has been replaced by new MPC. Same size but different design and color. I already have mine changed."

He held up a new issue MPC $10 bill to let them see the difference. "I can't change any more MPC, now that I've already changed mine. When you break from here, gather every bit of your MPC and sign them across the end of the front side," pointing to the correct location. "When you go to Disbursing to exchange it, you have to sign a statement that this is all the MPC money you have. No second chances.

"You can't come off liberty tomorrow and tell Mr. Barris you just remembered $3,000 in MPC you had hidden in your inspection shoes. Also, if you have more than $200, you have to explain why you have that much cash. Any questions? Dismissed."

No problem for me, thought Stewart, *I'm broke until Mr. Barris pays us.*

1300, March 23, 1951
USS Hoquiam PF-5
Moored Buoy X-2
Sasebo Harbor, Japan

"Liberty Call Liberty Call for Sections Two and Three. Liberty Party assemble on the oh one deck forward of Mount thirty-three."

Lee Harrison Stewart, RMSN, was ready to go. As a full Seaman, he wouldn't have to ride with the Apprentices — the Seaman Deuces — in the third liberty boat to the Fleet Landing. Second one, true, but being Seaman did have a tiny advantage. Barney, Red, and Roney joined him for inspection. The first party of Petty Officers had already left in the Motor Whaleboat. The new engine even ran quieter.

"You know you're buying the first couple of rounds, don'cha?" grinned Barney.

"Con mucho gusto, amigo," laughed Stewart.

"Oh shit, Stewart's gone linguist on us!" groaned Roney.

"Yeah, I know a lot of other foreign languages, too — umm — gesundheit, acktung, nein, nyet, non, combahwa, ah-no-nay — see, I'm a regular fucking fountain of languages."

The friends and shipmates stood there enjoying each other's company and making small talk as they waited for the liberty boat to return. After another three weeks up there, they were ready for female company again.

The sun was still in the sky as their Motor Whaleboat pulled into the Fleet Landing and they ran to the line of sailors and marines waiting in the official money exchange windows. Armed with Yen, the four friends stepped onto the wide street and looked around for a taxi.

"Charles," called a voice from across the street.
Another voice chimed in, "Lee."
Charles and Lee literally could not believe what their eyes showed them. In graceful Japanese dress, complete with parasols, there stood Charles's girlfriend, Kimiko Ansura, and Lee's girlfriend, Kiki Hatsumoto.

How the fuck did they know we were here?

That thought raced through their minds as they dashed through the traffic and up to the girls. Friends forgotten, Charles and Lee stood very close to their girls without touching. One does not get playful with Japanese in public. One does not grab his girl in his arms, lift her off the ground and kiss them, like he would back in the States. Kimiko and Kiki knew the boys wanted to, though.

They looked up as Barney and Roney closed in. Questions flew back and forth. Additional introductions and explanations followed. However, the overriding answer to the question—How did you know? — was not forthcoming.

The girls were delighted that Lee had been promoted and agreed to a brief party with the other friends. They, of course, would select the proper restaurant and bar.

"Barney," Lee whispered, "could you loan me eighteen hundred yen? I think tonight is going to get expensive."

"Sure, Lee. Kiki looks like she's going to eat you alive when she gets you alone."

Lee turned as someone tugged on his sleeve. Kiki was there in her pale green kimono and matching parasol.

"Lee, we need to go now. Kimiko knows where to go with your friends. We all have one beer together, then go to our rooms. Is that all right with you?"

Oh man, I'm going to devour her!

"Yeah, Kiki. I think this is going to take three taxis's to move us. Is this very far away?"

Kiki turned slightly and pointed up the hill where there seemed to be a low restaurant. They all walked up the many, many shallow steps.

Kiki lay curled against Lee, her head on his chest. The red quilt covering them against the cold night was pushed back far enough so they could see each other's face. It was all Lee could do to keep his eyes open. He was warm and exhausted from some kind of heavy physical exertion. Kiki appeared content as she watched his face. Lee had to go back to the ship in another hour. Cinderella liberty was still in effect for nonrated men, Seamen and under.

"Kiki," he asked sleepily, "how did you and Kimiko know we would be here?"

Lee knew the Hoquiam ship movements had been classified secret, so how could they possibly know? They only found out three days ago.

"We just heard about it in Yokosuka and came down on that stinky coal train to watch for you."

"But when did you find out?"

"Oh, we knew last week. Don't you know all the girls know when your ships come and go in Yokosuka, Kobe, and Sasebo?" Kiki laughed, "we saw three other girls from Yokosuka on the train to see their sailors on the Hoquiam."

Lee grunted softly and slipped into sleep as Kiki snuggled down on Lee's warm chest and traced circles on his chest with her fingertips.

0830, March 24, 1951
USS Hoquiam PF-5
Moored Buoy X-2
Sasebo Harbor, Japan

Six sailors and one chief stood in a row at attention outside the Executive Officer's stateroom. Lt. Marston, with fists on his hips, stood there puzzled and upset. Girl friends from Yokosuka of these seven, had appeared at the Fleet Landing yesterday afternoon, the day after the Hoquiam had returned to Sasebo from Songjin.

For crying out loud, we didn't know we were escorting the Navasota back into Sasebo until four hours before we left anti submarine patrol seaward of the bombardment group. How the hell could those girls have known?

"And you say they said all the girls in Yokosuka and Kobe and Sasebo know when their boy friends ships are due back?"

The sailors and chief nodded.

"And they knew last week?"

They nodded again.

"They just heard it around?" he asked incredulously, leaning toward them.

They nodded vigorously.

"Is there anything you can add to that?"

Stewart and the chief both raised their hands. Mr. Marston nodded to the chief.

"My friend says we're getting underway for Yokosuka on the 28th to get rid of something. We'll only be there for a couple of days and go back to Korea again."

Lt. Marston stared in surprise. My God, that's news to me.

He pointed at Stewart.

"My girl only said we were going to be here just about a week, sir. She didn't mention where we were going from here."

"All right — dismissed."

He absently returned their salute and went to meet with the Captain. This was a serious matter, possibly for Naval Intelligence.

He tapped on the Captain's door and stepped inside when invited to enter.

"Sit down, John," the Captain smiled, "I'm just going over the classified message board. Roger just decrypted our MOVORD."

Lt. Marston held up his hand like a traffic cop and put his other hand to his forehead as though deep in thought.

"Wait a minute, Captain. Let me guess and see how close I come with my Ouiji Board. We depart for Yokosuka on the 28th to get rid of something — maybe the KD catapult. But we will only be there for three or four days and we go back to Korea, probably to Wonsan. — How'd I do, Captain?"

LCDR Brown looked up from the message to John's face, then back down at the message form again.

"You haven't seen this message yet, John?" he asked with a very cold voice.

Lt. Marston shook his head as he watched his Captain. The Captain initialed the message and handed it to his Executive Officer.

"Mind telling me how you know so much without seeing the board?"

"Songjin, huh? Well, Wonsan was a stab in the dark, Captain." Then he looked directly at the Captain.

"We may have a problem for ONI. We have six sailors and a chief whose girlfriends were waiting for them when we got here. They knew in Yokosuka last week."

"Add one hot blooded young ensign to that list. I'll bring it up with Commander Fleet Activities Sasebo. I have a meeting with him this afternoon. See what he wants to do."

Lt. John Marston nodded, picked up his hat and went back to his stateroom and office across the passageway.

1415, March 29, 1951
USS Hoquiam PF-5
Underway
Arriving Yokosuka

"Sonar Bridge—Secure the BQF and raise the dome. We are going through the nets now."

"Sonar—Aye, aye, Mr. Dixon."

"All ahead one-third."

"All ahead one-third, Sir. Engine room answers all ahead one-third, sir."

"Very well."

The tremors decreased as Hoquiam slowed entering Yokosuka outer Harbor. Red got on the Bridge binoculars and sneaked a look up on the hill.

Yep, signal is there. They beat us back here.

He felt a presence and looked over his shoulder to find the Captain smiling at him.

"From the smile on your face, yours and Stewart's girl friends are already back?"

Red looked at the Captain sheepishly and nodded.

March 30, 1951
BuShips
U.S. Naval Station,
Anacostia, Maryland

The Bureau of Ships and Docks Mail Clerk wrote 3/30/51 on the internal route slip. She scribbled some code numbers on the slip and attached the U.S.S. Hoquiam's letter, dated 3/13/51, requesting a Ship's Allowance List. Then she tossed it onto the cart where the letter would remain until delivered to the appropriate office.

APRIL

0915, April 1, 1951
USS Hoquiam PF-5
Pier 7, Berth A
SRF, Yokosuka, Japan

"Captain, there's a small crane pushing a flatcar coming toward us. Thought you'd like to know," said Dominguez. The Captain smiled and thanked him. He grabbed his new combination hat with the scrambled eggs on the brim and touched the silver oak leaves. I'd hate someone to wake me up and say 'April Fool'.

The new Commander-who-is-Captain headed for the Bridge. He wanted to look down where Mount 32 belonged, as they removed the KD catapult. Too bad there's no time to install Mount 32.

Chief Swenson squinted at the Captain in the bright sun and saluted.

"You look good in scrambled eggs and silver, Captain."

The Captain grinned in appreciation, returning his salute.

"Thanks, Chief."

"Excuse me, Captain," called Curry, "I don't know if the catapult is coming off but looks like we get a present for your promotion to Commander."

The Captain arched his eyebrows and stepped over to the starboard side to see what Curry was pointing at.

Well, I'll be damned. We get a Watchcap for our straight pipe stack. Hoquiam is going to really look good now.

He reached down to the sound-powered phone selector switch and selected Engineering Log Room, buzzed, and picked up the handset.

"Engineering Log Room, Chief Dortas speaking, sir."

"Chief, find Mr. Hansen and both of you get up to the Bridge right away."

"Aye, aye, Captain," came the puzzled reply.

A few minutes later, Lt. Hansen and Chief Dortas arrived at a very unusual place for them—the Bridge. Almost always, they were at the opposite end—all the way down. The Captain beckoned them to the windscreen and pointed to the rail car.

"Hey, how about that." Lt. Hansen looked at his Chief. "You think the fires will draw any better with the Watchcap on?"

"Damned if I know, sir, but sure will look nicer on the ship."

They all watched as the glistening black, rakish hood—the Watch cap—for the top of their smoke stack was lowered, banged around to adjust for differences from the pattern, and bolted into place.

They were distracted by Japanese voices floating up from the deck below in front of the Bridge, and some strong sledge hammer strokes. The Yard birds were getting the catapult ready for removal. They watched the preparation with interest.

As the crane swung around over the catapult with cable and hook swinging, the Captain eased back to the

1MC, flipped all switches down, and announced, "If anyone is interested, SRF is removing the drone catapult right now."

They watched as the cable straightened, tensed and began lifting the hated red tube from their deck and dropped it onto the flat car. Removing all the gray and olive drab cases was anti-climatical.

April 1, 1951
USS Hoquiam PF-5
Bridge
SRF, Yokosuka, Japan

Red, Barney, and Stewart leaned against the starboard windscreen idly watching the crane and flatcar with the hated red catapult move away from the ship. Barney's brow, furrowed in thought, looked back on all the different tasks their ship had been assigned since commissioning last September.

"You know, guys," he said, "this old ship has done a lot the last six months. Escorted all kinds of different ships, passed hundreds of swept channel overlays, carried mail, cargo, Korean kids and troops, sunk a couple of junks and sampans, shot up several mines, scared the hell out of a couple of whales, played goat, and acted as an aircraft carrier. Maybe we ought to come up with a nickname for her — like the Trash Hauler or something like that.

"Come on, Barney, Hoquiam, an aircraft carrier?" joshed Stew, "That's a lot of hocky! Remember what Chief Billons told us back on that first day. The old Coastie crew called her the 'Hokey Pokey'. Maybe we ought to resurrect that old name."

"I don't think so, Stew," said Red slowly, "we ought to come up with something new. Maybe something Japanese or Korean. I don't think we'll ever sail this ship to Bremerton or Hunter's Point Naval Shipyards."

Stewart twisted around, looking at Red. "You think this is going to be some sort of Station Ship out here after the war is over, Red?"

"Dunno, Stew. That assumes we don't hit a mine and sink. The Japanese name their ships 'something Maru'." Red warmed to an idea. "Why not Hocky Maru, guys? Stew, you said this was a lot of hocky, and that's surely true. This old tub does get a lot of strange assignments and Hocky sorta fits Hoquiam. What do you say, guys?— Hocky Maru!"

Stewart squinted against the sun, looking at Red thoughtfully. "Red, you speak Japanese pretty well. What does Maru mean?"

Red chewed on his lip while he thought about it. "Well, it means going in a circle or round trip. It means getting there and back safely. That's the best I can say."

Barney and Stewart thought about that, lit up and smoked on the idea. Barney nodded and spoke. "Yeah, Hocky Maru. We been going in circles or here and back again with Korea, right?"

Stewart nodded. "That's it, back and forth."

"Okay. Think I'll go down and put 'Hocky Maru' on the back of my foul weather jacket," said Barney, "although I don't think that's the original intent of hocky, Red."

"Exactly, Barney,' grinned Red.

"Yeah, me too," chimed in Stewart.

Red rolled, now leaning back against the windshield, studying the hillside. "Kimiko and Kiki are standing up there, Stew. You got liberty or duty tonight?"

"Liberty, Red, Liberty. Give me Kiki or give me duty," Stewart laughed. Barney shook his head, stood up straight and went over to the port side to check for flag hoists.

0745, April 2, 1951
USS Hoquiam PF-5
Quarters at Fair Weather Parade
SRF, Yokosuka, Japan

They were standing at Parade Rest, waiting for Mr. Forsythe to appear. The men could smell rain coming and hoped to get inside before the rain got here. It would be close.

James sucked in his breath. "C Division, Aaa ten shun! Hand Salute!" The salutes came up sharply together. "Good morning, Mr. Forsythe. All hands present or accounted for." He turned his head sideways. "To!" Right arms whipped down to their dungaree side seams.

"At ease, men. I have some good news for you. Our stay has been extended for ten days for dockside availability. Commander Fleet Activities Yokosuka has taken pity on us and granted 75 slots for Rest and Recuperation

Leave, not to count against your annual leave. Is anyone interested?"

Every Radioman eagerly waved his hand in the air.

"Okay. I know this R&R is going to be in Nara, Japan. In case you don't know, that is the ancient capital of Japan. Lots of free sightseeing, great hotels, superior food, and not so great women. Total trip will be five days. Actually, you get three days in Nara. It takes a day to get there and a day to get back.

"Let's see. Stewart, you're the only one in the division with a girl friend, right?"

Everyone looked at Stewart as he nodded.

"Well, rules are rules. You can't take her with you, so don't ask. R&R is just for the servicemen who have been in combat, and we meet the Navy's qualifications for R&R. Finally, we don't know how many slots our division gets. Just so you know, I want to go and I don't know yet."

Mr. Forsythe paused. "Any questions?" His eyes darted left and right to see if any sailor had a question— no questions. "Relieve your quarters."

Everyone saluted and headed for the Radio Shack. As they passed through the watertight hatch, James was already thinking out loud, much to Roney's distress.

"Let's see," muttered James; "I've got to select based on time on the ship. So Roney is out, at the bottom of the list. That makes the rest of us equal. I suppose only half of us can go this time: only thing that makes sense. Okay, okay, I know what to do."

James grabbed scissors and a piece of paper out of the filing cabinet, and cutting six small pieces of paper, numbered each one and tossed them into his hat. He picked up his hat and shook it. "Okay. I think Mr. Forsythe is going to come in here in a minute and tell me to pick who gets to go. Nothing doing. This here is a lottery. Whoever picks the lowest numbers gets to go. I'll take the last one in the hat. Coyle, you're on fox, so you pull a number first."

Coyle raised his eyebrows as he continued to copy the message coming in.

"Reach up and pull one slip."

Without missing a beat, Coyle quickly grabbed a slip, looked at it, stuck it in his shirt pocket and continued to type. "Four", he announced.

Stewart reached up and grabbed a slip. His face broke into a big grin. "One!" he sang and watched the others. Masters pulled one. "Crap, six!" he said disgustedly.

Lloyd looked like he was drawing to an inside straight as he reached for his. "Ho ho. It's a three," he smiled.

Griffin half-heartedly pulled a slip and glanced at it. He had a fifty-fifty chance of going. "Five," he said glumly.

When it came to James's turn, he said with a big grin, "Shit! I already know it's two. So, it's Stewart, me, and Lloyd, for sure. Coyle, Griffin, and Masters got the high numbers and won't go this trip. If we get another offer later on, you guys are first in line. Okay?"

The unlucky three nodded quietly.

The door opened a little bit and Mr. Forsythe beckoned to James.

"How many spaces did we win, Mr. Forsythe?" he asked as he wended his way through the men to the door. "We already set up the order of who can go."

"C Division got one space for this R&R trip, so who got first pick?" Stewart chuckled in answer, his grin growing larger. Mr. Forsythe turned his head to Stewart.

"Pack your stuff, Stewart. You leave in two hours. Draw pay before you leave."

"Aye, aye, sir." Stewart flashed a smile and took off for his bunk. He hoped Red was there to pass the word along to Kiki that he would be back in five days. Clattering down the ladder into the compartment, he spotted Red packing his bag. He was going too. "Red, how are you passing the word to the girls?" panted Stewart as he stripped for a shower and fresh shave.

Red glanced at Stewart and continued to pack. "I'm not. Are you going?"

"Yeah." Stewart opened his locker and hustled to pack his gym bag with his spare clothes. He grabbed his shaving gear and clattered up the ladder in his zoris, in a hurry to beat the crowd. "If I don't see you sooner, I'll meet you at the gangway, Red."

Red glanced up sourly. He'd rather be with Kimiko for five days and wondered what might happen if he didn't go to Nara. Not worth getting busted over. Was too hard to make Third as it was.

A standard gray Navy bus took them to the Yokosuka train station. The Chief Storekeeper would take muster at every train change. Red frowned at that. The Hoquiam R&R group of 75 officers, chiefs and men caught the local to Yokosuka Junction and transferred to an electric express train to Zushi.

Stewart, one hand lightly holding the overhead bar and the other hand, his gym bag, bent over to look at the scenery flitting by outside the electric inter-urban train. Sailors from several ships had boarded the train at the Yokosuka train terminal. Their first destination was Zushi station: a very important rail junction of many passenger trains.

10:30AM, April 2, 1951
Zushi Railroad Station
Zushi Junction, Japan

When the electric train stopped, sailors and marines scattered at this station to different trains for different destinations. Lee knew he would wait two hours for his train to Nara. He and Red, now Charles, found a place to sit down, gym bags at their feet, to watch trains flying by in both directions.

Lee enjoyed trains from inside and out. What a variety he saw. There were pre World War Two coal-fed steam engines, patched together with a lick and a promise, hauling passenger and freight cars, puffing through the station, leaking water and wheezing for all they were worth. Decrepit electric cars with flat wheels appeared to be used on local commuter service. Freshly painted electric trains of several cars looked to be used for interurban service. Stewart had seen only one passenger train with an electric engine. Either that engine was new or it had escaped the bombing raids by the Air Force and Navy.

Men, unvaryingly dressed in black suits, ran across the platform from one train to another, or ran for the stairs to cross to another platform. This station had three platforms with tracks on both sides, as well as main line passing tracks. Older men and women too, dressed in traditional garb, scurried as fast as they could. Stew watched train attendants holding little white flags, push these people into already jammed passenger cars, then wave their flag at the train engineer.

Each R&R group was watched over by a Japanese guide. The guides wore different color headbands. The servicemen wore matching color shipping tags on their shirtfronts. Stew now saw men of every branch of armed services waiting for trains.

Lee Stewart didn't know his guide's name. He wore pressed black trousers, white long-sleeved shirt, open sandals, and a green headband. Lee kept an eye on him as he watched people and the trains.

R&R uniform requirements had surprised Lee. He was traveling in his dungarees and would wear them the whole time he was on R&R. Besides his toilet gear, Lee had rolled his raincoat and stuffed it in the tagged gym bag with an extra set of clothes. A tour guide trotted in their direction looking for blank green shipping tags tied to buttons on shirtfronts and gym bags. Spotting Charles and Lee, he trotted up to them, saying, "Sa-rors, you come he-ah now," as he pointed to a spot down the platform. "Train come soon, okay." Lee nodded, grabbed his gym bag, stretched and walked over to the group of fluttering green tags.

Lee swayed from side to side in the rocking car. He stared out the dirty window, chin resting on his fist, elbow against the window frame. His butt was numb from sitting on the slatted wooden coach seat. What a boring, dirty ride. This passenger train engine was probably the oldest engine in service. Grit and coal soot was everywhere. Worse, the train was a local, jerking and stopping at every station along the way. After the first two or three stations, they were all the same, one blurring into the next. Worse, their gym bags had disappeared while they snoozed.

7:45PM, April 2, 1951
Nara Railroad Station
Nara, Japan

"Fellas, if I can have your attention, please," smiled the soldier. "My name is Floyd, Specialist Fourth Class, attached to Eighth Army Special Services, Nara Detachment. I'm here to welcome you to Nara and get you situated in hotels around town." Floyd wore a GI rain slicker and pith helmet. He stood just inside the bus with a name-filled clipboard held in both hands.

He had every tired serviceman's attention. It was raining very hard and drumming loudly on the Army Bus. Between the bus's engine rumbling, many civilians chattering just outside the bus and clattering by in their getas, and the train announcer's voice booming and echoing unintelligibly from many station loudspeakers, Floyd was hard to understand. Stewart looked up to the ceiling to locate the leak dripping water on him. It really didn't matter that much. He had gotten soaked, as had the rest of the men.

"Your bags arrived ahead of you." A collective sigh of relief escaped from the twenty or so men. "They were collected and transferred to a through train. When they got here, we distributed them to hotels around town.

"Each hotel has everything you need, including a dining room to serve you all three meals each day. The rules are very simple and straightforward. You can't bring women into the hotels. Take your entertainment elsewhere.

"Check the front desk every time you leave and come back to the hotel. There could be messages for you. You have no curfew so you do not have to come back to the hotel to sleep if you don't want to. The front desk will have your travel orders ready at the end of your stay here. Have a good time."

Stewart looked out the bus window, through the rain, at people scurrying by, umbrellas at the ready. Checking his luminous watch, he couldn't decide whether he wanted to hit the beach, or hit the pad when he finally got settled in and had eaten dinner. Red was slouched down in his seat, staring at the seat back in front of him.

Lee turned to him. "Charles, do you know anything about Nara?"

"Not a fuckin' thing," he answered sourly.

"Hey, buddy, we're going to be here three whole days. Gotta think of something."

"I hate guided tours."

Lee looked at him. "Well, yeah—and that gives me an idea. How about some of these Army Civilian women? You suppose there are any of them down here?"

"Not a chance. They go for the officer shit. But we could see if the Ancient Castle is open to the public."

"Before or after pussy?"

"Between!"

"That's a big roger, Charles. Now, if this shitty rain will just stop."

The Army bus started with a jerk and moved away from the train station into town. Stewart continued to watch the street scene as the bus moved along.

Gee, certainly no bright lights around here. Maybe it's just the neighborhood.

When the bus stopped at the first hotel, Floyd called out three names. Three soldiers struggled out of their seats and got off the bus. A couple marines left at the next hotel. Four sailors, Lee included, were called for the third hotel. Charles shrugged his shoulders.

"I'll ask mister special services for the name of your hotel and meet you for breakfast, Lee. Don't eat until I get there. Okay?"

Lee nodded glumly. He expected to share a room with Charles. Worse, none of the other Hoquiam sailors got off with him. He walked shyly into the Japanese hotel, not sure if he would have to remove his shoes. *The last time I was in a hotel, it was the YMCA in Bremerton on my shipping over leave.*

This hotel lobby was long and narrow, not much more than a wide hallway. The man behind the counter pushed a registration card to him and handed Lee a fountain pen. No words were spoken. Lee wrote his name, rank, serial number, and duty station on the card and pushed it back to the man behind the counter. He looked at it and wrote some Japanese Katani characters on two slips of paper.

A bellhop or an assistant appeared at Lee's elbow, smiling and bowing. The counter man handed one slip to his assistant and handed the other to Lee. He spoke to Lee for the first time, "Disa hotel carda," he said and pointed to the Katani writing he had just written, "disa yo rooma numbah. Yo keep disa card. Okay? Yo givah caba drivah to bring hyah. Okay?"

Lee ducked his head, nodding several times. "Okay Joe, Okay, I keep this card and give it to a cab driver to come back here. Where is my room key?" Lee pantomimed with his fingers, inserting a key in a lock and twisting the key.

"No key, no key," he said, astonished that Lee should ask for a key, he shook his head strongly. "We watch rooms for yo. Yo see. Go now."

Lee looked at the other three guys waiting behind him, shrugged, and followed the desk manager's assistant.

The assistant opened the door and motioned for Lee to enter. A simple room, there were two single beds — both too short for him.

"Disa yo bed, okay Joe?" he said, pointing to one of the beds that had his gym bag on it. "Nudda man, he come to udda beda soon, lika yo."

Lee walked over to the other bed and checked the nametag.

Fuckin' doggy sharing my room!

"You got any longer beds, Boy-san? This bed is too short for me." Lee pointed his hands to the top of his head and shoes, then nodding at the bed, moved his lower hand almost to his knees.

"Oh, so sorry. Bedsa only disa long."

Lee suddenly realized there was no bathroom or shower.

"Boy-san! Where benjo?"

"Oh, yo come," he said, beckoning to Lee, bowing and smiling, and leaving the room. They walked to the middle of the long, bare wooden hall. He turned through a swinging door into a room with many American toilets, not Japanese benjo style holes. Two toilets were occupied.

Ignoring them, the assistant walked around a corner into a combined wash and shower room. Well, at least everything is free.

April 3, 1951
R & R Hotel,
Nara, Japan

Lee examined his Japanese self-winding watch for the fifth time.

Dammit, where the fuck is Charles? The hotel isn't serving breakfast at 1130. Wonder what is keeping him?

Lee joined the family style lunch at 1230 and ate his fill. By the time he finished two helpings and smoked a cigarette, it was 130PM, and still no Charles. Well, that's it. Guess I'll mosey around and see what kind of trouble I can stay out of.

"THIS IS A F R S TOKYO WITH THE MORNING NEWS APRIL FIFTH NINETEEN FIFTY-ONE, AIRMAN MIKE DILL REPORTING. IN THE NEWS, THE UNITED NATIONS COMMAND IN KOREA REPORTS THAT U.S. NAVY LST 799 RESCUE HELICOPTER RESCUED ITS FIRST PILOT YESTERDAY. THE RESCUE WAS ASSISTED BY ONE OF THE LST'S LCVP LANDING CRAFT. THE LST, NEAR WONSAN HARBOR, WAS ASSIGNED THIS MISSION THREE DAYS AGO."

1730, April 7, 1951
Radio Shack,
U.S.S. Hoquiam PF-5
SRF, Yokosuka, Japan

Stewart walked into the Radio Shack and dropped his gym bag. "Hey, what's been going on while I was gone?"

"Five days of the usual shit. How was R and R in Nara?"

"Okay, I guess, Lloyd. Don't know what happened to Red. Didn't see him after I got off the bus. Don't have anything to compare it with. Ass was hard to find and expensive; the food was okay but the Yokosuka Receiving Station feeds better. The trains down and back were slow and dirty. Oh yeah: at least a short shit like you would have been comfortable in that bed. I ended up sleeping on the floor. Fuckin' doggie bunking in my room said I was nuts. He thought his bunk was just fine but he was used to muddy foxholes in Korea."

"I'm going to Nara tomorrow for five days," said Lloyd, "wonder where they'll put me up? Oh yeah, your mail is on your bunk, Stew. Think you got another letter from that bad-ass girl in Astoria."

Oh Ho!

"Then, I'd better hustle down and check it out." With that, Stewart backed out of the door and headed below to his bunk. Several letters, including an official one from Clatsop County District Attorney's office, were there.

Yep, a letter from Betty, one from Mom, and—Wow, two from Ruth.

He tossed the D.A.'s and Betty's letter to one side.

Mr. Marston will open them and hand em to me, just in case there is bad news inside.

He opened the letter from his Mother and a money order for fifty dollars fell onto his bunk. Stewart realized from the first line, he hadn't written her for a couple of weeks. Newsy about Dad's job on the Siboney and her bowling league. Usual plea for a recent photo of him.

Should I send her the one of Kiki and me? Lots of explaining ought to keep her from getting too excited. Ah ha! Buy her a set of Noritake china for four, any patterned white would do. The fifty should cover it and shipping to Norfolk. I'll go to the Navy Exchange after lunch and find something for them.

The letter ended with a plea to write more often. He stuck the money order in his wallet and picked up the letters from Ruth.

March 15, 1951

Dear, dear Lee,
Hey, two dears!

Yes, I got my income taxes in before today's deadline. Mom and Dad were sweating it out right down to 4PM when the Post Office closed.
We don't have to file income tax returns out here.

Well, I have to tell you the bad news first. I met the wrong guy. He was bad and got worse when he started drinking. We got into a fight over his drinking and he beat me up. I tried to fight back. I ended up in the emergency center in down town Seattle.
Oh shit, Ruth!

Scared Mom and Dad half to death. He gave me many bruises all over, bruised ribs where he kicked me, and a very sore jaw when he punched me. Both eyes are black and blue. No broken bones, though. Dad was really grim with me and gave me a choice. I either clean up my act and select my male companions with a great deal more care, or move. They couldn't handle my being hurt this way.
Me neither.

My boss at Abercrombie was really sweet and gave me a week off as sick time, to recover. But he did give me some stuff to work on at home.

As far as you are concerned, the good news is Mom and Dad held you up as someone they wished I thought more about.

I like that.

That you were a good guy. (Little did they know about goings on in the cellar and in my room.)

Oh yeah, do I remember.

Lee, I am not ready to settle down yet. I still want to be independent and have fun. At the same time, I have never forgotten how sweet you are. Keep writing to me. And write me one letter that I could show to Mom and Dad. They'd like that.

Better yet, I'll write one to them.

I was really surprised to hear you snagged a Japanese girl who spoke good English. Don't you do something dumb like marrying her, Lee.

Not a Chinaman's chance in hell!

I would really be upset if you did that. Leave thoughts of her behind when you come home.

Ruth, what are you hinting at here?

Take good care of yourself. Newspaper stories are hinting you might rotate home in six months or so. See, I'm beginning to pay attention to Navy news. I really miss you, you big lug.

Wow! Down Junior.

RV

He sat thinking about Ruth for a few minutes. He wasn't ready for a commitment, either.

Hell, I'm only twenty. She cooked up some neat dinners for us on that weekend in Seattle. Her room is neat, and

Ruth is pretty squared away. Maybe she could be the one to ride the road with.

Lee sighed and picked up the other letter. Much thinner.

As he opened it, a photograph dropped out. It was a hand-tinted picture of Ruth in a flower print dress with trees and the Sound in the background.

March 21, 1951

Lee my dear,

I thought you might like to have a more formal photograph of me. Hope you like it.

Ruth, baby, you look good in anything, and this is very nice. This is going to hang on my locker door.

Would you send me one, please?

Ole whatshisname is making some liberty money by taking nice photo portraits for framing. I'll get him to do a couple. Folks would like one, too.

I feel much better now. Almost all the soreness is gone. Black eyes still show a little. The girls are worried I'll see that guy again and keep tsk tsk'ing at me. Fat chance of that.

Good!

I'm not even going to date for a while. I want to think about things such as what and where I want to be after a while.

Is this a broader hint? Is it time for me to start thinking seriously about her? I'm just not sure.

My love,
RV

In the warmth and misery of a love in the distance, Stewart stuffed the letters into his locker and locked it.

Grabbing the D.A.'s and Betty's letters, he headed for Lieutenant Marston's stateroom.

Stewart rattled his fingernails on the stateroom door and waited.

"Come!" He opened the door and stepped in. Lt. Marston looked up and smiled, then saw the envelopes Stewart held in his hand.

"Have you opened them, Stewart?"

"No sir, Mr. Marston. Brought 'em up here for you to open, like you said."

Lt. Marston took the letters, noted the time, and jotted that information on both envelopes. He reached for his miniature sumarai sword letter opener, and slit both envelopes. Lt. Marston glanced at Betty's letter and wordlessly passed it to Stewart. Stewart saw there was no return address and noted the cancellation cachet was some town he had never heard of, Blaine, Utah.

March 27, 1951

Dear Lee Stewart,

I never want to see you again. Because you didn't help me, my parents have disowned me and shipped me off to this godforsaken place in southern Utah. I'm stuck with a baby I didn't want.

I stuck a ring on my finger but the church elders who insist I attend church made me take it off. All the men in this village have been trying to coax me into bed, whether or not they are married. If you married me, everything would have been okay.

Oh sure, Betty!

The District Attorney is after Ralph Rogers now, and they may get some money from him through the Air Force. But I never want to see him again, either, after what he did to me.

So, fuck you Lee Stewart. I hope you rot in hell.

Betty

Stewart quickly read it and laughed.

"She's really pissed off—excuse me, sir—mad at me, isn't she?"

"I think pissed off describes her letter perfectly, Stewart," he smiled.

Stewart nodded, then asked, "Should I keep this letter, Mr. Marston, or throw it away?"

Lt. Marston took her letter and handed him the D.A.'s letter. He watched Stewart read the other letter before he answered.

March 15, 1951
Office of the District Attorney
Clatsop County, The State of Oregon
Commanding Officer, U.S.S. HOQUIAM
(PF-5)
c/o Fleet Post Office,
San Francisco, California
Re: Lee Stewart, RMSN

) The State of Oregon
)   vs.
)   Lee H. Stewart, a Radioman
Seaman,
) United States Navy

) currently stationed on U.S.S. HOQUIAM PF-5

Evidence and Miss Echols' confession that she wanted you to be her husband and father another's child, have led the County of Clatsop Children's Protective Service to drop all charges against Radioman Seaman Lee H. Stewart.
We regret the embarrassment and inconvenience this may have caused Stewart.
This case is dismissed and closed.
A.J. Crowlane,
District Attorney
Cc: Mr. and Mrs. Fred Echols, parents of minor child
Miss Betty Echols
Legal Dept., U.S. Naval Station Tongue Point, Astoria, Oregon
Commanding Officer, U.S.S. Hoquiam PF-5, c/o Fleet Post Office, San Francisco, Calif.
U.S. Naval Bureau of Personnel, Washington, D.C.

Lieutenant Marston watched the frown change to a smile and then a broad grin on Stewart's face.

No doubt a big load had been lifted from his mind, he thought.

Lt. Marston leaned back in his chair and eyed Stewart. "Stewart, I want to place all the material into a big manila envelope and seal it. That envelope should go into your file and stay, just in case she gets some cute ideas again. I'll date and write across the flap that this envelope is not to be removed or opened without your permission. What do you say?"

Stewart swallowed and nodded his head. "Do you think she'd ever try to get me again?"

"Oh yes, Stewart. She moved from Oregon to Utah, and you did attend her church. She could wait for everything to die down and try again. The church might be more sympathetic and listen to some new lies."

Stewart nodded. "Sir, thank you for all your help. I really appreciate this."

Lieutenant Marston liked his response and warmed to Stewart.

Indeed, he almost got royally screwed.

"You're quite welcome, Stewart. Now, if you will excuse me," and he turned back to his desk.

Stewart, walking lightly, turned into the Radio Shack to hear the latest stories. Lloyd was sitting on Fox with the cans down around his neck, sipping coffee.

"Running one of the long summary messages?" inquired Stewart.

"Nah, running about twenty repeats. That's almost as good as them running the call tape. I'm curious, Stew. What about those two letters? The D.A. and the girl, I mean."

Stewart laughed from the sheer pleasure of it. "The D.A. said that the evidence and Betty's confession cleared me. Charges are dropped and the case is closed. Betty, on the other hand, got kicked out of the family who shipped her ass to the backlands of Utah. Betty said it was all my fault for not marrying her, and I should get fucked. If Kiki is in town, I plan to do just that!" He rummaged through the coffee cups for his and poured one.

"I guess that's a big load off your mind, huh?"

"Oh, you betcha. Mr. Marston is going to wrap up all the papers, seal them in a big envelope and make 'em part of my official record, just in case she gives it the big try again. Got two letters from Ruth."

"That's that knockout from Seattle, right?"

"Yeah. She picked the wrong guy to run with. He beat the holy crap out of her, bad enough she had to go to the hospital for treatment."

"She's okay, though?"

"Yeah, and she sent me a great picture, all tinted and everything. Going to hang in on my locker door."

"Great. If you're not doing anything, there are three new messages that need to be written up and routed around on the board."

Stewart nodded and picked up the sheets of messages to find theirs. He found them and typed them up on the message forms. Completed, he placed them 'just so' on the clipboard, grabbed his hat, and left for the Wardroom.

As he stopped at the Wardroom door, Mr. Forsythe waved him in. He had a big smile for Stewart as he reached for the board.

"Welcome back. How was Nara, Stewart?"

"Let's see. The bed was way too short, so I slept on the floor, really upsetting the hotel staff. Food there was free but less than average. Couldn't get into the ancient castle, so I walked around the big park and fed the tame deer. Girls were so expensive, I passed. Besides, I think it's still raining." Stewart had been looking around the Wardroom and felt something was different.

"Esther, where's Esther?"

"It was bound to happen, Stewart. The O'Bannon's Wardroom has double our population, and they hit us when the Captain and the Officer of the Deck were the only two officers on board. Kinda dicey anyway, because we were still in dry-dock. Two of them held Lieutenant Unsenger prisoner on the Quarterdeck while the rest dashed in yelling like a bunch of Indians. Three went to the Captain's Stateroom and held him prisoner there. The other six walked into our Wardroom and sat down to enjoy our coffee while one unbolted Esther from the bulkhead. Then they left. But it was nice while it lasted."

Stewart shook his head and smiled at his division officer. "Guess that means the school bell has been taken down, too?" Mr. Forsythe nodded and Stewart left for the Signal Bridge. He had hydrographic messages for the Chief.

Red was sitting on the starboard flag bag sipping coffee.

"What the hell happened to you, Red? I waited and waited for you to show."

He shrugged. "I didn't want anything to do with Nara. When I got off at my hotel, I went in, got my bag, and took a taxi back to the train station." Sipping more coffee, he looked at Stewart. "I got the next express train about 11pm back to Zushi. Was with Kimiko by Noon. Sorry but that Army Specialist left before I could find out which hotel you were in." He laughed. "Kiki was pissed to find out where you were."

"Well, maybe tonight I can calm her down a bit," said Stewart, shaking his head.

1400, April 8, 1951
USS Hoquiam PF-5
SRF Yokosuka, Japan

Ding ding

"Hoquiam arriving." The 1MC clicked off.

The Captain smiled as he made his way up the gangway. He saluted the Colors and returned the Officer of the Deck's salute and stopped for a moment. He had some orders.

"The second group get off to Nara, yet?"

"No Captain. The bus is due in a half hour."

"Freeze the gangway except for trash and special runs, Mr. Barris, no R&R, as a matter of fact, announce that the second R&R to Nara is cancelled. Also, no base liberty. We're getting underway about sixteen hundred. Officers' Call in five minutes."

Mr. Barris saluted, beckoned to the Boatswain Mate of the Watch, and said, "Aye, aye, Captain", nearly in one motion.

"No one off the ship without my express permission, Boats."

"Aye, aye, Mr. Barris."

"Officers' Call Officers' Call. There will be a meeting in the Wardroom for all officers in five minutes." He paused for a second. "The second R&R tour to Nara,

Japan has been cancelled. I say again, the second R&R tour to Nara, Japan has been cancelled."

The officers settled in their chairs and waited for the Captain to speak. "Back to Songjin this afternoon, gentlemen. Get topped off and prepare the ship for sea. Get your people back. Departure at sixteen hundred," he looked at his watch, "in two hours. This time we join the bombardment group, even if we don't have Mount 32 yet. Are we waiting for anything special from SRF, or other places?" he paused for interruption, letting his finger point around to each department head. "Did we send any equipment off the ship for repair?" He looked around for comments. "No questions, then?" He pointed a knuckle at Lt. Marston. "Have Chief Swenson make sure we have the latest Hydrographic updates and new charts for our path and Korea. Dismissed."

The Captain got up and left for his stateroom.

The 1MC scratched into life. "Now hear this. Make all preparations for getting underway. Make reports to department heads. Make all preparations for getting underway."

The story continues in

KNOCK OFF SHIP'S WORK.